A BEAUTY DARK & DEADLY

HEATHER C. MYERS

CHAPTER 1

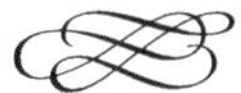

The first thought Emmy Atler had upon seeing him was how someone so beautiful could kill his wife and her lover. Because Jason Belmont was beautiful; any woman (and even some men) who could see (and anyone who could not see most certainly could feel) his beauty. While he was relatively short for a male, standing at five foot ten, he had incredibly angular features. His face was heart-shaped, with high cheekbones. His eyes were dark, deep, and soulful, hidden behind thick-rimmed glasses. Emmy made sure to note not to stare into those eyes in fear that she might lose a piece of her in them. His lips looked soft and shapely, his top lip only slightly smaller than his bottom lip. Oddly enough, it was Mr. Belmont's nose that Emmy was fascinated with the most; it was pointed and defined, the nostrils flaring out almost like the wings of a bird. His hair was dark and shaggy, constantly falling into his face on its own accord. It was longer than normal, coming down to about his chin. His shoulders were broad, hidden by an old, tattered robe. Emmy noticed that for a man of forty-eight, his body was still in good shape as evidenced by his clinging wife beater and loose pajama pants.

"I'm here to answer the ad," she said, mentally scolding herself for how small her voice sounded. Emmy was usually more forthcoming; she wasn't used to being intimidated by anybody.

However, Emmy was beginning to expect that Jason Belmont was a different man entirely. He had begun to develop a well-known reputation as an esteemed author after he published his first book. The man was talented, and because of that, he started making money. As always, however, night did accompany day. Jason began holing up in his home office, plagued with deadlines, appearances, and writer's block. The papers interpreted his isolation as a strain on his marriage and even managed to uncover his wife's secret, seven-month affair. Jason had to discover it in the papers. Next thing he knew, his wife and her lover ended up dead in a Motel 6 and he was being accused of committing the act. Two years later and after clearing his name, he took residence in his old cabin in Lake Tahoe.

He smiled at her, causing Emmy to look away. The sun seemed to shine differently when he smiled.

"You seem to be the only one to do so," he told her in a soft-spoken voice. Emmy had seen Jason being interviewed on television a few months back, and she found it rather baffling that the man had a voice that sounded articulate and mumbled at the same time. It was a low tenor and gave her chills; she hoped it was because she was intimidated by him.

"I guess that means that you're hired," he continued, opening the door wider – a silent invitation to come in.

She hesitated and glanced at her two suitcases idly on the cement porch on either side of her. It had been rather presumptuous of her to assume that she would get this job, but she highly doubted that anyone else would be applying, and upon seeing his surprised look when he first saw her, she assumed that he felt the same way.

As Emmy stepped over the threshold that would mark the beginning of the end for her, she began to reflect on why she had decided to take the cleared murderer up on his job offer.

Her grandfather was a wounded war veteran who barely managed to make ends meet with merely his disability check. He was the only thing Emmy had in the world and she loved him more than anything. She was currently a senior in college, about to graduate, but instead of finishing at the moment, she saw this opportunity to help him out and decided to take it. This, of course, was against her grandfather's strictest wishes. It broke her heart that she had to leave him, but the pay was good, and they needed it.

"Well, I assume you want the tour then," he said, glancing at the ground as he scratched the back of his neck.

"Actually, could you just show me to my room?" she asked. Even Emmy could admit that she sounded rather forceful and she quickly looked away to avoid that penetrating stare of his.

Jason paused for a beat as he stared at her intensely before he nodded once. This caused his hair to fall in his face and his hand reached up, his long fingers pushing the locks out of his face; a chain of events that Emmy expected to happen quite often.

"Uh... yeah," he said, and then began to lead her through the unkempt living room up to the base of the stairs.

Emmy watched his movements with interested curiosity. They were swift and fluid, however somewhat ungraceful as well. She noticed a rather large hole in the train of his robe, which was fluttering behind the man in hopes to keep up with him. To be honest, Emmy was somewhat surprised that she was carrying both of her suitcases. She had been raised by a man who had lived in the time where chivalry was an unwritten rule and expected the men of today to have some form of familiarity with etiquette, despite it being practically extinct.

As though Jason Belmont could read her mind, he stopped abruptly and spun around, causing his hair to curtain his face once again. Emmy had to strain her muscles to stop so that she would not run into him.

"I apologize," he said, after brushing his hair back. "I seem to have forgotten my manners." He looked at her bags before meeting her eyes. "May I?" he asked, raising his firm brow.

Emmy's face betrayed her thoughts by turning an unattractive shade of red. Deciding not to trust her voice, she nodded and handed him her bags. Emmy made it a point to avoid accidentally touching him, and once the two bags were in his hands, she mumbled a meek word of thanks. The corner of his lips curled up in response and again, he nodded, before turning and finally ascending up the narrow staircase.

Along with the house, the stairs were made of wood. Any pressure on certain stairs caused an alarming squeak of protest. The wall adjacent to the staircase was oddly bare, and Emmy wondered if pictures ever occupied the space. Everything in the cabin, while messy, reminded the young woman of loneliness. There was nothing that personalized the home, nothing that set it apart from the many cabins found in the Tahoe region. Murderer or not, the man was obviously very lonely.

When they reached the top of the stairs, Jason took a step to the right before stopping and spinning around, heading in the opposite direction. Emmy watched with a quirked brow from the top of the stairwell. He seemed uncomfortable in general, fumbling with her luggage, not because he wasn't sure what to do with his hands. As he walked, Emmy noticed that his eyes were prone to watching the floor, causing his glasses to slide down the bridge of his nose. Once she was sure the man was certain of his direction, she began to follow him.

The young woman felt about as uncomfortable as Jason Belmont did. She curled an errant strand of her hair behind her ear as she followed behind him, timid. She was beginning to get frustrated with herself; if any of her friends was asked to describe her, timid would definitely not be one of the words they would use. But this Jason Belmont made her more nervous than she would like to admit. Usually, she was quite good at quickly reading people and then adapting to whatever situation she had been placed in. The problem was, she couldn't quite read her employer.

He was unlike any other person Emmy had ever met before. Almost like some sort of enigma that she wasn't quite sure she wanted to figure out. In fact, Emmy wasn't exactly sure of anything since walking through his door. She wasn't sure if she was afraid that he was going to kill her or that she might be in love with him. Emmy was afraid, however. That, she knew.

"Well, home sweet home," he said, and then his lips curled up into a tightly forced smile.

Emmy glanced up at him and returned his smile with a fake one of her own. "For now," she murmured, averting her eyes so they focused on the wooden floor beneath her feet.

There was an awkward silence that hung in the stale air. Emmy cleared her throat and then pressed her lips together so they disappeared into a thin, white line. Her eyes glanced around the nearly empty room. There was a twin-sized bed with a crisp, purple comforter, pushed in the middle of the main wall. Beside it was a rather small nightstand adjacent to the left side of the bed, there was nothing else on either side of it. A triangular shaped window took up the majority of the connecting wall, sunlight seeping through the glass and causing the majority of the shadows to all but vanish. Across from the bed, there was a humble dresser just waiting for her to place her clothes in.

Another lonely room...

"Right," Jason said, raising his brow as more of his hair fell into his face. "Well, you should probably settle in. Uh... if you need me, I'll be in my office – that's the second door on the left. The first one is the bathroom, and my room is the last room down the hall." He turned to leave when something inside Emmy caused her to stop him.

"Before you leave," she called, her voice a bit sharper than she expected. He turned again and looked at her. Emmy regarded him for a long moment, searching his eyes before she could stop herself. Emmy realized she had temporarily forgotten what she was about to say. A blush cascaded over her face and she smiled in amusement as she shook her head.

"Before you leave," she stated again, looking back up at him, "you should – I mean, I don't want to tell you what to do or anything – but maybe you should tell me what you want me to do..." She let her voice trail off and then inhaled, pointedly avoiding 's eyes.

He watched her for a moment before chuckling softly. He raised his brow before pushing them together and then reached up to cup his lips with his index and middle finger.

"Uh..." he began, and then scratched the back of his neck, subconsciously revealing his level of comfort. "Well, cooking would be nice. You know, breakfast, lunch, and dinner."

"Yeah, I'm familiar with them," Emmy quipped before she had fully registered the thought. When she realized this, her face darkened considerably and she looked away once again.

* * *

JASON WATCHED HER, cocking his head to the side. Even through the dark strands of his hair, he could make her form out clearly. She was uniquely beautiful with long, wavy hair that reached the middle of her back, and incredibly expressive eyes. Her cheekbones and jawline were defined, with light freckles sprinkled on her cheeks and across the bridge of her small, upturned nose. She was somewhat short, at about five foot five; he had a good half a foot on her, which gave her a delicate undertone. He couldn't quite tell what kind of figure she had; her body was hidden under a loose grey hoodie, old blue jeans that looked quite comfortable, and worn converse shoes.

In all honesty, Jason was rather surprised she had shown up – that anyone had shown up, in fact. Despite being cleared of all charges, he knew that many people still believe that he committed the crimes. In fact, most of Tahoe shunned him, which was a reason why he needed Emmy; she could go into town and get what had been refused to him. Normally, he had no patience for any form of discrimination, but he thought if the community saw that he was trying to keep to himself and not bother anybody, they might start warming up to him a bit and let him buy food and other necessities.

It had been a week since he posted the ad in the local paper before she had knocked on his door. Even looking at her now, he was still slightly baffled that she had actually answered it at all.

"And cleaning," he continued, a very small, amused smile on his face. "As you can obviously see, the house isn't exactly in the best shape as it has been in the past." He paused for a long moment, peering at the young woman before him. He silently mused over how old she was. Obviously, she was young – definitely in her early twenties. Odd; his previous housekeeper had been a retired widow. She left after the murder charges were brought against him, just like everybody else had.

* * *

EMMY NOTICED Jason Belmont's eyes turn a darker shade than what she assumed was normal, and his lips were pressed tightly together. She wondered what he was thinking about, wondered what could make him so angry so quickly.

"Anyway," he mumbled through a sigh as he pushed his hair back with his long fingers. "I should leave you now." With that, the man turned around and disappeared down the hallway, probably to his office.

Emmy watched him until he disappeared before blinking a couple of times. She was really here, in his house, with this man. It was then that she realized how tense her body had become upon being in the same room with him, and knew that as long as she stayed here, she would be looking over her shoulder constantly.

She sighed then, trying to get a hold of herself. The room had suddenly become too hot, so she walked over to the triangular window and opened the glass. Immediately, a nice, crisp breeze blew in, pushing strands of hair over her shoulder.

Instead of retreating to the whole of the room, however, Emmy's curious eyes began to survey her view. There was a very small vegetable garden located in a pocket against the house. Her brows pushed together as she regarded the juicy tomatoes, the small patch of carrots, and the tall, gold maize. She had never been talented at gardening; that had been her grandfather's forte. Besides the garden, the cabin was surrounded by forest; tall trees that blocked the sunlight and provided a good portion of shade during the hot summer months. It also hid the cabin from view. It took Emmy a good twenty minutes of mindless searching until she spotted the nearly camouflaged red-bricked chimney upon first coming here. The main road was about a mile north, but there were many dirt trails leading every which way. Never good with direction, the young woman noted not to try and follow a trail by herself; despite how much it had been traveled by, she was certain that she would most definitely get lost. Finally, she could make out a very small sliver of a nearby lake, the sun's rays pressing down on the water and causing it to sparkle.

A dejected sort of grumble pressed itself against the inside of Emmy's throat. She had prided herself on being a city girl (although, if she was telling the truth, she was really more a suburb girl). Originally from Newport Beach, California, she moved up to live with her grandfather in San Francisco just after her high school graduation. Currently, she was taking classes at San Francisco State, majoring in sociology. Now, after she had decided to prolong her senior year to take this job, she found herself in a small town, practically isolated from the world. The fact that she was shacked up with a maybe murderer was definitely not helping things.

Emmy turned at that moment and decided that now was as

good time as any to begin to unpack. She entertained the thought of grabbing her iPod and listen to music as she did so but ultimately decided against it. Jason Belmont might sneak up behind her and slit her throat if she wasn't always on her guard. With that, she pulled both suitcases over to her dresser and began moving her clothes from the bags to the insides of the drawers. It took her about a half an hour to complete the transition, and when she finished, she pushed the empty bag underneath her bed.

There were still a couple of items left in the second bag, and she quickly pulled them out and put them around the room. A couple of books and a framed picture of her with her grandfather were placed on the surface of the nightstand. Her journal and her writing utensils were slipped in the nightstand drawer. Finally, her laptop was placed on top of the dresser. She highly doubted there was any internet access here, but she did have over three thousand songs on iTunes. Since she knew there was really nothing to do here, she would be listening to each song in a manner of days.

At that moment, she thought that she should call her grandfather and let him know that she was okay. She grabbed her purse while simultaneously slipping the second bag underneath the bed, adjacent to the first one. Once her cell phone was securely in her hand, she flipped it open and realized she had no service whatsoever. She whispered a swear word and set the phone on top of the small stack of books. Running her hands through her hair, she realized that she would have to ask Jason where the phone was (if he even *had* a phone), and if she could use it. Originally, Emmy had wanted to avoid the man as much as she possibly could, but she had promised her grandfather that she would call. Emmy never had and never would break a promise to her grandfather.

"Okay," she whispered to herself as she slowly rose from the bed. "You can do this."

Emmy proceeded cautiously out her door. She tried as hard as she could to make sure she didn't push down on the floor with all her weight so the floor wouldn't creak. Her heartbeat was hammering, but she couldn't rationalize why. He couldn't – *wouldn't* – kill her. He needed her help, which was why he had hired her. And even if he could get away with murder once, there was no way he could get away with it again. Plus, he had no reason to kill her. She was an innocent bystander. At least, with his ex-wife and her lover, there had been some sort of motive. He wasn't unhinged, per se... just uncontrollably upset.

Whoa, whoa, whoa, Emmy, she thought to herself and physically stopped in mid-step so that she might get a hold of herself. *Did you just defend him?*

It had to be the air, she reasoned and continued to head in the direction of Jason's office.

When she finally reached the second door on the right, she realized it had been left slightly ajar. She tilted her head to the side and tried to peer into the dark room. Emmy had no idea why the room was so dark; it hurt her eyes to type in dim lighting and here he was, sitting in pitch blackness. A soft scent bristled against her small nose, and she scrunched it in disgust without even thinking, immediately recognizing it. The man was a smoker. He was currently slouching over his keyboard, staring blankly at what appeared to be a blank word document. His thick-rimmed glasses had slid down the bridge of his nose until it was resting dangerously on the curves of his nostrils. He was chewing his bottom lip, obviously frustrated with himself, with the black, white screen, or maybe both.

Maybe now wasn't the best time to bother him...

"Did you need something?" Jason asked. He appeared at the door before Emmy even noticed and was now staring at her through the open space the door provided.

Her heart jumped into her throat as she pressed her lips together to contain her impending squeak. She glanced at him, the door now halfway open, as he regarded her with a curious stare. He didn't appear to be angry.

"I, uh," she said, her voice still shaky. Immediately, Emmy closed her mouth and her eyes, trying to calm herself down. She forced a tight smile as she reopened her eyes and looked up at him. "I don't have any service." This time, her voice came out a bit smoother. "On my cell phone, I mean. I was wondering if I could use your phone to call my grandfather and let him know I'm alive – *all right*! I mean all right." She didn't need a mirror to know that her face was changing into an unattractive shade of red, much like a chameleon might if he was sitting on top of a big, juicy tomato.

"Yeah, of course," Jason said, shaking his head as if the thought should have crossed his mind before. "There's one down the stairs on the coffee table." Emmy was about to turn and head down the stairs but Jason stopped her with the sound of him clearing his throat. She waited expectantly and he raised his brows. "This is actually really silly. I don't even know your name..." He let his voice trail off and continued to stare at her.

"Oh," Emmy said, and then due to habit, stuck out her right hand. "I'm Emmy, Emmy Atler."

Jason grinned at her, clearly amused, and then took her hand in his before shaking it. "Belmont," he said in what Emmy assumed was his most suave voice, "Jason Belmont."

The young woman had to refrain from rolling her eyes. Her father had been a James Bond fan, and whenever he introduced himself to any of her friends, he would use the same ploy. It had been embarrassing then, but now she missed it.

"It's nice to meet you," he said, breaking out of her revelries.

She slipped her hands from his. "Likewise," she murmured, and then turned, this time successfully heading down the stairs.

Emmy was not exactly paying attention to her surroundings. She only had one goal in mind, and that was to find the phone Jason had told her about and talk to her grandfather. Her grandfather had a voice that could calm her down, no matter how sad or how upset she might be. It soothed her to no end and especially came in handy when she had found out her parents had died. For the two months after she arrived, he would read stories to her before she went to bed, staying with her until she fell asleep. It didn't matter that she had been eighteen then and storytelling was reserved for children younger than her; all that mattered was that she was comfortable, *safe,* if only for a bit. Emmy, now, felt as though she needed her grandfather's voice. She had been on edge all day, every minute of being in this house, and hoped that maybe her grandfather would be able to help her.

The young woman took a seat on the couch and immediately noticed what appeared to be a groove in the shape of a body that seemed permanently etched in the couch. The man couldn't even sleep in his bedroom. What Emmy couldn't understand was, if Jason Belmont was so uncomfortable here, why didn't he just up and leave? He was a successful author; it wasn't as though he couldn't afford it.

Just like the author said, a beige telephone sat on the wooden coffee table. It was sort of old fashioned; the phone was not cordless or anything. Emmy didn't really care. As long as it worked, that was all that mattered. However, when she picked up the phone and placed it to her ear, the sound of silence greeted her. There was not even a dial tone. Furrowing her brow, she hung up the phone and then tried again. Still nothing. Her eyes began to search the phone's surroundings until she saw the cause of the problem. The phone line had been pulled out of the jack and was currently occupying the blue rug underneath the table.

Well, that was odd. It almost appeared as though Jason Belmont had pulled it out on purpose, as though he didn't want any phone calls. Maybe the ringing interrupted his writing, but then again, it wasn't as though he had been writing, from what Emmy could see. Maybe it was something else then...

It didn't matter, however. Emmy slipped the cord into the jack and picked up the phone once again. This time, however, the dial tone overtook the silence, much like church bells on a quiet Sunday morning. She smiled as her fingers hurriedly dialed her grandfather's phone number... her old phone number before coming here.

He answered on the second ring. Just hearing his voice caused Emmy's heart to flutter and a smile crossed over her features before she could actually respond to him.

"Papa?" she asked him softly, hopefully, as though maybe she was just dreaming. It was an odd feeling; she had seen him just this morning, and yet she felt as though she hadn't spoken to him in quite a while.

"Emmy?" he asked, and as he continued to speak, she could detect the hint of his notorious mischievous smile. "How's my baby doll? Obviously, you're still alive, so that's a good sign."

Emmy giggled at her grandfather's attempt at a joke and mindlessly brushed errant strands of hair from her face as she felt her body finally relax. "Yes, I'm here," she murmured almost wistfully into the phone. "I wanted to tell you that I made it and that I did get the job."

"Well, that's not really much of a surprise, now is it?" he asked. "So how is old Tahoe? I haven't been up there since you were, oh, maybe ten or eleven. I remember I would take you up there to camp, just us two. No parents allowed." Emmy smiled at the memories but said nothing in return. Currently, she didn't trust her voice. "How's that kook-author living up there? You know I've heard stories about him, Emmy. Everyone thinks you're crazy for going up there..."

"I know, I know," Emmy said through a sigh, making a conscious effort to keep her voice down. She didn't want Jason Belmont to overhear her conversation, or worse, creep up behind her and scare the life out of her. "I don't exactly know what to make of him, Papa. I mean, from what I've seen, he's just uncomfortable. He's unkempt and he walks around in this old tattered robe and his hair isn't brushed and he smokes! I get this weird vibe from him, but I don't know if it's good or if it's bad." Another sigh escaped from her lips as she glanced around suspiciously.

Yup; still alone. "But, having said that, he's been polite. I kind of... I kind of feel bad for him."

"You always feel bad for people," her grandfather said, chuckling, and though Emmy could not see him, she was sure he was shaking his head. "Well, I should let you get going. Now, you be careful Emmy. And you call me if you need anything, day or night, you hear?"

"Yes," Emmy replied. "Oh, and Papa; my cell phone doesn't get any reception up here so I'll make sure to call you tomorrow and give you the number here if you ever need me." He chuckled again, and her heart clenched. She knew she would have to hang up soon, despite the fact that she really did not want to. "I, uh..." Her voice came out shaky, but not because she was afraid. She swallowed, trying to collect her bearings. "I miss you, Papa."

"And you know I miss you, baby doll," he told her, his voice growing softer. "Call me when you can." He paused, and in the silence, Emmy prayed that it might just last forever so she wouldn't have to hang up. "I love you, sugar."

"I love you too, Papa," she told him and waited until she heard the click of the phone on the other line.

Emmy released a deep breath before hanging up. She pushed herself up from her sitting position and glanced out the window. It surprised her how dark the night looked, and she decided that now was as good as ever to begin cooking dinner. The young woman padded into the kitchen as she blinked away the tears that had accumulated while speaking with her grandfather, and stopped when she reached the fridge. Upon inspecting the food receptacle, she concluded that it contrasted heavily with the nearby sink due to the fact that the refrigerator was remarkably empty while the sink held numerous dishes. Emmy idly wondered just how long those dishes were sitting there, but figured she would have to wash them sooner or later.

Once the dishes were in the dishwasher and Emmy had thoroughly washed her hands, she opened the door to the refrigerator once again. After another brief inspection, Emmy decided that eggs were the best and decidedly only option for dinner. She grabbed four of them and carefully rested them on the counter before rummaging through an assortment of cabinets, looking for a frying pan and a spatula. Once everything had been found, she cracked the eggs into the pan and disposed of the white shells in the nearby trashcan. Scrambled eggs had always been a favorite of Emmy's, and if there had been cheese, she would have sprinkled some on the finished product. Alas, she knew that she would tire of eggs if she would have to eat them constantly.

"No," she muttered under her breath as she grabbed two plates from the top cabinets. "I'll have to go to the store tomorrow."

But for now, dinner was served.

CHAPTER 2

Dinner went as well as anybody could expect. It was silent, something Emmy was rather thankful for. Jason Belmont seemed surprised that Emmy made him dinner in the first place, and for the first few moments, he did nothing, really, except stare at his food and then ramble a string of 'thank yous' together. Despite the fact that Emmy was afraid of him, the man was beginning to fascinate her with the little things he did. During dinner, instead of focusing on the plate in front of her, the young woman watched intently as Jason Belmont ate his dinner in a rather peculiar way. His fork was held with the fingertips of his right hand, and he would raise the eggs level to his mouth. However, instead of moving the fork to his mouth and placing the food on his tongue, he would move his head a few inches to the fork, and then dab the food with his tongue, as though he was checking its temperature, before placing it in his mouth. A couple of times he caught her staring at him, and immediately she would look away, blushing as she picked at her food. He never did call her on it, though, and for that, she was thankful.

It was hard for her to get to sleep that night. The most physical reason for this was because she wasn't sleeping in her own bed.

This bed was stiff and crisp, although not entirely uncomfortable. She kept tossing and turning, trying to find the perfect position to fall asleep in when, for whatever reason, she grew uncomfortable and had to shift. It also didn't help that the bugs outdoors were rather obnoxious when it came to making noises. Even as she thought about it, she knew it sounded silly, but the squeak of the crickets and the buzzing of the flies seemed much noisier to her than the soft hums of vehicles as they drove by. Yes, she was definitely much more used to the city than... here. And then finally, somewhere deep, down inside of her, she was afraid Jason might slip into her bedroom and do something to her. Suffice to say she did not get much sleep that night.

When she woke, she woke up tired and sore. She quickly threw on some clothes before quietly heading downstairs. It was deathly silent; not even the bugs outside seemed to be up. No matter; all Emmy was planning on doing was going to the store. She had already spoken to Jason about it, and he had promised he would leave some cash on the sink. Before she left, she quickly fixed up some coffee and poured it into a thermal cup so she could take it along with her. She placed the pot back in the machine and contemplated for a moment whether to turn it off and let it get cold, or keep it on, assuming Jason would wake up sometime soon. Finally, she decided that he might like some coffee and ultimately left it on.

After grabbing a hoodie and slipping it on, she pocketed the cash Jason had left her, grabbed a purse, her wallet, and her coffee, before heading out into the morning. The cold surprised her; it was much brisker than she had originally anticipated. The cold pinched at her skin so hard that her cheeks reddened, and she quickly placed her lips on the thermal cup and took a long sip, selfishly downing the hot liquid in hopes to warm her insides. While it worked initially, the feeling was temporary, and Emmy had to make do with walking the mile to the main road rather quickly. Once the first ten minutes had passed, she began to get used to the temperature and even found herself enjoying the walk.

Once Emmy hit the main road, the young woman turned right and headed down the side of the street until she found the next trolley stop. She glanced at the times listed and then pulled out her cell phone to compare. She had a good twenty minutes until it would show. She sighed and took another sip of the coffee; it had grown lukewarm during her walk, but she didn't want to drink it all while it was hot. Oh well. She didn't necessarily mind lukewarm coffee anyways.

The trolley came a few minutes late, and Emmy made a mental note to bring her iPod and some sort of book the next time she decided to venture into town. She took a seat in the middle and yawned as the trolley began to ascend up the curve of a hill. Tahoe had many different hills and mountains, and while one could argue the adventure of traveling up and down these hills, Emmy was somewhat paranoid about it. Some of the mountain roads were rather high, some of the turns were rather sharp, and some streets had little to no guardrails, allowing for the opportunity of driving off the road. Emmy swallowed as she glanced out of the trolley and at the scenery. The fact that she was on an open trolley really wasn't helping either; she could feel the wind in her face, blowing through her hair just as it blew through the leaves of the trees.

Just don't look down...

To keep from doing such a thing, Emmy straightened up and began to focus on the occupants of the trolley. One could easily spot a tourist in Tahoe; they were always wearing bathing suits under their clothing, either flip flops or hiking shoes, and there would be at least one person in a party who wore a ridiculous hat. They were always loud when discussing plans, would hold their cell phones out rather obnoxiously looking for service that wasn't there, and reek of sunscreen. Most were also burned because they were unfamiliar with the fact that because they were in the mountains, they were actually closer to the sun. Tourists usually annoyed Emmy whether they were in Tahoe or Frisco, but they served their purpose as a good distraction from her paranoia until she reached her intended destination: Raley's.

When she walked into the supermarket, the first thing Emmy noticed was the Halloween decorations. She pursed her lips in a tiny frown at the thought; it was only mid-September and already they were thinking about Halloween? Her grandfather, on the other hand, would wait until Halloween day to buy to buy his candy, and still used the same outdated Halloween decorations he had bought back in the late eighties. The thought cheered her up a bit and caused her to chuckle, and she grabbed a basket before heading into the heart of the store.

Now, what was she looking for? What did he like, exactly? Maybe she should have asked for his input about what he wanted. It was, after all, his residence, and she was supposed to be cooking for him. She stopped in the middle of the cereal aisle and pulled out her phone. Should she call and ask? Would he even be up? Did she want to wake him up? Who knew how he would react if he felt that he didn't get enough sleep. Plus, she quickly remembered, that she didn't yet have the number to his home. Okay... then she would have to use her best judgment and hope that she was correct.

There were a couple of other women in the cereal aisle, and as Emmy silently made her way down, her eyes skimmed over the brand and store names of the cereal. Would he get upset if she bought brand name, and thus, more expensive cereal, or did he actually prefer the cheap store knockoffs? Her head was swimming with unanswered questions, causing a very soft but very noticeable pulsing in the temples of her head. Great, she was going to have a headache on top of all top of things. She stopped finally and decided to get some Raisin Bran. Raisin Bran was always good; it was one of her favorite cereals.

This isn't about you, Emmy, a little voice reminded herself and she frowned once again.

Okay, so then what would Jason Belmont want? Cinnamon Toast Crunch? Cheerios? Everyone loves Cheerios. What about Honeynut Cheerios? She began to tap her index finger on her chin and decided that she would grab a box of Honeynut Cheerios as well. As she began to walk down the aisle, she began to feel an impending stare burn in her back. She continued to walk, this time more slowly, to make sure that her paranoia concerning her new living arrangements wasn't merging over to other aspects of her life, such as simply shopping for food. But the feeling continued to follow her until she reached the very end of the aisle. One glance wouldn't kill her... She physically stopped in her tracks, and then, very slowly, she arched her neck so that she could glance behind her. Sure enough, the two old women sharing the aisle with her were staring intently, and when Emmy caught them, they immediately looked away and started chatting, as though nothing happened.

Furrowing her brow, Emmy continued to head to the milk. Well, that was odd. She knew that many of the residents here could spot tourists just as easily as she could, and figured they must think of her as just another tourist. However, she had been to Tahoe enough times with her grandfather early in her life to know that the locals didn't stare at tourists. If they were going to gossip about tourists, they would do it when said tourists weren't around. No; this was blatant staring and Emmy had no idea as to why.

When she reached the milk, she grabbed two cartons of 2% before deciding to head down the pasta aisle. Pasta was one of her favorite foods, whether it was with red tomato sauce or white alfredo sauce. She grabbed a few packs of different pasta (such as noodles, shells, and bowties) and both types of sauce. Now, what? Maybe she should pick up some bacon and sausage. They still had eggs... would he want eggs again, after just having them for dinner? She placed the heavy basket on the floor and thought intently for a minute. What about pancakes instead? A smile eclipsed her face as the idea popped into her head. She loved pancakes and had not had them in so long.

When she turned to head down the adjacent aisle, she realized three other people staring at her. Subconsciously, Emmy glanced down. There was nothing on her clothes. She touched her face; she doubted anything was on her face... What was wrong with her? Why, exactly, was she attracting all these stares? Hurriedly, the young woman spun around and headed down the next aisle, searching for Bisquick and syrup in hopes to get out of the store as quickly as possible.

Emmy grabbed the Bisquick, making absolutely sure that it wasn't the kind where one merely added water but needed eggs and milk as well. The syrup, thankfully, was near the Bisquick and she grabbed a bottle. She stood up and did a quick, mental checklist before deciding that she was finished. It struck her odd as though, that she was actually looking forward to heading back to Belmont's residence, but at least there, he wouldn't stare at her. In fact, it would seem he avoided her, which was fine by her.

"Emmy?"

The familiar voice caused all hope of escaping unscathed to shatter into a million pieces. Emmy struggled to refrain her shoulders from slumping forward, and she surprised herself by being able to hold her rigid posture.

"Emmy Atler?"

It took Emmy a couple of times before she successfully plastered a very tight and very fake smile on her face. Once she did so, she sharply turned around to face one of her college acquaintances, a term she used very, very loosely.

During her freshmen year, Linda Carson was referred by the student body as one of the 'Plastic Girls,' not because she was fake, but because she had access to her own credit cards. She didn't just have one either, she had about three or four, all lined up for her disposal. It didn't help that she was also incredibly beautiful. Linda was five foot nine, with the legs to prove it. Her face was evenly structured, and with big, blue eyes and rich, chestnut brown hair that went just past her shoulders, she looked like an angel. She was also incredibly fashion-forward. Because she had numerous credit cards burning a hole in her Louis Vuitton wallet, she was always out shopping for the latest trends no matter what the cost. Boys had constantly thrown themselves at Linda's perfectly pedicured feet, and despite the fact that her boyfriends did not have a good survival rate. Oddly enough, Linda had befriended Emmy, and the two remained friends throughout freshmen year. They really didn't talk about anything with substance; mainly just boys and clothes, but Emmy had never been happier. She actually trusted Linda with everything, including her crush-to-end-all-crushes, Cody Finch. That was when she heard Linda had asked him to go to home coming with her during their sophomore year. It was then that she realized that Linda had personally befriended Emmy on the obvious fact that Emmy was less than she was. While Linda's hair was either incredibly straight or perfectly curly, Emmy's hair had somewhat frizzy waves she had never been able to tame. While Linda's face had makeup that enhanced the best features from her face, Emmy preferred not wear any such makeup; instead, she would sleep in until she absolutely had to get up. While Linda had the most expensive, trendiest, and newest clothes in time for every season, Emmy continued to wear the same general outfit throughout the year – a t-shirt with a hoodie over it, jeans, and converses. While Linda's body was tight and toned, Emmy's was slender and soft. When Emmy found out about Linda's façade and had seen her with Emmy's crush-to-end-all-crushes, she refused to speak to Linda again. She hated to admit it, but in a way, she was glad to have an excuse to come up to Tahoe.

And yet, despite her best efforts, Linda was standing in front of Emmy, with that same smirk she had been known for. As always, she was dressed incredibly well, even though it didn't go well with her surroundings. Wearing a cropped jean jacket, a black, spaghetti-strapped tank top that revealed a wonderful pair of assets, and a mini skirt over black tights, she looked completely out of place. On her feet, she wore four-inch stiletto boots, making Emmy subconsciously wince in pain. However, the irony that came out of this situation was the locals were staring at her and not Linda.

"Emmy!" Linda exclaimed, clapping her hands together as a brilliant smile lit up her face. Emmy still couldn't decipher if the smile was genuine or not. "It really is you! My, it's been so long! *Too* long!"

"Uh, yeah," Emmy murmured as she braced herself for Linda's trademark hug. She pressed her lips into a tight line and awkwardly returned her former classmate's hug. When Linda finally released her vice-like grip on Emmy, she took a step back and flattened the wrinkles of her shirt. "What are you doing here, Linda?" Emmy asked uneasily. "I thought Berkley started a couple of weeks ago."

"Oh, I already graduated," Linda said, flicking her wrist as though it wasn't that big of a deal. "I wanted to get out of college as fast as I possibly could. You knew that. But anyway, I came up here because my father has some work he has to finish up, and I decided to tag along. I've never been to Tahoe before, and I heard it was gorgeous, which it is, but it's also really dirty." She then took a step toward Emmy and leaned forward, as if the two were going to share a secret much like old times. "I mean, look at this store, Emmy. Where's a Ralph's when you need one? And there are no malls up here whatsoever." Emmy was going to re-ask her question with more emphasis, especially since Linda obviously did not like it here, but Linda tossed her hair over her shoulder (today it was straight). Emmy knew Linda well enough to know that she was not finished speaking. "Anyway, I've been here for a few weeks now, and it was only recently that the locals started talking to me. But after finding out that you and I went to school together, they said something about you going to work for the psycho killer Jason Belmont." She looked at Emmy pointedly, tilting her chin down and placing her hand on her hip, expecting Emmy to confess.

It took Emmy a couple of minutes to finally reply due to the fact that sometimes, Linda spoke faster than most people could comprehend. "Yeah, actually, I am," she said, nodding her head. "I mean, you know my grandpa, so-"

"Who cares, Emmy?" Linda said, pushing her brows together. "There's nothing in the world that would make me go live with that creep. You couldn't *pay* me to."

Emmy furrowed her brow, and her eyes flashed in anger, something that went completely over Linda's head. "Yes, well, we can't be as lucky as you, can we Linda?" Emmy asked. "I don't have four credit cards to pay his bills with, and if I did, I would owe even more than what we do now. This is the only option, and to me, it's worth the risk knowing my grandfather won't have to worry about his bills."

Linda glanced to the side of her as her mouth contorted into a dismissal form. "Well, I just wanted to tell you that all the locals are talking about you," she said. "So don't say I didn't warn you." And with that, Linda spun on the heel of her boot and disappeared down the aisle.

Emmy blinked once and then grabbed her basket and headed to the check-out. A couple of the clerks watched her walk up, and she timidly coiled a strand of hair behind her ear. Emmy avoided any and all eyes that seemed to be watching her. She hated this kind of blatant, shameless attention, especially when she really didn't do anything. She took this job to help with her grandfather's medical bills, not because she liked the guy or thought he was innocent. Emmy wasn't trying to play rebel; she just *needed* the money. Maybe they thought that she was betraying them in some way. Maybe they thought that she was aligning herself with him instead of them.

Before she could dwell on such thoughts, she realized the line before her had cleared, and the clerk was waiting for Emmy to take the items out of the basket so she could begin to scan them. An impatient cough only provided evidence for this hypothesis, and Emmy nearly dumped the contents on the conveyor belt. She cleared her throat and her eyes began to scan the headlines of the gossip magazines, despite the obvious stare from the cashier.

"So," the cashier began, once Emmy indicated that she preferred paper over plastic bags for her items. "I hear you're working for that Jason Belmont."

Emmy looked at the middle-aged woman's somewhat tired expression, and she pushed the edge of her lips up in what she hoped was a friendly smile. "Uh, yes," she replied, nodding once. "Yes, I am."

"So, how's he treating you, dear?" the cashier asked, her brown eyes trying to find any sort of proof of injury on the young woman before her. "He hasn't hurt you, has he?" She began to type with one hand on the register once she finished scanning all of Emmy's items. "Hasn't threatened you?" Her thin brow perked up, and she paused for a beat, before dully reading the total. "Thirty-six fifty-seven."

Emmy reached into her wallet and handed the cashier the two twenties Jason had left her to use. "Actually," Emmy said, surprised she was actually going to say what she was about to say, "he's been really nice." She smiled politely and waited for the woman to type in the amount she had given her, and hand Emmy her change. Customers and other cashiers had begun to give her more attention, as though they each heard her response to the cashier's biased question.

But the cashier just stared at her with obvious doubt and annoyance etched in her face. "You had better be careful now, missy," she said finally, her acrylic nails pecking at the buttons on her register. "That Mr. Belmont may be appealing to the eye, and I'm sure he has some charm in him, but that doesn't mean he didn't do you-know-what." She handed Emmy the necessary change and stared pointedly in Emmy's eyes. "You had better be careful," she finally repeated, "or else you may be next." With that, the cashier plastered a smile on her face and whipped her head in the direction of her next customer.

Emmy frowned, and grabbed the paper bags and headed outside. Much to her dismay, they were a bit heavier than originally expected, and she had to shift them around a couple of times before she got to the trolley stop. Luckily, it came rather quick, and once she was situated on the red and gold piece of transportation, she let her body relax. She wasn't exactly sure how she felt; the cashier, as well as the majority of occupants living in Tahoe, obviously believed that Jason committed the heinous act, and Emmy had initially believed that too. While she still did believe such a thing, she had begun to grow defensive of her employer during her conversation with Linda and the cashier, which she couldn't quite understand. Nevertheless, what she had said was true; he had been hospitable to her.

When the trolley got to her stop, she grabbed the bags, and with a determined heave, lifted them up and headed off the car. Surprisingly enough, Jason Belmont was waiting for her. Her heart clenched and she felt her fingers tighten around the bags, but he offered her a humble smile. His hair was still as unruly as she remembered it, maybe even more so, and his glasses occupied the tip of his nose, but he was not wearing his robe, and he had changed clothes. Instead, he wore a simple grey T-shirt and a new pair of black sweatpants along with flip-flops on his feet.

As Emmy stopped and gave him a questioning stare, Jason simultaneously scratched the back of his head and pushed up his glasses up the bridge of his nose. "Well, you see, I figured you would come back with your hands full," he explained in his soft-spoken voice. "I should have let you take the car, but it must have slipped my mind, so I decided to help you carry them back to the house."

"Did you bring the car?" Emmy questioned, raising a brow.

Jason was about to reply, but cut himself off. Emmy carefully placed the bags down and watched him as his deep blue eyes trailed along the surrounding trees. It would seem that he was searching for an answer in the wilderness, but he couldn't find the one he wanted. "Well, no," he said, shaking his head. He began to chuckle softly and shook his head. "That would have been a better idea, wouldn't it?" He looked at Emmy, who had let a very tiny, amused smile slip onto her face. He smiled at that. "Here," he said, walking over to her, and grabbing the heavier paper grocery bags. "Let me help you."

"Thank you," Emmy said in a voice above a whisper. She watched him turn around and begin to head back towards the house for a moment. She wasn't exactly sure what to make of him. Everybody believed that he was going to hurt her in some way, and yet, to be honest, he seemed timid. She couldn't exactly picture this guy killing a fly, let alone two human beings.

That doesn't mean I trust him, Emmy reassured herself, and then picked up the remaining bags and followed him deep into the forest, on the way back to his home.

Oddly enough, the way back to Jason's home was faster than the way to the trolley station. It was quiet for the most part. Emmy preferred to watch the man walking ahead of her instead of conversing with him. She always figured that the way somebody acts says much more than words ever could. However, as she watched him, she wasn't exactly sure what to make of him. He walked normally enough, even with his long fingers coiled around the paper handles of the heavy bags, but there were times when he would pause, stop walking altogether, and glance around as though the whispers of the trees called out to him in a voice only he could hear. Sometimes he would glance over his shoulder at Emmy, to make sure she was still walking behind him, and each time he saw her, his eyes would widen slightly, as though he was surprised that she was still behind him, then smile in relief, turn back around and continue to walk.

When they reached the house, Jason put the bags down and reached into his pocket for the keys. Emmy briefly wondered why he would even lock his house; people were afraid of him and wouldn't dare set foot inside his residence, but she made no comment on her observation and followed him inside. They walked into the kitchen, where the two both placed their bags on the counters. Emmy began to take the items out of the bags and put them away. She didn't know for sure if she had placed them in their correct spots, but she had put away groceries enough times to know that while she might not have been completely correct, she wasn't completely wrong.

"Is there anything you prefer for breakfast?" Emmy asked softly, avoiding eye contact with him as she put the syrup away. "I picked up some pancake ingredients at the store..."

As Emmy turned around, she watched as one of the most breath-taking smiles that she had ever seen eclipsed his heart-shaped face. It was sort of shy and very boyish, but his deep blue eyes seemed to sparkle along with it, and it revealed straight, white teeth. Even his nose seemed to want to bask in his smile's light; the wings that represented his nostrils seemed to flare slightly. Emmy immediately looked away, down to the wooden floor beneath her as her face flared up.

"I *love* pancakes!" he exclaimed enthusiastically. "I remember when I was a kid, my mother made the best pancakes ever. Each Saturday morning, if we woke up at the same time as we did for school, she would make us pancakes."

"'We?'" Emmy asked before she could stop herself.

"Oh," he said, almost nervously, as though he wasn't quite used to talking to people about his family. Maybe nobody even asked him about them. "I have three younger sisters."

Emmy smiled but said nothing, and she began to grab a skillet, a bowl to mix the ingredients in, and measuring cups, preparing to cook pancakes.

"What about you?" Jason asked after a moment, his eyes watching Emmy intricately from behind his thick-rimmed glasses. "Uh... do you have any brothers and sisters?" It sounded as though he was even more uncomfortable asking about people than someone asking him.

Emmy remained silent for a long moment, cracking a couple of eggs in the Bisquick. She pressed her lips together as she poured the milk into the mix, and grabbed a fork to stir it up. Despite advances in technology, Emmy preferred to manually stir any concoctions that needed such stirring because it gave her something to do.

"No," she said and glanced up at the man standing behind the counter, looking at her with an interested expression on his face. "No, I don't have any brothers and sisters."

Jason opened his mouth to say something, but upon a second thought, decided against it, and closed it. He took a seat at the dining table and pulled out a crinkled sheet of paper. He tried to smooth it out against the table, but he failed miserably. Finally, he stood up and grabbed one of the numerous pens that seemed to be lying around different places in the house. Once the pen was between his fingers, he plopped back down and began writing whatever was in that head of his. While Emmy flipped the pancakes on the skillet, she glanced at him. He seemed so intently focused, and though she tried to make out his writing, it was too sloppy and too small to decipher anything.

"What would you like to drink?" Emmy asked as she turned off the stove.

"Oh, milk is fine," he said without looking up at her.

"I love milk too," she said with a quiet smile. Then, she abruptly shook her head, ridding all thought of similarities between her and Jason from her mind.

In a manner of minutes, the two were seated with plates of pancakes and glasses of milk.

Jason looked up at her and slipped both the crumpled paper and pen in his pocket. "This smells..." He let his voice trail off as he inhaled, and a peaceful smile took over his features. "I haven't had pancakes in a long time." Emmy already had quite a big bite of the flapjacks in her mouth so she didn't reply, but she acknowledged his silent compliment with a nod. "When you went into town," Jason said as he doused his pancakes with syrup, "I'm sure the locals gave you some sort of hassle for being here, with me." He looked at her directly, in such a way that Emmy could not look away from him, even if she tried.

Emmy swallowed her thoroughly chewed bite of pancake, and took a long gulp of milk before answering. "Yeah," she said, and then licked her lip to rid it of any leftover milk residue. "They wanted to warn me about you, I guess." She paused, and then took a deep breath, preparing for what she was about to say next. "I said that you were nice." She quickly stuffed her mouth with another bite of food so she wouldn't have to explain herself, and looked away.

If she had looked up at the man before her, she would have seen that breathtaking smile back on his face.

CHAPTER 3

"I want to show you something," Jason stated once he had finished his pancakes. Emmy looked at him, unable to keep the obvious suspicion off of her face. However, she remained silent and stood from the table, collecting both his and her dishes. "There's a small garden, off to the side of the house," he continued, as she placed them in the sink. "I want to teach you how to keep it."

Emmy still kept quiet, but turned to face him, and nodded once. He nodded in return, and stood as well, wiping his hands together a few times. His eyes, for whatever reason, were focused on the wooden floor. It was a simple place, on the floor; there was nothing special about it, and yet the way Jason was staring so intently at it that Emmy could not stop her eyes from following his. It amazed her how well his focus was when it seemed to concern nothing too important.

"Come," he said finally, flicking his wrist in a sloppy come-hither motion that lacked any and all sensuality that usually accompanied such a movement. However, Emmy highly doubted that he even intended to add a double meaning to his gesture, but she was still wary about following him into the garden. She hadn't seen any sort of neighbors residing next to the man; no one would hear her if she screamed... But at least she would be outside. If she needed to run, she would have a better chance of escaping than if she remained inside.

She followed him nonetheless, and he led her outside. They walked around the frame of the house, and Emmy was surprised to see the sun so high despite the morning. She took off her hoodie and hung it on her arm while she continued to follow the man around to the side of the house. When Jason got to his intended destination, Emmy took a moment to observe her surroundings. She could easily see the triangular-shaped window – her window – from where she was standing. Her eyes scanned the garden itself; there were carrots, tomatoes, and corn. The corn seemed to be a couple of feet from the pocket garden while the tomatoes and carrots coincided rather beautifully. She pushed her brow, however. Shouldn't he have picked these vegetables by now?

The young woman turned to ask the man just that, but he had disappeared. She could not make him out through the forest. Her heart clenched once, twice, before a trifle of fear wrapped its cold fingers around it and squeezed. She gulped and spun wildly, hoping that maybe her eyes deceived her the first time around. But no, he was not in the camouflaging greenery. Maybe she could call out to him? But what would that accomplish, exactly? Maybe she should run, make a get away as quickly as possible.

Just before Emmy could follow through with her plan, Jason walked around the side of the house with a couple of trowels and a basket. Upon seeing him, she wasn't sure if she should continue with her thoughts or relax. All he had were garden tools and a basket to collect the vegetables. She let out a heavy, abrupt breath before she began to resume her breathing as normally as she could. It took a moment before fear begrudgingly released her from its grasp, and Emmy was somewhat back to normal. Her face was surely red, and she was certain her eyes were still ridden with the terrifying emotion (fear always left the eyes last), but she was safe, at least for now.

Jason pursed his lips and cocked his head to the side as he studied Emmy's somewhat unstable appearance. His eyes scanned every crevice of her skin, as though he was looking for some kind of cause of her reaction. Upon finding absolutely nothing, his eyes reached back into hers, and for whatever reason, Emmy felt herself calm down substantially. Despite the looming rumors that surrounded the secluded author, his eyes were incredibly warm. When they rested on her, Emmy felt safe, which made absolutely no sense, since she was afraid of him. This was a dangerous contradiction, one that could surely place her in a compromising position. She had known from the moment she first looked into them she would have to be aware of them. Now she wished she was still naïve concerning them because they could easily be her downfall.

"Are you all right?" he asked her softly, taking a step toward her. He sounded so genuine that her previous silent accusations seemed ridiculous. And yet, she had to make sure that she couldn't let her guard down. Not around him.

"Yeah," she said, her voice still shaky. There was a cool breeze that gently seemed to massage her hot face, hoping to calm her further. "Yeah, I'm fine."

"Good," he said, smiling. There was something else she needed to be wary of. That smile of his would be a deadly distraction while his eyes took advantage of her disoriented state. What a death – to be killed by beauty. She watched as he looked down at the tools in his hand before looking back up at her. "I'm sure you know what these are," he said with a tone that sounded as if he was teasing her, making some kind of joke. "These are trowels. You use them to dig a hole in the soil to put seeds in, or to dig a stubborn vegetable out." He handed her one, and as before, she took it, making sure she did not brush his fingers with hers. "Today, I want to pick the ripe vegetables."

"Isn't it a little late to do this?" Emmy asked him before she could stop herself. She paused, pressing her brows together. Jason remained silent, as though he knew she was not yet finished with her question. "What I mean is, shouldn't you have already picked the vegetables?"

He smiled at her and nodded a couple of times, causing his messy, dark hair to fall in his face and his glasses to slide down the bridge of his nose. Since he could not readjust both things at the same time, he pushed his glasses up the bridge of his nose and then did the same to his hair. "Yes, actually," he said. "But I prefer them to be picked a little later than usual." He then knelt down and began to inspect his tomatoes rather carefully. After a moment, Jason glanced up at her for a moment. For whatever reason, Emmy felt compelled to kneel down next to him, but as she did so, she made sure there was a safe distance between them. "Now," he continued in his soft-spoken voice, "you can never, ever plant corn and tomatoes together. The combination just doesn't work. However, you can plant tomatoes and carrots together, which is why the maize is a good distance away from the tomatoes and carrots." He paused as his eyes followed the soil that held the roots of the vegetables in place. "There are two types of ways to plant seeds; in flat beds and in raised beds. Personally, I prefer raised beds because I feel that the outcome is much more superfluous than flat beds, but again, that's just me."

It took a moment for Emmy to realize he had stopped talking and instead, focused his attention back on the garden. His voice was comparable to a haunting melody that one would not normally indulge, but could not yet help. It was like a smooth glass of rich, velvet wine that one knew was bad for them, but just the scent caused temptation to win the fight. It was the sole shining light in a dark web, bidding the helpless fly into its clutches before killing them softly. Emmy had been distracted by his voice, and, therefore, did not really hear what he had told her, but let his voice temporarily mystify her senses. This situation she was in was becoming more and more complicated; she was uncovering more and more alluring traits in this man that would surely fog her perception of him if she let them get the better of her. Briefly, she went over her mental check-list of do nots- DO NOT look straight into his eyes, DO NOT become blinded by his smile, DO NOT listen to him speak. This was going to be incredibly exhausting, and it had barely been her second day on the job.

It was then that she noticed that he was staring at her with a slight frown on his soft lips, and his brows were gently pushed together. It was a look of helpless confusion, and with those eyes of his, he reminded Emmy of a lost puppy, simply looking for a home. Emmy had to quickly clear her throat. Why was he looking at her in such a way? Had she caused him some sort of distress? Maybe he thought that she wasn't paying attention to what he had said, which wasn't exactly off the mark...

"You have a lovely garden," she said and offered him a weak smile. His brows slowly relaxed, but the frown remained present on his face. Emmy decided she didn't much like his frown, not because it detracted from his face, but, in reality, added to it. It was like looking at a painting from a different angle; beautiful, yet different at the same time. "Why do you have one, if you don't mind me asking?" She had to ask him something. Yes, she knew very well that it went against her own rule of engaging him in conversation, but she had to make that frown disappear at any cost.

"Well," he began, and his brow re-furrowed. While the frown did not completely vanish, as Emmy was hoping, it turned into a pensive pursing of the lips rather than of confusion. "It was originally my wife's." His brows now pushed together, and Emmy was certain that if she looked directly into his eyes, she would see moving silhouettes reflecting whatever memory seemed to have taken a hold of him. This was crucial for her to study; did he feel guilty at his wife's death, as though he knew what happened to her? Was he angry at her? At himself? But what she found was sadness. And she couldn't really interpret sadness in any way to claim his guilt or innocence. Maybe he missed her, whether he was the cause of her death or not. He attempted a smile right then, the right side of his face cocking up into a small grin, but he wasn't looking at Emmy; he seemed far away from his garden. "She never liked Tahoe. She rather would have stayed in Seattle; she absolutely adored the rain. It was hard for her to find a job, and Stacey always had to do something with her time, so she decided to take up gardening – she had always wanted to. And she got really passionate about it and taught me. So I've been keeping it up ever since..."

He didn't finish, and he didn't need to. His voice just trailed off, as though trying to merge with his unspoken thoughts.

Emmy had no idea what to say. She had never been all that great at reassuring her friends and believed that silence was usually a better statement than words could ever be. At the same time, however, Emmy felt compelled to rid Jason of the new look of sorrow that had taken over his delicate facial features, especially considering she had indirectly caused him to look so forlorn.

"Well, she taught you well," Emmy said, staring intently at the vegetables that occupied his small garden. "They all look very delicious."

From the corner of her eyes, Emmy saw the man smile, albeit lightly, and his eyes were like a pool of blue that were attempting in vain to drown his painful memories, but, at least, he was trying to smile. Emmy wasn't exactly sure at that point if she preferred the frown over the smile. She didn't like either of them, really, because his eyes expressed all that he could not say. In fact, she was surprised he had revealed so much about his wife, and in turn, himself to her, a mere stranger. Maybe he needed to speak to someone. Maybe he needed a lifeline.

But Emmy couldn't be that for him.

"So how do you like Tahoe?" he asked her as he began to pick certain vegetables with a tool Emmy hadn't noticed before. The vegetables he did choose to remove, he placed in the basket he brought.

Emmy wasn't sure if she should be helping him, so she pretended to look carefully at each vegetable, but despite how juicy they looked, she refrained from picking them. Jason seemed attached to his garden, and she did not want to upset him if she picked the wrong vegetable in the wrong way. Her eyes studied each one, and she began to play a game that would help her learn more about the art of gardening; she tried guessing which vegetables he would pick.

"It's quiet," Emmy said, and before she realized it, she felt a very small smile gently touch her lips. He stopped what he was doing and glanced at her, the same kind of smile adorned on his face. She dared to raise her eyes in order to meet his, but she couldn't hold his stare and had to look away. "I'm from Newport Beach – Southern California. I moved up here after I graduated high school to be with my grandfather in San Francisco. I really like the suburbs, the city; the noise lets me know that there are other people around me, and I feel safe."

"Are you afraid of being alone?" Jason asked her, peering at her. He took the round tomato and gently placed it in the basket so it would not bruise, but instead of continuing to remove the ready vegetables, he placed his hand in the soil and pushed his weight on it so that he was looking at her fully now.

"No," Emmy said, shook her head, keenly avoiding his eyes. "I mean, I don't think so. I would be fine living in an apartment by myself if I knew there were people around. As long as I heard cars driving by, day or night, I'd be fine."

He chuckled and shook his head. "You're odd," he murmured, his eyes glancing at the soil that surrounded his hand. Emmy could not help the surprised outburst of laughter that flew past her lips if she tried. No one had called her odd since middle school, maybe high school. It sounded so weird coming from this man. Jason watched her and started laughing with her. It was a sound unlike anything Emmy had ever heard before; light and crisp, like the wings of a butterfly. And when merged with hers, it sounded like a song too long unsung. Abruptly she stopped; it was too much to take right now. He soon followed suit, but he was still smiling.

"I came here for the seclusion," Jason said, finally looking away from her and at his garden. "There were too many distractions in Seattle and I felt blocked. I would sit in front of my computer and stare at the blank screen, but no matter what, nothing would come. Words that used to flow so freely from my fingertips reached some sort of obstacle." He paused, his brow furrowing, and he gently nibbled the bottom of his lip. "Stacey was always off somewhere, doing... something. I got the seclusion I wanted, but my muse seems to have left me."

Emmy had always been curious about how the process of writing worked. There were so many ideas out there, and it was interesting to see which author accumulated which idea, put it on paper, and sold it. She was also incredibly interested in the whole inspiration thing; she would never admit it aloud, but she loved the sort of story where a love story inspired a romance or vice versa. But she supposed music would suffice, maybe even something elemental, like rain. Or visual, like fresh snow. She wondered what his muse had been, before, of course, it had left him.

"Can you get it back?" she asked, cocking her head to the side.

He turned and looked at her. "Some authors will say that lack of inspiration is an excuse of justifying not writing," he told her, "and I agree with them to a point. But having a muse makes it so much easier. When you have a muse, it feels like your sole purpose on this planet is to write this story. Nothing can stop you. No distractions will sway you. It's one of the best feelings of the world." He paused, and the happy light that cascaded his eyes dimmed a bit. "But once you lose that muse, you're stuck. Words come out, but they feel like they came from someone else. It's crap. It's horrible, and you wonder how you came up with something so bad when just the day before, words came freely, like a fountain of water forever producing liquid. I don't know if you can ever regain the same muse once it's lost, but sooner or later, one comes back, and the process starts over again."

"How long have you gone without one?" Emmy asked curiously, genuinely. Whatever fear she had had long disappeared. He was distracting her, but at this moment, she did not seem to care.

"A very long while now," Jason replied, sitting up now and running his finger through his hair.

"Maybe you're concentrating too hard," Emmy mused aloud, her eyes returning to the colorful vegetables. Jason looked at her with an interested gaze, but said nothing. He seemed to have known that she was not yet finished with what she was going to say but did not press her. He had incredible patience, she noticed. "Maybe a muse is kind of like a butterfly. You have to hold on to it, but hold too hard and you'll kill it. I think you should do something that has nothing to do with writing. Maybe then you'll find your muse." With every word, Emmy's face began to get darker and darker with redness because, in all honesty, she had no idea what she was talking about. But whenever she had to write something for her creative writing class, she found that distancing herself from writing actually helped her write.

Jason looked at her, somewhat intently. A few of his long fingers gently caressed his chin and his lips pursed, but not into a frown. His eyes seemed to consume hers, and Emmy found that try as she might, she could not look away. If it were any other person looking at her like that, she might feel uncomfortable, but ironically enough, she didn't. Despite her own warnings, she found that she liked the way it felt when his eyes were upon her. She also liked looking at him. His obvious beauty provided millions of different things for her to continuously notice; it reminded her of a painting, where each time she looked upon it, she noticed something different yet just as beautiful. The guilt that usually accompanied these feelings was lacking, for whatever reason, so she tried to conjure up some and failed to do so.

"That's a good idea," he murmured, and Emmy could have sworn he was blushing, something that, until now, Emmy had deemed impossible. She even blinked a couple of times, making sure that it was not her mind playing tricks on her. "I'm completely embarrassed that I didn't think of it sooner." He smiled softly then and his fixated back on his vegetables. "Maybe I'll go into town..."

"The people in town don't like you." The phrase slipped out of her mouth before she could stop it. Without even thinking, the young woman clamped her mouth shut with her hand, hoping that it would prevent any further embarrassment, and prayed that she would still have her job in the next five minutes. Her cheeks had colored substantially, and she was sure that if she shaped her body into a round circle, she could very easily blend in with the tomatoes.

Well, it's true, a very quiet voice inside an isolated place in her mind tried to reassure her. *Nobody likes him. It's not your fault...*

"No," he stated simply, quietly as he pushed his glasses back up the bridge of his nose. "They don't like me, do they? Which is why I have acquired you as my ally. They don't know that you're working for me, and as such, they won't give you that much of a hassle."

"You're wrong," Emmy said, upon realizing that, no, he was *not* actually mad at her. "I don't think they like me either. Somehow, they found out that I was working for you and they weren't really friendly when I confirmed it."

"Well, that places us in the same boat," Jason murmured, dropping a carrot into the basket. "At least we're together then."

Emmy forced a smile and nodded a couple of times, but otherwise remained silent. A cool breeze had crept upon them and was gently caressing the waves of her hair, beckoning them back over her shoulder with gentle whispers. The leaves of the trees ruffled each other as the branches swayed, the crisping sound of the leaves providing the melody to an otherwise silent song. The sun, now up, hid behind the tops of the trees, only allowing a few rays to break through the forest's shield. It would seem even the sun was upset at the thought that Mister Jason Belmont had a companion in his seclusion.

"Well, I think we've salvaged as much as we can right now," Jason stated, and pushed himself up into a standing position. Emmy followed suit, and as she stood, her limbs burned in pain; she must have sat there in that position for longer than she first assumed. Who knew that spending time with Jason Belmont could pass the time?

Emmy wiped off the back of her jeans, trying to rid herself of any dirt before grabbing her warm hoodie. She followed Jason as he headed back towards the house. As she watched him, she began to notice habits of his. For whatever reason, his head was always down, either because he was trying to decode a pattern in the ground, or because his hair provided an excellent sort of hiding place. His right hand securely held the basket, and Emmy could see that despite his oddities, he was quite strong, as evidenced by his prominent bicep. Even Emmy had to applaud such fine sculpture. However, his other arm was relaxed by his side save for his wrist; it was tense, and as a result, his hand stuck out and his index and middle finger rubbed against each other. Maybe he was in dire need of a cigarette. Finally, his steps were bigger than necessary, but not dramatically so. Emmy figured he must have spent a good portion of his life in New York, for he had adopted a determined sort of stride. All in all, it was fascinating for Emmy to watch all of Jason's oddities; he could very easily be a character of his own story, and what a fascinating read he would be.

When they reached the house, Jason quickly turned around, surprising Emmy so suddenly that she nearly ran into him. Her instincts were nothing to brag about, but she was sure that after cohabiting with this man, they would be sharpened. She managed to stop herself just in time and did not fight off the questioning look on her face as she regarded him with silence.

"I would like to cook dinner tonight," he said, and with that, he turned around and headed back to the kitchen, expecting no such questions to arise from such a simple statement.

While Jason headed into the kitchen, Emmy decided that this would be the perfect time to take her own tour of the house now that its owner was temporarily distracted with his task. She stood idly in the living room, her hands on her hips, wondering if Jason could cook. Would he ask her for help, or would she be free to do as she liked for the better part of an hour? Her eyes surveyed the empty room and a frown found its way onto her face. She had already known that he was isolated, but beside the necessary furniture, the room was vacant. There wasn't even a television, which wasn't exactly a bad thing, but it just furthered his disconnection to the outside world. How would he keep in touch with what's going around him? Taking a few steps toward the couch, her eyes rested on the large piece of furniture. It was an eyesore, from the bold pattern to the scattered rips and holes. There were two cushions that might have originally blended well with the couch, but through time, had transformed into something quite different and awful as well. There was a groove in the couch, probably caused by Jason sleeping there rather than his bedroom. The telephone was still resting on the coffee table, and there were a couple of shelves on the wall opposite the couch, filled with books. As Emmy stepped closer, she realized that they were *his* books, Jason's books.

She couldn't stop herself. The young woman reached her arm

out and plucked a book with her fingers from its resting place. It looked like some sort of spy psychological thriller. Flipping it open, she flipped through the first couple of pages but stopped when she caught sight of the dedication page. There, in italics, it read, *To my loving wife Stacey, May you always be my muse.* She pursed her lips; how could this woman find comfort in another man's arms? He obviously loved her very much, had a very good career, and was very handsome. Yet, as usual, she knew there was more to their story than such simplicities and quickly snapped the book closed, as well as any further inquiries her mind might make.

Emmy turned and walked down a very small hallway. There was no other bedroom downstairs, but there was a bathroom, and right across from that, a nearly empty closet. All that was inside were a couple of coats and an umbrella.

Well then.

Emmy then decided to head upstairs. A squeak cried out from under her foot as she stepped on the third step, but this time, her focus was on what she wanted to accomplish. Instead of heading into her room, however, she took a right down the hallway. Passing Jason's office, she continued to walk down the hall. There was a larger bathroom, complete with a bathtub/shower instead of just a mere toilet. Just across the hall was his room, and much to Emmy's surprise, the door was halfway open. Her brows perked at the mere notion of peeking into the very private room of a very private man.

Don't do it, Emmy, a voice cautioned, but her feet refused to listen, and continued ever-so-delicately to head into the room.

Emmy slid through the opening and was surprised to find it rather ordinary. Even she couldn't deny her disappointment; she was hoping for unclean blades and blood splatter, maybe even a stained raincoat similar to Patrick Bateman's. Her eyes moved swiftly; there was a very unkempt king-sized bed in the center of the room, a window with a lovely view of the forest, a bookshelf, a desk, and a closet. However, her search did not go completely unwarranted. On a nightstand adjacent to the left side of the bed, there was a framed photograph faced towards the bed.

You're on thin ice, Emmy, the voice murmured. *What if he catches you here? What will you do then?*

"I'll jump out the window," Emmy murmured back, as her feet, on their own accord, of course, continued to head in the direction of the photograph.

She took a seat on the bed as well as a deep breath before reaching for the picture. Her fingers shook, and she wasn't sure if it was due to excitement or fear. However, neither emotion seemed to stop her, and she continued to wrap her fingers around the simple black frame and held it so that she could see it more clearly. It was a wedding picture. There was Jason, much younger, but still incredibly handsome, smiling a smile Emmy had never seen and hoped to never encounter. It was one of pure happiness, blinding in its beauty. If she wasn't already in love with him, she would most certainly be if she saw it even for a mere second. Standing next to him in a simple white wedding dress was Stacey, or so Emmy assumed, and she was just as lovely as he was. She had dark, curly long hair and a very petite frame. Emmy began to feel self-conscious just looking at it, but she couldn't bring herself to feel any jealousy at Stacey's beauty because her crystal blue eyes and her bright smile revealed a kindness about her. No wonder he had fallen in love with her, and no wonder why she had fallen in love with him.

So what happened?

"Emmy."

Emmy jumped and nearly dropped the photograph onto the floor. Her heart rivaled that of the newest sports car in the fact that it jumped from steady to accelerating in two seconds flat. He was right behind her, probably staring at her back, deciding which artery he could pierce. She pressed her lips together and placed the frame back onto its place, on the nightstand. Slowly, she forced herself to turn and regard him. Her fear was not easy to mask, and as such, decided not to even try.

"Dinner's ready."

That was all he said before he turned and walked away. Emmy didn't know how to react because for the life of her, she had no idea how he reacted to seeing her in his room with a very intimate photograph.

CHAPTER 4

The next day, after breakfast, Jason headed upstairs to no doubt to continue to stare at another blank screen for the majority of the day. Since being caught in his room looking at his wedding photograph, Emmy had been on her guard, waiting for Jason to lash out verbally, or worse. However, during dinner and breakfast, he was completely like himself; calm and awkward, if a little more quiet than usual. When she was sure that he was upstairs, she decided to head outside and check on the garden. After grabbing the basket Jason used yesterday, she slipped out the door as quietly as she could and walked around the side of the house. The weather was beautiful today though a bit chilly if Emmy was being honest. Luckily, she had planned for the cold and had thrown on her hoodie over her clothes. The sky was painted with heavy white clouds that successfully hid the majority of the sun, but it would seem that the sun did not mind too much. There was no breeze, but due to the forestry surrounding the small house, there was a lot of shade.

The garden looked as it had yesterday. She set down the basket and then plopped down next to it, curling a strand of hair behind her ear. Her eyes flitted over the vegetables, staring at them idly, not exactly sure why she was out here. No, that was a lie. She was outside because she felt that she needed to get out of the house. There was a tension, however slight it might be, that had grown between Emmy and Jason due to her reckless behavior last night. At least here, she did not have to worry about such tension; she actually enjoyed being outdoors.

However, as her eyes skimmed the garden once again, she realized that she had no idea how to decipher a ripe vegetable from a nearly-ripe vegetable from a not-even-close vegetable. Emmy didn't want to guess and choose wrong, ruining his garden in a way, and preventing any chance to let the vegetables in need of growth to ripen. Pursing her lips, she sighed through her nose, and then finally let out a frustrated sigh. Well, now what was she to do? She didn't want to go back in the house, in fear that Jason decided to get angry with her when she walked through the door, but she had nothing to do outside. She would never venture into the forest for fear that she would get lost, and she didn't want to head into town because she was in no mood to get lectured about being in the company of an alleged murderer. To put it frankly, she was stuck.

A snap caught her attention, and Emmy jumped, startled, and peered over her shoulder, expecting to see Jason Belmont with an ax or a butcher knife, standing right behind her. But no, she could see nothing. How odd. Emmy craned her neck and shifted her position so that she could easily look behind her. However, with the forest so thick and the sun mostly blotted out, it was hard to see through the shadows and darkness. If there was something in the forest, she could not see it.

Emmy yawned and then looked up at the sky sleepily. She wondered how her grandfather was, if he was getting along okay without her. But he wasn't really ever alone now, was he? He had Bingo, their chubby Australian Shepherd that was incredibly loyal and protective. The majority of his fur was black, with brown scattered throughout his fur. White consumed his chest, as well as the tips of his paws, and like all Australian Shepherds, Bingo had no tail, but a tiny little nub in its stead. Emmy was very close with Bingo, just as she was close with her grandfather. She felt tears prick the inside of her eyes as she reflected upon them; she missed them dearly.

Another snap caused her shoulders to jump and a tear to slip down her cheek in surprise. Quickly, she wiped it away and she stood, preparing to defend herself from whatever it was that caused the noise. Her brow was furrowed, and she felt herself become slightly angry that someone or something had unnerved her as she was thinking about her close-knit family. She did not appreciate people sneaking up on her when she was in such a vulnerable state; she preferred privacy due to the fear that people might know exactly what she was thinking, and she did not want people to know.

She whirled around, staring back in the forest, but there was just blackness, thickness, forestry. Her eyes flashed frustration, and her fingers curled so that her hands were balled into fists. Was Jason playing tricks on her in retaliation for yesterday? Was he trying to scare her? If he was, he was going about it the wrong way, for Emmy was becoming quite angry instead of quite scared.

"Show yourself," she murmured as her eyes narrowed. "Let's get this over with."

Then, a shuffle pierced Emmy's ear, as though feet were treading on autumn leaves. Emmy felt her body tense due to her flight-or-fight reaction, and she realized, although it was slightly off-subject, that she was going to fight rather than walk away. This caused a very small, proud smile to slip onto her face. If she were being honest, she would have thought she would run rather than fight only because she didn't really engage in fights, and really didn't like to when she had to. She was quite good with persuasion, however, and she was also relatively quick on her feet. But here she was, her body rigid, prepared to take on whatever it was that had been scaring her.

The shuffling continued to get louder and louder until Emmy saw a silhouette start to emerge from the trees. However, it was rather short, and for a moment, Emmy thought it might have been a child that had gotten lost on a trail and ended up in a forest. It continued towards her, and to her surprise, a very skinny dog came out of the darkness. It (for Emmy had yet to notice if the dog was a boy or a girl yet) was brown, with different sizes of blotchy, black spots plopped onto different places of its fur, like big, black ink spots that stained his fur from a careless master. Its eyes were brown and his ears were squared shape, in the same manner as a Chow's. Its tale was long and skinny, and upon noticing Emmy, it pointed straight out, its ears perked up, and one paw was held up as though it was unsure of what to do. Should it venture towards Emmy, or head back into the woods? Emmy wasn't quite sure what sort of dog it was, although she was certain it was some sort of mutt. At first, she believed the dog belonged to Jason, but upon further inspection of its skinny body, she noticed bones protruding from its skin and figured that this dog was indeed a stray.

Her first instinct was, of course, to feed it. Looking at her with those big brown eyes, the dog was already melting Emmy's heart, although if Emmy was being honest, such a thing concerning any dog, any animal for that matter, was quite easy to do. However, her mind began to argue with her pulled heartstrings, reminding her that if she did do such a kind act of charity, the dog would begin to expect such a thing and come back to the house. Normally, this wouldn't have bothered Emmy all that much because she loved dogs too much to care if a stray continued to come back, begging for food (she might have even preferred that it did), but this wasn't exactly her house, and as such, it really wasn't her decision to commit to the dog. First off, who knew if Jason would actually *want* a stray dog lounging around the perimeter of his home, or if he even liked dogs, for that matter? Not that he would notice, however; he was always up in that office of his, staring at nothing, and probably developing cancer by doing so. Secondly, it was also Jason's food she would be using to satiate the dog, and she wasn't sure Jason would approve if he saw that Emmy was using the food he paid for to aid a dog that didn't actually belong to him.

Well, it didn't actually matter, though, did it? She was going to feed the dog no matter what. Emmy ran her tongue over her lips and the dog tilted its head to the side. Their eyes were still locked, and Emmy moved her arms. The dog raised its brow at this, but did not move, and slowly, Emmy put her arms down, hoping the dog would know the signal to stay. Then, Emmy slowly began to back up, wary that she would scare the dog before finally turning around and all but bursting into the house.

Her feet led her directly to the kitchen, and she threw open the refrigerator. What would be fit for a dog to eat? All right, immediately cross of fruits, vegetables, and chocolates... no eggs, obviously... Did they have sandwich meat? She moved some things around in the fridge and found the last of the round slices of turkey. After she grabbed them, she closed the refrigerator door and was about to head outside when she realized she should probably give it some water as well. For a moment, she placed the turkey package down and grabbed a small bowl from the cupboard, quickly filling it up with water. When she was satisfied, she grabbed both items and headed back outside.

Much to Emmy's astonishment, the dog was still in the same position it had been when it first noticed Emmy, and upon seeing her coming back, its hair, along with its body, tensed.

"Here, doggie," she murmured softly, hoping that she would not scare it. "I've got some food for you... Would you like some food?"

Emmy froze in her former position outside, not quite sure if she should approach it or if she should wait for it to approach her. She bit her lip and then carefully placed the water bowl down on the dirt next to her, and then slipped the turkey out of the package. While she didn't move from her stance, she reached out her arm as far as it would go, hoping the dog would catch its scent and come closer to her. Upon seeing the food, the dog shifted its brown eyes from Emmy to the meat, and unconsciously licked its lips. However, it did not move, at least not yet; it was as though the dog was as unsure as Emmy was.

The dog lowered its head, and Emmy could see its nose twitching, so she was sure it could smell the food she was offering it. Boldly, she took one step forward, hoping to go unnoticed by the dog, but failing miserably. Seeing her move caused the dog's body to snap into action, and tense again. However, it would seem to dog's curiosity currently outweighed any fear it might have had. Emmy, of course, was frozen on the spot, not exactly sure if she should move again or not. They stayed like this for a long time, for in a frozen position three minutes feels like three hours. A little voice in Emmy's head, however, was growing impatient.

Why don't you just throw a piece of meat at him? it suggested. *Then maybe once it realizes your intentions, it'll be more comfortable with you.*

That sounded like a good idea, so Emmy threw one piece of turkey at the dog. The dog's ears jumped upon seeing the flying meat, and it caught it in its mouth, devouring it greedily. Immediately after swallowing it, the dog darted off, back into the dark forest. Before Emmy fully comprehended what she was doing, exactly, she began to follow him, insistent on feeding him the second piece of meat. Two would surely not fatten him up, but then again, two pieces were better than one. However, as though the dog knew she was following him, it continued to run. And for whatever reason, Emmy began to follow it into the forest she promised she wouldn't enter, at least alone.

--

How long had he been sitting there? How long had his screen been a pure, white blank page? His long fingers were draped over his lips, his back was somewhat slouched, his thick-rimmed glasses slid down the bridge of his nose until it hung on the flare of his nostrils, his brows were pushed together, and his lips, though covered, were pursed. This was his usual position, or, at least, it had been for the past few months. He had a couple of pages with introductions and dialogue, but for whatever reason, they were never good enough. How many thrillers had he written before this? Shouldn't this come easy to him, or had he used all he had concerning somewhat similar plots? Maybe he should switch gears, write a horror story instead of his usual choice of genre?

His dark eyes rolled over to his window, the sunlight hidden by blinds with only rays peeking through the spaces. Jason stood up, and using his fingers, he pushed the middle portion of the blinds down until his eyes sought out what he was looking for. Emmy Atler was outside, looking at something in the forest. He couldn't quite make out what she was looking at exactly, but he didn't particularly care. If he was being honest, he really liked simply looking at her. She was very attractive, and yet he doubted that she even knew it. The clothes she wore were more for comfort rather than style, and her hair was either tumbling down her back or tossed in a messy ponytail or a bun. Her reaction to his presence was quite amusing, if not fascinating. He was pretty sure that she had heard of his trial, of the charges brought against him (and later dismissed), and she was obviously frightened of him. How could she think that he would ever hurt her? That would be like harming a butterfly, something so fragile and yet so beautiful.

He wasn't exactly sure how she perceived him, however. When he had walked into his bedroom and found her sitting in his bedroom looking at his old wedding photograph of him and Stacey, he startled her unintentionally. He wasn't sure how he felt, seeing her there, watching her look at something that he felt was incredibly private. Jason wasn't angry or offended, but he did not want her to see that photo. There were times he missed Stacey, but then he remembered what she had done to him, how everything he worked so hard for crumbled into pieces right before his eyes. When she died, she took his muse with him. In fact, he wasn't exactly sure why he still had the picture out. And Emmy looked up with those big eyes of hers, full of fear, that any anger that might have bubbled inside of him, immediately dissipated. How could he be angry with her?

Jason released the blinds and sat back down. He brought his chair closer to his desk and began typing. Characters never came easily for him; it was plot he was good at, but for whatever reason, a description flew through his fingertips, and his typing became almost furious. It was of a woman he was writing about; she was lost, alone, and very beautiful, but naturally so. Whatever sparked this burst of inspiration, he did not know, but as soon as it hit him, it spread like wildfire, and soon, he had an idea which was coming alive on his page. The screen was not blank anymore.

It seemed like hours when he finally finished the first chapter, but he smiled, feeling incredibly accomplished. He hadn't even taken a cigarette break. He sat back, his eyes scanning the screen as though he couldn't quite believe that he had written anything, let alone a full chapter. A small smile had touched his lips and his fingers interlocked and rested behind his head. However, he still wasn't exactly sure how this story was going to turn out, but that didn't bother him as of yet. Briefly, he wondered what time it was. He really should keep some sort of clock in here, but he didn't want to get distracted by the ticking of a clock. It was then he remembered there was one in the very corner of his laptop. Hmm... one o'clock. At that moment, his stomach rumbled noisily, reminding him that he needed to eat. Maybe Emmy had lunch ready and didn't want to disturb him.

After saving his document at least three times, Jason stood up. His legs hurt, and he made a note to himself to make sure to get up and walk around a little as he wrote. However, it was easier said than done, because once he was in the zone, it was hard to remind him of anything else. He stood for a moment, letting feeling resume in his lower body, and stretched as he felt a yawn coming on. Then he pushed his glasses up the bridge of his nose and ran his fingers through his hair before heading down the stairs.

When he entered the kitchen, however, Emmy was not inside cooking, as he expected her to be. He furrowed his brow and then headed into the living room. She was not there either. Maybe she was in her room...? It was then that he noticed how quiet his house really was. He had always been used to the silence, but now that there was a second person living with him, the silence seemed to get louder. He headed upstairs, checked every room, but Emmy was not there.

Where, then, could she be?

Maybe she was outside? He ran his fingers through his hair once again and pushed his door open, stepping outside. The sun's rays, though somewhat hidden behind the tall trees that surrounded his quaint home still made his eyes wince. He scrunched his nose, and raised his arm over his head, hoping to block out the blinding rays as he took a couple of steps, moving his head to the left and the right, but seeing no young woman or any sort of evidence of if she had been here. Chewing the bottom of his lip, he finally let his arm fall back to his side once he got used to the light and took a couple more paces to the right. He decided to circle the house, making sure to cover his entire basis, and made a personal decision to not think about what to do if it turned out that she was not there. Jason took his time as he traced the perimeter of his house. Instead of keeping his eyes on the ground, as he usually did, his blue eyes scanned whatever was directly in front of him.

When he got to his garden, Jason stopped walking. No, she was not at his garden but it appeared that she had been. A bowl of water was sitting there temporarily forgotten with dust particles already gathering on the surface. He knelt down and pursed his lips. Underneath the bowl of water was a discarded empty turkey package, as though Emmy had wanted to make sure the package didn't blow away. She probably wanted to throw it away instead of littering. He smiled at the sheer thoughtfulness of the action, but he wasn't as happy as he could be. Emmy was still gone, or at least, she wasn't found yet, and he wanted to know why, where she was, and if she was coming back.

Jason tilted his head so that his focus was on the forest in front of him. She couldn't possibly be in the forest, could she? She was new to his property, new to Tahoe, really. It would be dangerous for her to go running off into the forest without someone who was familiar with the terrain, without him. He felt his stress level raising a fraction, and pushed his fingers between the locks of his hair, but instead of running them through, he gripped them albeit somewhat gently. Should he follow her? How did he know she really was in the forest? And if she was, why would she go in there if she knew she could most probably get lost there? Did she choose to leave? Was she forced...? No, she would have screamed, wouldn't she? And he didn't see any signs of a struggle.

Jason chuckled at his law enforcement-like thoughts. He had written too many thrillers, hadn't he? He shook his head and decided to finish his circle of the house. Maybe she had just wanted to go for a walk, and she hadn't asked him because she hadn't wanted to disturb him. If this was so, the thought made him smile. Stacey was almost always bothering him, at least twice, when he holed himself up in his office to work. While some writers might not have been thrown by this, he was. He needed peace and quiet to fuel his concentration. She would ask him minuscule things, such as what he wanted for dinner, if he was going to the grocery store, and other questions that could have waited until he was done. He had told her not to bother him, but maybe that was in her nature, maybe she just really needed loving attention from him. And maybe if he had given it to her, she wouldn't have run off with... But he didn't want to think about that anymore.

As he headed back inside, a sudden thought struck him. Emmy... hadn't run away from him, did she? He headed up the stairs and into her room. No, all of her stuff was still here. Jason meant to leave upon realizing this, but instead of taking a step back, he took a step forward. Her room was very clean, very empty in a way. A laptop was on a dresser, and a couple of books, a framed photograph and a cell phone were all on the nightstand next to her bed. He took a seat on the bed, facing the beautiful view out the triangular-shaped window, and was immediately hit with a very subtle scent of vanilla and cinnamon. This was what she smelled like, he realized. A soft smile touched his lips. He rather liked this scent.

Jason's eyes caught sight of the photo and decided to have a look at it. He rationalized that she had pretty much done the same to him, and it was only fair that he check her out as well. Jason shook his head; he did not usually do things like this. In fact, he was a very private person himself, but his desire seemed to outweigh propriety at the moment, and he took the frame in his hand so he could look upon it more thoroughly. It was of her and her grandfather, and judging from the deep, royal blue robe and a matching, square cap with a tassel hanging from the center of it, it was her high school graduation photograph. Her colorful eyes were heightened due to the black eyeliner, and her lips were pulled into the most genuine smile he had ever seen. She looked so incredibly happy, and he wanted to see such a smile in real life. Better than that, he realized he wanted to be the cause of such happiness. The two seemed to be on a field, probably a football field, and the picture was probably taken after the ceremony due to the similar situations concerning her colleagues seen in the background and posing for similar pictures.

He let out a sigh and placed the photo back down on the nightstand. Jason had never really thought about love, or even attraction since Stacey had left him. He had isolated himself from society, couldn't stand the questioning and the judgmental looks anymore. If people didn't want him around, if people didn't want him shopping, or getting gas, or anything like that, then he was happy to withdraw in seclusion. He wanted to write in private anyways, and it was nice not to have the phone constantly ringing or people continuously knocking on his front door. How long had it been since Stacey's... disappearance? Two years ago? How different he had been then. In all honesty, he never thought he would meet somebody. He thought love would elude him, and was quite content with the thought. How could anyone love him given the general perception people had of him?

And then she walked through his door. Emmy was unlike anyone he had ever met. It was true, however, that it did not exactly appear that she was falling head over heels for him, but the fact that she took his job, the fact that she had stood up for him at the supermarket, that all meant that she wasn't going to hold society's perceptions of him against him per se. Maybe if he showed her who he really was, she might actually like him, they might actually be friends, maybe even more... He chuckled at this thought. Yeah, as though somebody like her could actually be interested in someone like him. Someone who went on trial for killing his estranged wife and her lover. The thought was actually a joke. Shaking his head, he took a seat slowly at his kitchen table. He had walked to the kitchen after exploring her room. A part of him hoped she hadn't run away. She was his key to society, and now that she had entered his life, he hoped she wouldn't quickly depart it.

--

Currently, Emmy Atler was somewhere where she was not expected to be; she was in a tree, her eyes scanning the surrounding forest. She had sticky turkey in her hand that she had actually put in her mouth so she was even capable of climbing the tree, and still it was there because both of her arms were securely wrapped around the trunk of the tree. When she was younger, she had been an expert at such at such physical activities, and whenever her grandfather had visited, he always took her to the local park (Mariner's Park in Newport Beach) where he made sure she did a round on the monkey bars and a climb in the trees. Her parents were worried at such daring behavior for a girl of seven, but her grandfather had always assured them that she would always be safe with him, no matter what. And to this day, it had remained so.

The stray dog that had run from her had yet to return, and she had been searching for a good half an hour. The turkey was starting to stain her tongue with its taste, and in all honesty, Emmy had never really favored turkey, especially not old turkey that had been soaking in the sun for a good portion of time. Quickly and carefully, Emmy whipped the turkey from her lips and dropped it on the ground. She made a face as she tried to rid her mouth of the residue the meat had left and then began to cautiously make her way down. It would seem the dog had disappeared, had left her to fend for herself. All she had wanted to do was feed the stray some food. Now, as she looked around, she realized she should have thought a bit before heading off into the forest.

Emmy glanced around, hoping for some sort of helpful hint that might lead her back to Jason Belmont's house, but all she could see were trees. And though she should know better, it appeared that all the trees looked remarkably similar. She nibbled on her bottom lip as her eyes scanned her surroundings once again. There was no doubt about it; she was screwed. She took a step forward, and then another, but stopped and shook her head, second-guessing her initial choice of direction. Emmy ran her fingers through her hair and knelt down, feeling a sense of hopelessness surround her. What was she going to do? Tears began to blur her vision, but for some reason, they would not fall.

"Hello!"

The young woman froze. Was that a voice she just heard? It had sounded clear, distinct, with sophistication added to her tone. She wasn't hearing things now, was she? She wasn't hallucinating, was she? She turned slowly, wishing she didn't have to humor the voice, still unsure of its origins, but she froze when she saw it was not in vain.

There was a woman, probably in her late fifties or early sixties. She was dressed as though she had been raised in Tahoe, with durable clothes rather than fashionable. Her long, grey hair was swept up into a high ponytail and there was basic makeup on her face. While her demeanor might come off as somewhat astute, her honey-colored-eyes were filled with warmth as she gazed upon Emmy with a sense of sympathy.

"Hi," Emmy said, letting out a breath. She silently prayed that this was not some sort of hallucination and that an older woman really was in the middle of the forest with her.

"Are you the woman who took the job for Jason Belmont?" the older woman inquired. Emmy raised a brow, unsure of where this conversation was leading, slowly, she answered with a nod. Her body was tense, not certain if she should stay where she was, or make a break for it and take her chances deeper into the forest. However, the older woman smiled at Emmy's answer, accumulating even more warmth to her face. "I am glad to hear that. I was wondering if you might like to join me for a cup of tea? Afterwards, I would be happy to escort you back to his residence."

"I really should go..." Emmy said, not quite meeting her eyes, but the woman interrupted her.

"I insist," she said, her face still friendly. "I know Belmont just as I'm sure as you do. He's probably sitting up in that office of his, smoking a cigarette, and staring at a blank page. He probably won't even know you're gone." She paused, and perked her brow as she said, "Please?"

CHAPTER 5

Emmy watched with wonder as the woman led her through the labyrinth that was also known as the forest Emmy had so recently been lost in. The woman, who had introduced herself as Mrs. Franzsky, seemed to have lived here her whole life. Not even the similar surroundings seemed to daunt her; when she walked, she did so with determination and ease, as though she knew exactly where she was and how to get to where she was going.

Emmy wasn't sure if she should envy the older woman or not. While it was valuable to understand and be thoroughly familiar with the surroundings, the experience was not gained overnight. Mrs. Franzsky must have gotten lost in these woods a time or two, probably even more than that. And now she was here, leading Emmy through bushes and thistles, around thick trees, and warning the younger woman to be wary of upturned roots so she wouldn't trip over them. Emmy quickly lost track of time as she followed the older woman; how long had she been wandering around, looking for the stray dog? How long had she and her rescuer been in the forest, attempting to make an exit? How long had she been away from Jason's home, and would he really not notice her missing presence?

Now's not the time to worry about that now, Emmy, she thought to herself. *Just concentrate on familiarizing yourself with the forest.*

Mrs. Franzsky led Emmy to a quaint cottage, somewhat similar to Jason's home. However, this cottage was made more of stones while Jason's was a combination of wood, plaster, and brick. The cottage was smaller than Jason's home and did not appear to have any sort of garden attached to any side of the house. However, while there was no garden, there was an abundance of colorful wildflowers in a variety of different colors, still in bloom. It definitely gave the cottage a sort of Renaissance vibe, and Emmy felt warm, welcomed, immediately at home in this place.

After fishing for her keys and unlocking the door, Mrs. Franzsky opened the door to her home and held it open so Emmy could enter first. Once the young woman was safely inside, she followed suit and shut the door behind her. The first thing Emmy noticed upon walking into the cottage was the large fireplace in the center of the living room. Emmy had always had a soft spot for fireplaces; she loved scooting as close as she could to the flames at night, with a good book and reading for as long as her eyes would let her. And judging by the books that seemed to overload her shelves, it would appear Mrs. Franzsky dabbled in the same pastime Emmy did.

"Have a seat," Mrs. Franzsky instructed warmly, gesturing at the couch across from the fireplace. "I want to hear all about you! My, my, when I saw the ad in the local paper for this position, I didn't think anybody would actually agree to take it." Her eyes narrowed immediately as she took a seat across from Emmy, in a nice, cushy armchair. "You aren't any sort of reporter or private eye or something, are you? Because if you are, then let me escort you right back out now. I don't take too kindly to people trying to exploit my neighbor when all he wants to do is write in peace."

"Oh, no, no, no, ma'am," Emmy said, shaking her head as a faint blush crawled onto her cheeks. "No, I'm not a reporter or a cop or anything like that."

"Then why'd you take the job?" the older woman asked, arching a perfectly plucked brow and looking unabashedly at the young woman before her.

"I need the money," Emmy replied honestly. She wasn't ashamed or embarrassed. "My grandfather is a war veteran. He uh..." She could feel her eyes water, and realized how much she really missed her grandfather. Now, she tilted her head, causing waves of hair to tumble down in front of her face to hide the redness that tainted her cheeks. "Well, he can't exactly go to work, and it's uh... well, it's been hard – nearly impossible, really – to pay all of his medical bills along with the other bills that go along with owning a house."

Mrs. Franzsky's face softened, and she handed Emmy a box of tissues that were conveniently placed next to her on a light stand, which also housed a couple of books. "And Jason's offer was quick and paid well," she finished, and nodded as though she understood the girl before her. "Yes, that would make the job more appealing. You've been over there a few days now?" At Emmy's affirmative murmur, Mrs. Franzsky nodded again. "And how has he been treating you?"

"He's very..." Emmy looked up at the ceiling, as though maybe the right word would be up there. "...quiet," she decided. A smile touched her face, satisfied with the diction. "Yes, quiet. He keeps to himself. But he's never been... mean, or anything." She chewed her bottom lip, unsure of how to word her next question. Then, she just decided to be direct. "Do you think he killed them?"

Mrs. Franzsky laughed at Emmy's abruptness, a gleam that glinted respect towards the young woman. "My, my, I have no idea," she said, shaking her head. Not one strand slipped out of her ponytail, however. "Jason, before Stacey died, was such a warm, friendly person. He worked at home and loved leaving little surprises for Stacey whenever she came back from work. He was such a romantic. A few months leading up to Stacey's death, he began to change. I'm not sure if it was because he found out about her affair, or if it was due to the pressure of his new book. From what I hear, he would be holed up late at night, well into the morning. Who knows when that man would sleep? Who knows if he did? But his sudden reclusive behavior caused Stacey to crave her lover more than ever, and as such, she became more careless. When Jason found out, even if he did do it, his heart broke into a thousand pieces. It was reality for him, and ever since the trial, he's fallen into the same sort of destructive pattern." Again, she paused, pursing her lip. Her eyes were intent, thoughtful, as she gazed at the floor beneath her booted feet. "But, I must say," she continued, locking eyes with Emmy, "if he did commit such an act, the two deserved it, I believe."

Emmy's mouth fell open on her own accord, and though she probably should look somewhere else to show some sort of shame at her blunt response and unwavering look, she couldn't bring herself to look away. "I..." She shut her mouth, as though she was attempting to swallow the pointed question that desperately wanted to escape. However, despite such an action, it managed to slip past her lips, fully intent on being heard. "I'm sorry, but are you saying they deserved to die for an affair...?"

There were television shows, movies, and books that used this sort of plot thoroughly, but it was hard for Emmy to wrap her head around this sort of thing in real life. No matter how sweet and how quiet Jason Belmont was, no matter how horrible and conniving his wife and her lover had been, no matter how hurt he was, there was no reason for them to die.

Surprisingly, Mrs. Franzsky did not get defensive, as Emmy originally expected she would. Instead, she smiled a bit and raised her brow, as though even she could not believe that was the stand she was taking. "You haven't been in love ever, have you?" she asked the young woman softly. Emmy felt her body straighten, surprised at such a personal question, and chose to shake her head very slightly. "Love is an interesting feeling, Emmy. It takes the most rational person and makes them... well, goofy, I'd imagine. Personally, I was the good girl, back in my day, and my husband... well, he was the bad boy. Tale as old as time, eh? Good girl falls for bad boy?" Emmy allowed a polite smile to touch her lips but made no comment. "There were many things I thought were so important to me before I met him. Obviously, my family and my education, but selfishly, my collection of Barbie dolls was so incredibly important to me. Well, one day, I went to go watch him race. (Street racing was a big thing back then, you know.) I never really paid much attention to racing, but he had invited me, and so I went. Well, something went wrong. He got into a serious accident and was in the hospital for two weeks. The only time I left his side was to go to school and to go home and sleep. The first few days, they had no idea if he was going to make it; nobody did. I knew I loved him when I wouldn't hesitate to give away my very last Barbie if he would only open his eyes." Her eyes had filled up with unshed tears at her recount of the story, but a smile decorated her face. "And he did." She stopped and scrutinized the young woman in front of her. "I guess what I'm trying to say, dear, is that love changes a person in the best and worst way."

Emmy let everything Mrs. Franzsky told her sink in. She breathed in and out, deeply, trying to process her thoughts and filter out any rash defense phrases. Finally, she said softly yet firmly, "While I understand your point of view, love is not an excuse for murder."

"Oh, of course not!" Mrs. Franzsky agreed in a voice that suggested such a thought was rather preposterous. "Love is definitely not an excuse for such a vile act, but when you feel such an array of emotions that true love comes with, the feeling of killing someone who threatens that love is a tad more understandable." Her eyes twinkle mysteriously, and Emmy could swear she was fighting off a smile. "Now, I have a question for you, my dear. Let us say you are in love with somebody, truly, madly, and deeply. Would you fight for it? Would you fight for your love?"

This time, Emmy had to look away from Mrs. Franzsky's stare. While it was true, Emmy had never been in love before, but there was a hopeless romantic inside of her rationale, kicking and screaming and clawing to be released. She liked to think that when she did fall in love, and when she found the same person to love her back, she would give herself completely, and no matter what, she would fight for him. She would protect him, and maybe even die for him. But she had yet to experience such an intense feeling, and as such, had no idea what she would really do in such a situation. Surely she would not resort to murder...? No, of course not. But, then again, who knew?

"Listen," Mrs. Franzsky said, seeing the conflicting look in Emmy's eyes. "I'm not trying to defend him because, as we both know, murder is inexcusable unless one is defending their family. But I think I could understand his reasoning, if he *did* do such a thing." Mrs. Franzsky then waved nonchalantly, as though she was carelessly trying to wave a fly away from her. "It does not matter, now does it? We don't know if Jason did such a thing, and really, it's none of our business. The only thing that matters is that he's treating you right. He's a very calm and gentle man, Emmy, but very, very lonely. I'm sure you know what I'm talking about since you've been there for a few days now. It breaks my heart seeing the way he lives, without anyone there with him. You working for him is good for him; friendly interaction is always good for an isolated person. And maybe it will turn out to be good for you as well." She shrugged nonchalantly, but her eyes twinkled mysteriously. "You never know."

Emmy pressed her lips together, tilting her head slightly to the side. She let Mrs. Franzsky's words sink in for a moment. Maybe Mrs. Franzsky was right. Maybe she should be nicer to Jason, go out of her way to...

"What do I do?" Emmy asked. It was a stupid question, she

knew, but she couldn't read this man and didn't know what made him happy. Would she have to read one of his books and then tell him that she liked it? Would she have to learn more about gardening and eat more vegetables – the latter sounding much more difficult to do than the reading. She wasn't good at small talk and couldn't pretend to like someone when she didn't. But perhaps... perhaps she could be more open to him.

Mrs. Franzsky laughed at Emmy's question, but not in a mean way. She reached out to touch Emmy's forearm as she did so. "Oh, dear," she managed to say once she finally stopped laughing. "I don't mean to laugh, really I don't. Are you being honest, though? Do you really not know how to make someone happy? I'm certain you do. Don't think too much on it. What is it with you young girls and overanalyzing every little thing, trying to be what you think is perfect or ideal, afraid to fall or to make a mistake. Start out small: Smile at him. Compliment him. Tell him, 'Good morning.' Make him a cup of coffee when he doesn't ask for one. And, more important, talk to him. But not about him. He's very reserved, you see. Talk to him about *you*. I guarantee he'll open up to you. Slowly." She paused, her eyes looking over to the ancient grandfather clock that stood just off to the side of the old-fashioned television. "Well, dear, you should probably get going. It's just after five. Shouldn't you be starting dinner?"

"Five?" Emmy snapped up from the chair and dashed to the front door. "Um, I'm really sorry, Mrs. Franzsky but I have to go. It was really nice meeting you!"

She opened the door and burst out into the unfamiliar greenery. How far away was Jason's home? In what direction? She stopped running, already lost, already panicking. She should have done her research, should have become familiar with the area before she so foolishly lost herself in the woods. There were bears here. When her grandfather took her camping, it was common to see warnings plastered all over the campgrounds and the two would be able to hear them walking around at night. She didn't want to be eaten by a bear. She twirled around, trying to find something familiar. A path, maybe. A noise. The shape of Jason's home. Where was the dog, anyways? Was it okay?

Something grabbed her shoulder and she jumped, letting out a shout.

"Emmy?"

The mumble, articulate, soft-spoken voice.

Before she could think to stop herself, she turned around and flung herself into his arms. Emmy managed to keep herself from crying in relief as she clung to him. He smelled like cigarettes, pine trees, and something musky, something unique to just him. It was familiar and safe and she clung tighter to him, burying her face into her chest. It was only when Jason placed a cautious hand on her back, his arm cradling hers, that she realized what she was doing. Her first instinct was to pull away, to throw some distance between the two of them, but Mrs. Franzsky's words stopped her. Maybe physical contact was another thing to add to the list, because as he relaxed into her grip, he wrapped both of his arms around her and pulled her even closer to him, tucking her head under his chin. She would never admit it, but this was… nice. His hands made her feel secure. Could these hands be deceivers? Could the same hands that held his wife like he was currently holding Emmy be the same hands that killed her? It was impossible. It had to be impossible.

"I thought you left."

It was a whisper, a caress that barely made any contact with the wind, but she heard it, clear as the crickets that squawked in the woods.

Emmy tilted her head up to look into his eyes. As she did so, the bridge of her nose brushed his jawline and her lips were close to his own. His lips looked soft, actually. Much softer than she would have ever believed. Were they as soft as they looked...?

She blinked, making traitorous, dangerous thoughts vanish. "What do you mean?" she asked as soft as possible.

He wasn't looking at her. His eyes were focused on the lower half of her face, but she wasn't sure why. It took him a moment before he realized she had spoken, had asked him a question, and he immediately picked his eyes up so they locked with hers.

"I thought you left," he said again. "I thought you weren't coming back."

Emmy's heart clenched at the worry drenched in his words and she had to clench her jaw to keep herself from saying something stupid, like a reassurance that she wouldn't leave him. In fact, she dropped her hands from his baggy t-shirt and forced herself from his grasp so there was space between them.

"We should head back," she murmured.

"Where did you go?" He began walking south, deeper into the woods.

Emmy had to curl her fingers into fists to keep from reaching out to latch onto his robe to ensure they wouldn't get separated. Instead, she kept close to him, her eyes keeping a firm watch on the back of his head, his hair flaring out in its odd way. The light of the moon shone down on it, casting an almost-halo over him.

"I," she began, but shook her head, transfixed. He was beautiful, even from behind. The more she studied him, the more interested she became in looking at him. "I saw a dog. It looked like a stray. I was going to get it some food, but when I went back out, it was gone. I climbed a tree, tried to look for it, and met Mrs. Franzsky."

"Ah," he said, as though that explained everything. The way he said it, Emmy thought he might be smiling. "Yes, she's quite a talker, isn't she? Nice, though. Very nice. She's one of the only people who still talks to me. Well, besides you."

Emmy had no idea how to respond to that, so she remained silent. The walk back to the cabin was about half a mile. All the while, Emmy's head kept turning every which way, keeping an eye out for both bears and the dog. When they reached their destination, neither was spotted. Her heart sank. She hoped it was okay out there, but judging from its slight stature, if it didn't get food soon, it wouldn't last long.

"You realize," Jason said as he held the back door open for her, "that if you were successful and gave the dog food, it would be back every day."

Emmy walked over to the cabinets that hung over the stove and had to stand on her toes to open them. Her eyes latched on a couple of cans of baked beans and snatched them. "Oh," she said, once she rolled back down to the flat of her feet. "I'm sorry, I didn't even think of that." It was a lie and she knew it. She set the cans on the counter and closed the cabinet back up. "Of course, you wouldn't want to be responsible for a dog."

"I never said that," he corrected, his voice gentle. Jason took a tentative step towards her and when he saw she wasn't retreating, walked towards a drawer next to her hip. He slid it opened and handed her a can-opener. "Do you have a dog?"

As Emmy proceeded to open the cans, she noticed he hadn't stepped back. He was so close that she could reach out and touch him. Her hands shook as she twisted the knob. What was she doing? She wanted to run, to take her chances in the woods, to be with her grandfather once again. Another part of her, another irrational and far too compassionate part of her wanted to stay, to get to know the elusive, brooding author better. She wanted to ask him questions and answer his and pretend, for just a moment, that he hadn't been accused of killing his wife and her lover. There were moments when she let herself be too reckless, when she let herself start to like him, to linger in his warm embrace, but she always remembered what he was. How could she forget?

But...

He hadn't tried to harm her, at least not yet. He hadn't even yelled at her and he had good reasons to do so, what with her sneaking in his room and then disappearing without first telling him that she'd be gone. Perhaps she could give him a tiny chance.

"Yes," she said, her lips daring to creep into a smile. Once she popped the lids off, she turned on the stove and placed a pot on the burner before pouring the beans in it. "An Australian Shepherd." She threw the cans away in the nearby trashcan and tucked a strand of hair behind her ear. "His name is Bingo. He's the smartest dog in the world."

"Really?" His eyes looked soft, a warm blue rather than a dark one. He was smiling, too a smile just as small as hers, but his came accompanied with dimples.

As they waited for the beans to cook, she nodded her head. "He can jump through hoops and listen to commands," she explained. "He doesn't need a leash."

He didn't say anything in return but continued to stare at her, his eyes carving something into her skin. What, she wasn't sure, but she felt herself flush as she looked away. Her hand reached up and started playing with her hair, her eyes looking at the food.

"I'd like a dog," he said, causing her to look back at him. "I've been alone for a while. It's nice to not be alone anymore."

Emmy cleared her throat. "Well, dogs make the best companions," she mumbled. Had he complimented her, or was that metaphorical? Whatever it was meant to convey, she felt herself start to shift her weight from her left leg to her right one and then back again. She reached for a serving spoon and stuck it in the pot of beans, needing something to do with her hands so she wouldn't have to look at him, wouldn't have to think about him. She started to stir, slow and methodical.

"Why don't you take a bath?" Jason suggested.

Emmy furrowed her brow, turning her head.

"I'll take care of dinner," he continued. "You should have some time to yourself to relax. By the time you're done, dinner will be ready."

"If you're sure..." She let her voice trail off. Was this some kind of trick? Was he trying to tell her in a nice way that she smelled?

"You deserve to relax, Emmy," he said in a way that sounded

like there was more to his words than he was letting on. "I don't want you to be tense all the time."

He couldn't force her to not be tense. Not when there were still questions regarding the real story about his wife and her lover. A bath wasn't going to fix that.

He offered her a smile, and while she wanted to return it, she couldn't. If she had tried, her face would resemble a grimace rather than anything sweet.

She headed up the stairs and down the hall where the bathroom was. Emmy couldn't help but glance in Jason's room, directly across from the bathroom, but this time, the door was firmly shut. He had learned his lesson. Not that she would have dared to go in there again. Not after what happened last time.

After stepping inside the compact room, she made sure to lock the door behind her and proceeded to fill the tub up with hot water. It took a while before the water was hot enough for her, but once it was and she had stripped off her clothes and pinned her hair up as well as she could with three bobby pins, she eased herself into the water and a sigh escaped from her lips. Her head instantly rested against the cool porcelain rim, and her eyes fluttered shut on their own accord. Perhaps she did need a bath, now that she thought about it.

Even from the second story of Jason's home, Emmy could clearly hear the crickets from outside. A small square window with a screen over it was placed just above the rectangular mirror. It was too dark to see out of it, and while there was no breeze, every now and then, she could feel the coldness that permeated the night drift in, mingling with the steam rising from the water, and causing Emmy to feel conflicting temperatures.

She should call her grandfather. It had been two days since she last spoke to him, but it felt like an eternity. She missed his voice.

Her thoughts continued to rehash everything that had happened to her so far, from the judging stares she received at the store and Mrs. Franzsky's advice. She had no idea how to treat

Jason, no idea what to be around him, and as such, she was an awkward ball of confusion, tugging at her hair and pulling at her hoodie, her eyes cast downwards or to the side, just as long as she wasn't looking at him.

He was probably used to it.

Everybody probably treated him that way.

Guilt seeped into her stomach and she had to open her eyes, as though to acknowledge it. Emmy couldn't make Jason happy. She couldn't pretend to not be affected by his potential murderer status because she was a horrible liar, and Emmy had a feeling his eyes were sharp enough to recognize any attempt at it. Still, he was a person and a jury found him not guilty. She would continue to keep on her toes but she couldn't keep avoiding him, looking past him, seeing through him as though he was transparent, as though he wasn't even there. She didn't want to call him a friend, but she could be warm to him. She could be nice to him.

When the water started to cool, she stepped out of the tub, making sure to not drip any water onto the wood floors. She wrapped a towel around her frame before she remembered she hadn't brought any clean clothes for her to change into. She glanced at her clothes, but her newly clean body physically shrunk back at the idea. Chewing on her bottom lip, Emmy's thoughts raced. She might be able to reach her room where she could throw on pajamas and be down before Jason wondered where she was.

Emmy crept to the door after making sure her feet were dry so she wouldn't slip and after unlocking it, opened it only to see Jason standing just outside, his fingers curled into his palm, poised to knock. His eyes took her in, everything from the drops of water on her shoulders, the strands of hair molded to her face while the majority of it became frizzy due to the steam, the fact that she was practically naked in front of him. His mouth had dropped open, obviously in utter surprise, and it took only a beat before Emmy realized what was happening, stepped back into the bathroom, and slammed the door shut.

"I, um." She could practically hear him push his glasses up the bridge of his nose. "Sorry. Uh, I was worried about you. It's been a while. The food was getting cold."

As soon as she heard his footsteps walking away from her, Emmy started laughing. She slapped her palm over her lip, but it did nothing to shield her ears from the sound. Her face turned red and her muscles pinched at her facial action; she hadn't smiled much in the past few days so laughing was downright unfamiliar.

Why was she laughing? He had seen her with just a towel. Yet, the situation they had found themselves in had been awkward and Emmy could not help but release the tension that had been building since she had left her grandfather. Laughter had been an interesting but not unpleasant choice of expression. It reminded her how much she enjoyed laughing and wanted to do it again. Hopefully, soon.

CHAPTER 6

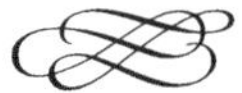

Emmy woke up to the sound of scratches on the front door, the creak of it being opened, and slobbering. She knitted her brows together as she threw her legs over the bed and stretched as she stood. Before she went to see where the noise came from, she threw her hair in a messy ponytail. Her feet were wrapped in socks and proceeded with caution as she stepped out of her room. Since the cabin was made from wood, each step danced on the threat of causing a squeak to cry out and let anyone who might overhear become aware of her whereabouts. She wasn't familiar enough with her new environment to know where to step, but each step was slow and deliberate to avoid it as best she could.

When she reached the top of the stairs, her eyes took in a sight she never would have thought she'd see: Jason was kneeling down, still clad in that robe, his chin length hair standing in every direction, in front of the open door, where the dog from yesterday was eating what Emmy could only assume was the leftover beans from last night on the front porch. She could hear the slobbering, the lapping of the water Jason had offered the animal, Jason's low murmurs as he petted the dog between the ears.

A warm feeling gripped hold of the insides of her stomach, and as she continued to watch, her body leaned against the frame and one arm crossed her chest to hold onto the other.

There was something gentle about him in that moment. He knew the dog would be back every day, now that Jason had offered it food, water, and affection. Of course, just because he had been nice to an animal did not mean he wasn't a murderer or had redeemed himself, but the fact that he did so while he thought she was still asleep, as though he had nothing to prove to anybody, did something to Emmy's thought process. She couldn't hate him. Perhaps she could not even dislike him, even if she wanted to, even if it was the safer option. But he couldn't be a monster, not if he genuinely cared about this animal.

He shocked her again when he stood back up and took a step back. He waved his right arm – drowning in the sleeve of the robe – indicating the dog could come inside. Emmy's eyes narrowed at the scene. She thoroughly believed that animals were good judges of character, even better than other humans. If the dog chose to take its chances out in the woods, with the bears and the cold, it would tell Emmy that while Jason was generous, he wasn't safe. The dog waited for a moment, its big brown eyes looking from Jason to the inside of his cabin, its eyebrows twitching with each glance. Finally, it eased its way into the home and began to pant, as thought it was already comfortable with its new home.

"Good boy," Jason said and she could hear the smile in his voice as he closed the door behind him. He took care not to step in the small, plastic bowl that was still occupied with water and patted the dog's head once again.

It was only then that his eyes noticed Emmy standing there. She wasn't quite as quick to react as she hoped to be, and instantly picked up the shoulder of her sweater and fixed it so her skin wasn't showing.

"I thought we could keep him," he said, indicating the dog.

Emmy wasn't sure what to make of the statement. The fact

that he used we instead of I caused her heart to harden. But not as much as it should have.

"I'll get dog food the next time I go to the store," she replied. She began to walk down the stairs and she offered him a smile. It was small, but it was real, and he smiled in return.

She experienced a different feeling when he smiled at her, like light shining through the cracks of the walls around her heart, and she had to look away in fear that his mere smile might cause them to crumble. "Have you decided on a name?" she asked, looking back at the dog, her voice sounding strained. The dog looked happy to see her again, wagging his tail, his eyebrows pushed up as high as they could go. She smiled at the sight and couldn't help but pet him once she reached him.

"Not yet," Jason said. He didn't talk fast often so at least she could understand what he was saying. "I figured what with you being an expert in dogs you'd have some suggestions."

The two began to walk into the dining room, the dog right on their heels. Emmy made a note to pick up the plastic bowl and replace it with a bigger one in the kitchen.

"I'm no expert," she said. She was surprised to see Jason up so early. Normally she had a couple of hours to herself in the morning where she could plan on what to make for breakfast and make him coffee so he had food and a hot drink by the time he woke up. Now, he took a seat at the dining table, the dog already lying by his feet, while Emmy walked to the cabinets.

"My grandfather's the real expert," she went on. Oatmeal sounded good. She remembered her grandmother's oatmeal, made from scratch. Papa would always put much more sugar than Grandma would allow and more than enough cream. Emmy was in charge of the raisins, and after mixing everything together, got the best oatmeal she ever had. Maybe she could try making some for breakfast. "He researched dogs before settling on Bingo."

"Bingo?" His tone was light and amused.

Emmy felt herself smiling as she grabbed the oats from the

back of the cabinet, strands of her hair falling into her face. "Australian Shepherd," she said. She grabbed another bowl and, after filling it up with water, began to boil the liquid. "He wanted the smartest dog he could find, and managed to find a breeder who just had a litter of puppies. Bingo was the only one who didn't jump up and bark and that was why Papa picked him."

"Papa?"

She flushed at her slip of the tongue. "It's what I call him," she murmured, turning away from Jason in order to find the sugar. "My grandfather, I mean."

"You sound close," he mused.

"He's my..." Emmy paused, setting the sugar next to oats. She turned so she could look him in the eye. "He's my everything."

His tilted his head up, his eyes still locked on Emmy. He looked almost wistful, but his eyes had a touch of sorrow embedded in them. "I don't think I've ever been that close to anyone in the world," he said, more to himself than to her.

Emmy turned back to the pot and found the water was already boiling. She poured her guesstimation of four cups of oats in the water before capping the canister and putting it back in its proper place. She opened the fridge and found cream but no raisins.

"We have no raisins," she stated before she realized what she had said.

We.

She had said we.

She needed to stop that before it got out of hand and she didn't even realize it. Clearing her throat, she closed the fridge, rubbing her palms on her cotton-clad thighs. "I'll just put it on the list," she said.

Silence hung between the two of them. Even the dog had stopped panting and was resting his head on his paws. Emmy could see ribs protruding through his skin. She would make sure to get extra dog food so he could put some fat on his bones.

"So you named Bingo?" Jason asked as she stirred the oats.

She glanced at him over her shoulder, nodding her head. The sleeve slipped down and revealed her bare shoulder, which she readjusted as quickly as she could. "I was in first grade," she gave as explanation. "My grandfather said I could name him. Bingo stuck."

"First grade, hmm?" He caressed his bottom lip with the pads of his index and middle finger, appearing to be deep in thought.

"Trying to figure out my age, are you?" The words were out of her mouth before she realized she had teased him. She glanced at him, a sharp movement that was only supposed to last a second in order to gauge his reaction to her familiarity with him. It lasted more than a second, however. His blue eyes were warm again, and more than that, they sparkled, something she hadn't encountered before this. It was hard not to look at him, especially not with those dimples winking at her.

"I know better than to do that," he said.

The coffeemaker beeped and Emmy shut it off, grabbing a mug from one of the cabinets positioned above the stove. She poured him a glass, filling it up about three-quarters of the way before stopping, and adding a bit of cream. He liked his coffee predominantly black, but because he was impatient and wanted to drink it when it was hot, she would add cold cream to cool the liquid a bit.

She blinked and nearly dropped the mug.

"Are you all right, Emmy?"

His voice caused her realizations to disappear and her grip on the mug tightened so he wouldn't notice her fingers shake. How did she already know that about him? A man's coffee order was only supposed to be known by his wife or his barista. *Although,* she reasoned as she handed him the mug, *you are kind of like his barista.* True, but she had never expected to learn his preference so fast. Something about the knowledge felt intimate, and she wasn't comfortable that it was now ingrained into her mind.

She never answered his question, and instead turned back to the oatmeal. It was almost done.

"I'm twenty-two," she finally said.

He nearly choked on his coffee.

"Are you okay?" she asked, hurrying over to him. "Was the coffee too hot?"

He shook his head as he coughed. Emmy reached over and began to pat his back. She wasn't sure if her gestures were helping, but he wasn't pushing her away.

"No, it's not that," he murmured once he could, capturing her eyes again.

He wasn't wearing glasses, she noticed. Why had it taken her so long to realize this? She gulped, realizing that his eyes looked bigger without his glasses. They seemed soulful, human. She was suddenly aware of how close she was to his sitting frame, her hand still resting on his back. Immediately, she dropped it and headed back to the stove, turning it off. It didn't take long before she had two bowls of oatmeal on the table, a cup of coffee for herself, and the sugar and cream between the two.

"I hope you like it," Emmy said as she sprinkled sugar on food. "My grandma used to make it for me when I was young."

"Wait." He stood up, causing the dog to pick his head up and watch his new master head over to the same cabinet where Emmy found the sugar. He grabbed something and walked back to Emmy's chair. He leaned over her shoulder so his hair touched her cheek. When he spoke, his breath invaded her bare shoulder. "May I...?"

Emmy couldn't find her voice, but she nodded.

He sprinkled something on her oatmeal before pulling away and sitting back down in his seat, letting her breathe again.

"It's cinnamon," he explained, doing the same to his own oatmeal. "A little trick my grandmother taught me."

This time, Emmy couldn't stop the smile on her face if she tried. She poured a good amount of cream and after stirring, began to eat. It wasn't her grandmother's oatmeal, but it wasn't bad, and with the addition of raisins, it would be better.

"So," he said, looking up at her. "A name for a dog. Any suggestions?"

"Well, what do you want to call him?" she asked, tilting her head to the side. Why did he want her opinion on this anyway? She knew if she did contribute to naming the dog in some way, she'd get attached and it would be harder to leave when it was her time to go. However, she also knew that whether she chose the dog's name or not, she'd end up attached to him anyway. There was no shorter way to her heart than animals, especially dogs. "I can't explain how it happened with Bingo. As silly as it sounds, the name just came to me and it fit. He was Bingo, he was always Bingo, and I was lucky to figure out his name."

"So he's hiding his name then?" He seemed amused by this and looked down at the dog. He was smiling again – he seemed to be doing more of that as well – and then, glancing up at Emmy, said, "That sounds a lot like Rumpelstiltskin, wouldn't you say?"

"You're going to name your dog Rumpelstiltskin?" Emmy asked, hiding her smile with a big bite of oatmeal.

"He is a bit of a trickster, isn't he?" Jason asked, flicking his head so some of his feathered bangs might get out of his eyes. No such luck. "And he's hiding his name from us. We could call him Rumpel for short. What do you think?"

There was the 'we' again, and this time, he coupled it with 'us.' He also wanted her opinion before he made the ultimate decision.

"Oh, it's not my dog," Emmy said, pointedly looking down at her food. "You should name him whatever you want to."

He was silent and Emmy had to physically stop herself from looking up at him. She wouldn't be able to stand it if there was discernible sorrow in those eyes. "Rumpel it is, then," he said.

"Rumpel it is," she repeated in a soft voice. A tiny smile touched her lips as she watched Jason rub the dog's head.

"It's a good thing we got to him now," Jason said, picking up his spoon once more. "Tahoe gets cold, even in the fall. I expect it'll snow in November. If he hadn't found us, I wouldn't be surprised if he froze." A pause, a held breath, a swipe of hair brushed behind an ear. "Would you like to take a walk?"

Emmy had just finished breakfast and dropped her spoon in the bowl so it clattered like a broken melody. She picked her eyes up and dared to look at Jason. His eyes, still warm, were looking at her in a way she didn't fully understand. Studious, but there was something more to it, only emphasized by the soft smile on his face.

"All right," she agreed, standing up to place both bowls in the sink.

Jason followed suit. "I'll get changed," he said.

The thought of Jason in actual clothes instead of sweats and a bathrobe was hard for Emmy to imagine, but she found herself looking forward to it only because she was curious to see what the end result would be. She followed him up the stairs, but hung a left and stepped into her room. She opened her dresser drawers and pulled out a change of clothes, deciding that she would do laundry once the two returned from their walk.

Emmy slipped out of her pajamas and threw on a pair of skinny jeans and a small, maroon baby tee with a small pocket on her left breast. After dousing her skin with sunscreen and throwing on a light button-up sweater, she pulled on her trusty converses and braided her hair loosely so it fell over her right shoulder. Stray strands of hair curved around her face but she didn't push them away.

When she stepped out of her room, she found Jason leaning against the hallway banister, waiting for her. She was surprised by how normal he looked in regular clothes. He decided on a plain grey t-shirt and a worn pair of jeans. Instead of tennis shoes he had on an old pair of brown loafers. His hair looked as soft as ever, and fell into his face. If Emmy was being honest, she might admit that perhaps he looked better than she thought he might.

"That's a lovely color for you," he murmured. For whatever reason, Emmy felt herself blush at the compliment and mumble a half-hearted thanks. "Are you ready to go?"

She nodded.

The two headed down the stairs and headed out the door. Jason whistled and Rumpel darted after the pair, walking in between them as they left the house behind.

"The woods can get a bit confusing," he explained as they headed further into the forest. "I wanted to show you around so you'd be more familiar with them and, in case you get lost again, you can navigate your way back to the house."

Rumpel's ears were perked up as he sniffed the dirt intently. Emmy didn't know what the dog had found, but he seemed happy chasing down the scent, scurrying out in front of her and Jason in order to further his investigation. From the corner of her eye, she noticed a genuine smile touch his features. He was content, she realized. His features weren't as hard as they had been. Her eyes found the ground and she decided she'd rather focus on learning about the paths in the woods than the lines on Jason's face.

"This trail leads directly to the back door," he said, pointing a long finger at the trail they were currently on. "It also leads directly into the woods and lasts until it curves west and meets Mrs. Franzsky's home. If, for whatever reason, you're in the woods, try and find this path and, if it doesn't get you home, it'll get you to the road. From there, you can just turn around and follow it back."

Home. There was that word again. Emmy never really felt at home anywhere except with her grandfather. Jason's house would never be her home. Her parents' home in Fountain Valley never felt like home. It was always with Papa. Wherever he was, she was home.

"How long does it last?" she asked, tilting her head up to look at his profile. She was certain when he was younger, his face was taut, sharp, and somewhere along the road, he had somehow broken his nose once, maybe twice. Now, his features were softer, but just as prominent. His cheekbones were high and defined, his jawline firm and masculine.

"The path?" He looked straight ahead, as though to calculate it in his head. "Well, as you know, you can get lost out there if you get off the path, and it might take days to find you if the bears don't get you first. If you take it to the main road, you'll be on it for... oh, I'd guess a couple of hours, at least. But if you have the time, it's a beautiful walk. The woods can be beautiful, especially with the sun peeking through the leaves."

Emmy felt her lips twitch up, her eyes back down on the dirt. It was starting to make a home on her shoes, just another sign of where she'd been, a promise of where she was going. "You have a way with words," she told him. It wasn't exactly a compliment, at least not in her mind; it was a fact. He still seemed pleased, however, as his fingers made a home in the roots of his hair in order to brush the locks out of his face.

"I hope so," he said. "I am a writer."

Rumpel was a few feet away, still chasing after the scent.

"Aren't you worried he's going to run away?" Emmy asked. She knew Bingo didn't need a leash, but he had been with Papa since he was six weeks old and one of the first things Papa did was put Bingo through an etiquette school. Rumpel had been with Jason for all of an hour at best and might dash off for greener pastures at any moment.

Jason shrugged, scrunching his nose and shaking his head. "Nah," he said. "He found us. If he wants to leave, I don't want to force him to stay." He paused as his words settled into the pores of her skin. "I'd love to keep him, I'd love for him to stay. If not, all we can do is hope he comes back."

Emmy glanced at him, using her hair as a shield so he wouldn't see her looking at him. There it was again. That thing he did with his words where she was certain he meant something more than what he said.

"You must have a lot of faith in him."

"No, it's not that." He stopped and so she did too. They faced each other. Jason had to raise his arm at a diagonal in order to block out the rising sun. "I can't stop someone from leaving, whether it's the dog or my wife. All I can do is wait for him to come back, and if he doesn't, I move on."

She pursed her lips, tilting her head to the side. She felt the sun's rays caress the top of her head and she found it nice that she was warm.

"It's scary," she said in a low voice, her eyes on the tips of her shoes. The white color was rubbed down, like craters pocketing the moon. "Not knowing."

"Yeah," he said with a curt nod. "The waiting's dreadful. But the moment he comes back, it makes everything worth it."

She looked back up again, only to find him still looking at her, and the two shared a smile.

Emmy let him lead her down the path until they reached the entrance to the woods. She zipped up her sweater a bit more as the tops of the trees began to blot out the sun. Her eyes took in the grass, the darker soil, the sounds of buzzing and flapping wings and bird calls, though, for the life of her, she couldn't distinguish one bird call from another, except seagulls. And crows.

"Sometimes, when I'm stuck with my writing," he said, "I come out here. It helps me think. Walking helps my brain come up with ideas."

"The woods inspire you?"

He nodded. "Being alone in the woods, I can think," he said. "I can walk for hours and hours and come up with the plot to a novel." He turned back to her, his left eyebrow cocked. Emmy couldn't move one brow in favor of the other but she wished she could. Jason made it look so easy. "Would you like to continue?"

The wolf was offering to lead her to his cave. Jason had been in Tahoe for a while now. The murders were two years ago, and he summered here with his wife beforehand. He knew the woods like the back of his hand. It was probably how he was able to find her so quickly after she had left Mrs. Franzsky's home. As such, he could lead her anywhere he wanted, and she'd be dependent on him, to lead her back to his cabin, to not try and kill her.

But, a voice reasoned, *there's really no reason to think he wants to kill you. If he had, you'd probably already be dead by now.*

Her guts churned like they were going through a meat grinder.

Plus, what's the difference between killing you in the woods and killing you in his home?

The woods didn't require an excessive amount of clean-up. He wouldn't have to carry her body anywhere; he could bury her in the soil. No one would ever know. No one would ever find her.

"You can say no," he teased, but she could detect disappointment in his brown eyes. They weren't warm anymore. Just sad. "I just wanted you to know about the path, in case you ever got lost again. Perhaps next time we can take a walk through the woods?"

The fact that Jason was actually out and walking, dressed in actual clothes, must mean a lot. It had to. The first couple of days here, she had barely seen him, and it was the first day he wasn't shrouded in that awful bathrobe. She hadn't heard him talk this much, either, not even when he was telling her about his vegetables. He was reaching out to her in his own way. Was she really going to shut him down?

"That would be nice," she answered, and was surprised at how sincere she sounded.

Rumpel made his appearance. He hadn't found whatever it was he was looking for, but he was back beside Jason, licking Jason's hand. Emmy rubbed her lips together as she took the sight in. If the dog could come back even with the option of freedom, Jason couldn't be so bad. He was found not guilty, after all. Maybe he really didn't do it.

"I should probably go to the store when we get back," she said as they turned back around. The cabin was about five hundred yards away. She slid her hands into her back pockets. "Is there anything else you'd like me to pick up?"

"You should probably get some laundry detergent," he said, "in case you wanted to do laundry."

Emmy found herself chuckling at his joke. It wasn't that good, but something about the way he said it, how self-deprecating it was, made her laugh.

"Ah, I knew I could make you laugh eventually," he said. His eyes were bright with triumph and his dimples were on full display.

Emmy blushed and looked away. The next couple of steps were dragged feet and kicked-up dust.

"Don't forget dog food," he continued.

Rumpel's tongue was sagging out of his mouth, his eyebrows going up and down and up and down, almost as though he knew the couple was talking about him and the prospect of food.

"And anything you might prefer," he finished. He reached out and grabbed her bare wrist, coiling his fingers around her skin and pulling to a stop. She had to stop herself from yanking back her hand as though she had been burned. "Listen Emmy" – her name sounded different when he said it and she didn't know why – "I know it's difficult and perhaps too much to ask for, but during your stay, I would like you to feel at home. Feel free to get whatever food or drinks you want. Take as many showers and baths as you need to. Call your friends or your family, even if they're on the other side of the country. Go into town and see a movie, if you'd like."

He still hadn't let go of her wrist. His fingers were sure to leave prints behind. She might not be able to see them, but she would feel them, long after he had released her.

"I just" – he looked away from her and to the left, where the field that served as a buffer between his home and the woods extended to the horizon. Emmy wondered just how much of it he owned – "I know that you're probably not here because you want to be. And I understand that. But I want you to feel comfortable here. I want you to be happy."

He continued to look in her eyes and she was compelled to hold his stare. It distracted her from the tingling underneath his fingers.

"I," she began but stopped. She couldn't, wouldn't, lie to him. Not only because Emmy had a feeling he'd be able to tell, but because it just felt... wrong. For whatever reason, lying to Jason felt wrong. However, he was waiting for some kind of response. She wasn't sure what to say. Instead, with her free hand, she curled a strand of hair behind her ear and pressed her lips together. Then, the words found her lips and compelled them to speak. "I'll try."

He nodded his head once and finally released her. Her arm fell back into its proper place at her side, but the goosebumps still lingered. Not because he had touched her, though, but because he let her go. Because her skin was cold now, so she pulled the sleeve of her sweatshirt down in order to alleviate the problem. It didn't work. She was still cold, even when they reached the sun and the house, even when she was safe in his car, driving to the store. She didn't want to think about it anymore.

CHAPTER 7

The nights grew colder with each passing day, and Emmy was surprised to find a heavy blanket folded up and placed just outside her room when she woke up the next morning. Her lips curled up as she retrieved it and brought it back to her bed. She was already layering her clothes thanks to the decrease in temperature, but this would definitely help keep her warm.

Another week went by, and whether Emmy would admit it or not, she and Jason and Rumpel had developed a comfortable routine. Since Emmy was prone to be the early riser, she would let Rumpel out to do his business and chase any deviant squirrels while she made coffee. By the time Jason woke up, breakfast was ready. When breakfast finished, the couple and the dog would go on a walk around the property. Jason had yet to venture back into the woods, and for that, Emmy was grateful. She wasn't sure she was ready to explore them with him just yet. Normally, they were silent, but the silence was companionable rather than awkward. Every now and then, Jason would ask her something, she would respond, and a conversation would develop. Lunch followed after that, and then Emmy would run errands, or, if there were none, she would tidy up the cabin. Jason would go back up to his room and write until dinner. When dinner would finish, Emmy would shower and then turn in, while Jason would stay up, late into the night and early morning. Emmy never knew how long Jason stayed up, but she could hear him typing away on his keyboard, even with her door closed.

On a particular morning, Emmy was roused from her sleep thanks to a chill. Knowing she wouldn't be able to get back to sleep without the aid of some warm milk, she crawled out of bed, pulled on a jacket, and headed down the stairs. She yawned, her hand coming up to scratch the top of her head. It took about twenty minutes for her to warm up the milk, drink it, and then put everything away.

As she headed up the stairs, a shout nearly caused her to lose her balance and tumble down the stairs. She managed to grab the banister just in time, all the while wondering just what was going on. The shout sounded human. It had to be. Was Jason shouting at Rumpel? Rumpel always did sleep curled against the back of his legs. There were times she wondered if the dog would do her the honor of spending the night with her, but she wasn't ready to leave her door open just yet.

She crept in the direction of Jason's room, trying to figure out what was going on. The shouting had stopped but there was talking going on, and... whimpering? Was Jason really doing something to the dog? Because, in all the time Emmy spent with the two, she was certain they both loved one another very much. Yes, in this instance, she knew that Jason was capable of love. It was clearly written in his brown eyes. There was no way he would harm the Rumpel in any way.

Then why the whimpering?

Emmy continued down the hall until she was directly in front of Jason's room. She hadn't been here since she had gotten caught looking at a picture of his wedding. In fact, she had pointedly avoided his room for that very reason. He had never brought it up, and for that, she was thankful, but she didn't want him to do so now. Unlike Emmy, Jason left his door open so Rumpel could go in and out as he pleased. Still, Emmy could barely make out anything from where she stood beside random silhouettes that could be... anything, really.

The whimpering, and then talking, continued.

Emmy was caught in the doorway, still unsure of what to do. She wanted to go in there and make sure everything was all right but she was rooted in place, afraid that he might yell at her for disturbing him.

Something touched her hand, and she had to bite her bottom lip to keep from yelping in surprise. Her heart continued to race even after finding out it was Rumpel. He looked much healthier. Fat began to coat his body, but if he wanted to survive the bitter Tahoe winter, he'd need to pile on some more. He was looking up at her with big brown eyes, his eyebrows jumping up and down, as though they were trying to coax her into doing something. As she stared at the dog, she realized she could still hear the whimpering, which meant the sound was coming from Jason.

Was he... crying?

Or was he sleeping?

Emmy didn't want to interrupt him if he was crying. It was just after three in the morning, and it wasn't any of her business to walk in and disturb him. He'd be embarrassed, she'd be mortified, and the awkwardness that had been slowly fading away would come back full-force.

But if he was dreaming...

He sounded so sad.

Rumpel headed back into the room, but once he was fully immersed in the shadows, he stopped and turned, waiting for her to follow.

If Jason was crying, Emmy would just tell him the dog heard a strange sound and led her to him.

She inhaled deeply, preparing to hold her breath until she found out the source of the noises. Using as light a foot as she could muster, she proceeded to step into the room. It wasn't as dark as she had originally anticipated, what with the full moon shining through the window just above the head of Jason's bed.

That was where she found him. He was sleeping. Once she reached the side of the bed, she dared challenge his slumber by taking a seat on the edge, all while twisting her torso so she could continue to keep her eyes focused on him. Wrinkles permeated his skin, more so now than when he was awake. Judging from the furrow of his brow, the pursed lips that would either mumble something incoherent or let out a whine, he was having a nightmare. Beads of sweat littered his brow, forcing the locks of hair to cling to his skin. Emmy couldn't help but drop her index finger to his face with the intent to brush away the hair, but she was stopped before she could do anything by a hand that shot up and gripped her wrist. His eyes snapped open into hers, and for a moment, neither spoke. Neither breathed. They simply stared at each other. She was trapped and she knew it, but the heat he was inflicting on her skin made it slightly more bearable than she ever thought was possible.

"You were speaking," she managed to say though her voice was laced with breath and warm milk.

He didn't say anything, just continued to search her eyes. She didn't pull away though she knew she probably should. She couldn't blink, couldn't catch her breath, couldn't look away.

Finally, he dropped her hand and reached up to brush his hair away himself.

"I, I'm sorry." She looked down at her hands in her lap. They were suddenly cold and she rubbed them together, giving her something to focus on.

Rumpel hopped up on the other side of the bed and curled up against Jason.

"Don't apologize," he murmured. He was rightfully tired but somehow was able to coat some sincerity in his words. "I was having a nightmare." A pause. Emmy dared to breathe. She didn't know why she was so keen on hearing what the nightmare was about, but it didn't matter: She didn't want to scare him into shutting up by saying or doing anything he might deem as threatening. A strained smile touched his face but didn't reach his eyes. Even his dimples looked like they didn't want to accompany it. "Just my past, catching up to me."

It was the only explanation she would get. Letting out a shaky breath, she craned her neck so she could look at him again. "Is that a good thing or a bad thing?" she asked.

"The past is the past," he said. His exhaustion made his voice thicker so Emmy had to pay attention in order to understand what he said. "It's neither good nor bad but defines who you are. You can't change it. It's not one thing or another, it just is."

Emmy let his words sink in by looking out the window, at the moon glowing on the field. She could make the edge of the woods just off to the side, but Jason's view was grass and wildflowers rather than trees and bushes. It was nice, she realized. This stillness. This serenity. The silence. She could get used to this.

At that thought, her head snapped back down to Jason. "Are, are you all right?" she managed to ask. She had no idea why she thought she could ever get used to living out here in the middle of nowhere with a stranger – although now he was more of an acquaintance, wasn't he? – who might or might not have killed his wife and her lover, where the closest person around was an old woman half a mile away. If she screamed, no would hear her.

It must be the exhaustion. It has to be. That, or the altitude. She was up higher here than in San Francisco.

He chuckled at her question. This time, his smile was real, but since it wasn't bright, his face merely glowed rather than lit up. Still, it was better than that fake one from before.

"I think I should be asking you the same question," he said. "You look like you've just seen a ghost. This is different for you, isn't it?"

Emmy wasn't exactly sure what he meant. There were a slew of answers she could respond with, ranging from "Yeah, I've never really lived with a murderer before" to "My parents

telling me to turn down my music because the neighbors might call the cops but now I'm living somewhere where I could blow out the speakers and no one would be able to hear" but she decided to answer with something honest but vague, as usual.

"I'm still getting used to it."

"You will," he said, his eyes softening as he continued to stare. "Or, at least, I hope you do."

Emmy swallowed and pulled her eyes away from him to rest on the dog. "My grandfather always made me hot chocolate after I've had a bad dream," she said. "Would you like me to make you some?"

This caused his brow to furrow. "Do we even have hot chocolate?" he asked.

Emmy nodded. "I picked some up the last time I was at the store. I hope you don't mind. It's just, it's getting colder and since I'm not much of a tea drinker and don't want to drink coffee right before going to bed, I thought hot chocolate would be the safest bet."

"I don't remember the last time I had hot chocolate," he admitted. "Did you get marshmallows?"

Emmy felt a smile threaten to break out onto her face. "Mini marshmallows," she said.

"Then let's have at it, shall we?"

When he moved, Rumpel jumped up, as though they were all going somewhere together, and soon, the trio was heading down the stairs, Jason in his robe, Rumpel wagging his tail, and Emmy bringing up the rear, watching the sight with surprised amusement. Jason made sure to turn on the lights so nobody would trip or run into things.

"I'll make a fire," he said as he headed into the still-dark front room.

Emmy nodded but didn't respond. She grabbed the same pan she had boiled milk with and proceeded to do the same thing. From her position in the kitchen, she had a good view of Jason, currently opening a trunk placed just off to the side from the fireplace. She watched as he rolled his robe sleeves up to his elbows in order to grab a piece of wood without worrying about getting any residue on the material. He placed the wood down in the fireplace and then fumbled through a few matches before lighting the wood on fire. Just as he stood back up, Emmy whipped back around and focused back on the milk. She didn't want him to see her staring. In fact, she didn't want to realize she had been staring.

It took her another few minutes before she poured the milk into mugs, added the chocolate mix, and stirred everything up. Since she wasn't sure about his preference concerning the marshmallows, she decided to bring the bag so he could do what he wanted. It took her two trips, and then both Emmy and Jason were sitting on the couch, his feet on the low coffee table, her legs tucked underneath her, both with mugs in their hands, and the marshmallow bag between them. The fire crackled into the distance, the bright flames illuminating the otherwise dark room. Rumpel was on the floor, resting in the space between the couch and the coffee table.

"I love marshmallows," Jason said as he opened the bag of marshmallows. Emmy was holding onto his mug so he wouldn't accidentally spill his drink. Not that it would affect the couch much, but Rumpel probably wouldn't approve of being showered with hot liquid. "I have to have at least ten in my hot chocolate."

"I actually only like a few," Emmy said though he hadn't actually asked her her opinion. It was as though she wanted to share something about herself with him. How odd. "I'm not a big fan of them outside of hot chocolate, except with s'mores."

"I love s'mores," he agreed. "We should make some soon. You can get chocolate and graham crackers at the store, I have plenty of metal hangers, and we could roast them right here." He began to pour a generous amount of the marshmallows into his drink.

Before Emmy could stop herself, she smiled and said, "That sounds nice."

The fire reflected in Jason's eyes as he took a sip of his drink. "It's a date."

This time, Emmy didn't look away from him despite the fact that before, his words would have her murmuring excuses about needing sleep and retreating as fast as she could. Instead, she let herself stare at him, being blatant about it while doing so. She didn't know why she was so relaxed right now when she was only inches from him, when they were actually enjoying themselves together, sitting before a fire and drinking hot chocolate. The scene was one Emmy would have laughed at if anyone had foretold it. But now, as she experienced it, she could admit that this wasn't so bad. In fact, it almost felt... right.

There was something about Jason, something about the way he looked in the light of the flames. It was as though the fire stripped him of any disguise he might be wearing until his shell was cast aside and he remained. His feathered hair framed his face, the locks going every which way. His eyes were warm again, and she wasn't sure if the light reflected in them, the drink, or the moment was the cause of it. And his smile was sincere. The more she looked at the curve of his lips, the more she found herself mimicking the action. He really wasn't so bad looking, she realized. Not when he looked like this. Even with that horrid robe and bedhead, he actually looked... beautiful.

Emmy slowly swallowed the gulp of hot chocolate in her mouth in lieu of spitting it all out.

Her mind was turning traitorous on her. Where had that come

from? She couldn't argue that he was attractive. In his own way. She couldn't deny that. She'd be lying to herself if she did.

"What?" he asked, a ghost of a caress, one key of a piano. He tilted his head to the side. He wasn't wearing glasses again. "What is it? You're staring at me." He said it as though he was amused by her but somehow she could tell that he was worried about her unusual scrutiny.

"Your eyes," Emmy said as explanation. "When the light hits them, they look like the sea."

He was silent for a moment and Emmy took the time to take a long sip of the drink. Unlike the previous thought in her head, this time, she didn't flinch at her words. It wasn't as though she was paying him a compliment; it was mere fact and nothing more. She didn't think she had ever seen varying degrees of blue all wrapped up in one iris, but there it was, in Jason's eyes. It was as though she was looking into a kaleidoscope of the color that changed depending on his mood and whatever light he happened to be in. Right now, his eyes looked nothing short of captivating, like the fireworks at Disneyland.

"Is that a good thing?" He placed his empty mug on the surface of the coffee table before leaning into the couch, keeping his eyes fixed firmly on hers.

Emmy shrugged, taking another sip. Her torso was angled so it was facing him, and her legs were tucked underneath her. "It's a fact," she mumbled, unsure if her answer would satisfy him.

He glanced away, at the fire, but a thoughtful smile touched his face. He placed his arm up on the back of the couch. From the corner of her eye, Emmy could see his fingers rest near her shoulder, could feel the heat radiating from the digits and onto the bare skin of her neck. Every once in a while, he would move his index finger and she would hold her breath, both anticipating and worrying it might accidentally brush her neck. She wasn't sure how she would react. She didn't want to know how she would react.

"No one's ever said that to me before," he said, more to himself than to her.

Emmy leaned forward, placing her mug – still half-full – next to his before leaning back, shifting her position so her entire body was facing his, her shoulder pushed against the couch, her cheek resting against the scratchy material. She couldn't not look at him, not with the flames setting fire to his features, and she didn't particularly care if he caught her again or not. She must be tired.

"Do you want to talk about your dream?" Emmy asked. He looked surprised that she would endeavor to start a conversation but didn't comment on it. Instead, he mirrored her positioning on the couch so now he faced her, and instead of resting his head on the couch, he placed his elbow on the back and his palm on his head. "Whenever I had a bad dream, I would tell my grandfather about it. Speaking about it made me realize just how unreal it was and it was easier for me to go back to sleep."

"Not really," he said. It was the first time he refused her, and she found a swell of disappointment fill her stomach like cough syrup on her tongue. "Just being with you right now, talking about anything else, helps."

Emmy flushed at the words, her eyes darting to the fire to escape his. The words were too intimate, too... *something*. The look on his face was too sincere, his voice too soft, his dimples too charming. It wasn't fair. He wasn't supposed to make her feel this way, as though she wanted to know more about him, more about who he was, as though she wanted to take care of him and make him hot chocolate and have him make a fire every time he had a bad dream. She was supposed to be afraid of him and he was supposed to be cold and reserved and drop hints at how he really did get away with murder and if she didn't watch it, she'd become a victim too and no one would ever know. The feelings she should be having for him were slowly slipping from her grasp, like the sand in an hourglass, and she wasn't sure how to get them back.

She wasn't sure if she wanted to.

They were silent for some time. Emmy couldn't be sure the length of time they spent sitting on the couch together, the embers finally starting to dim in the fireplace, staring at everything but each other, but eventually, her eyes began to close and she couldn't stop sleep from overtaking her if she tried.

* * *

THE MINUTE her head hit his shoulder, Jason did everything in his power to keep from jumping in surprise. He had been looking out the window, wondering if a storm would hit soon. The angry clouds were certainly heading their way, and he had lived here long enough to distinguish when it would rain, when it would snow, or when the sun would shine better than meteorologists said they would. Not that he had any other choice, since he didn't have a television or even a radio beside the one in his car. After what had happened, he wanted to take a break from civilization, and judging from the way he was treated when he did go in for groceries and other such needs, civilization needed a break from him.

It couldn't last forever, of course, but he decided to prolong the inevitable by putting an ad in the paper for a live-in maid. He didn't think anyone would actually show up. It was just an excuse to go a couple more weeks without socializing unless it was absolutely necessary.

And then she showed up. She was his link to the outside world. His connection to a world he hadn't wanted to be a part of, and the more time he spent with her, the more he realized that while he wasn't ready to go into town just yet, he wanted to be a part of her world. She made the sun shine brighter and his heart accelerate at a rate he wasn't used to. He smiled just thinking about her and found himself wondering what she would think of certain topics and how she would look if she wore her hair up.

It wasn't a shock to know she had her guard up when she was

around him. He couldn't blame her. It made the times when he bent them, however slightly, that much more worthwhile. When she talked to him about herself, especially about her grandfather, he thought she was doing him a grand honor by allowing him to have a small peek into her world, a world he knew he could never be a part of, no matter how badly he wanted to. She was young, beautiful, and full of life. He was old, beastly, and couldn't even leave his home.

He was surprised she had stayed around this long. He was surprised she hadn't left. The thought of her doing so caused his heart to constrict quite painfully. He had been blessed by her presence and to lose that happiness was something he didn't want to think about. Not when she was slowly starting to trust him.

Jason hadn't meant for her to know he had nightmares, but now, he was glad. She had made him hot chocolate and was sitting so close to him that when she fell asleep, her head hit his shoulder. When he refused to answer her question, she didn't press him like Stacey had. She let him be silent when he needed to think. He didn't want to tell her about the wicked man he was. It was selfish, but he wanted to keep her for as long as he could, and revealing the content of his nightmare would only push her away. She was good and pure and everything he wasn't, and he wanted her to shine down on him, to drench him in even the tiniest rays of her light. It was too much to hope for, but all that he wanted. He couldn't make up for his past, but maybe, just maybe, he could get some form of redemption.

The idea clouded his eyes and caused his body to tense.

Jason couldn't allow himself to hope for something that would never happen. It was a waste of his energy when he knew, without a doubt, that someone like her would ever fall for someone like him. Maybe before, before the tragedy and the scandal. He had actually cared about his appearance back when he did book tours and went to award banquets and charity events. Now, he let his hair grow out so it danced below his ears and fell into his face, as though shielding his eyes from whatever he didn't want to see. His nose had been broken in a bar fight back when he was in college and had lots of mates, lots of female prospects, the world at his feet and the dream of being a best-selling novelist in his back pocket. Now, he had no friends, no female prospects, the world was in his rearview mirror, and his dream had been realized but didn't shine as bright as it once had, back when he had new eyes. Back then, he lived in jeans and t-shirts, and when he would go to important benefits or meetings, he had slacks and a collection of button-down shirts. Now, he only wore his robe, a gift from his ex-wife during their first Christmas spent together as a married couple. It was old and ratty, with holes and the stench of sweat, blood, tears, and loss within the fabric. But it was safe, comfortable, and he didn't feel the need to change it.

He hadn't written anything in a while. Well, that wasn't true. He wrote, but it wasn't good and it never made any sense. A lot of the time, he strung words together to form sentences that sounded right in his mind but, when read aloud, sounded off. Unnatural. His agent was patient and then distant and then stopped calling. Jason knew Bram hadn't given up on him, but he wasn't going to waste his time and effort on a recluse like him. While Jason had savings and didn't need the money thanks to the royalties his books brought him, he wanted to be able to tell stories again. Just because the dream had dimmed didn't mean it had faded. This was what he wanted to do for the rest of his life, but he couldn't find the right words. The right words couldn't find him. And he wasn't ready to go searching for them. He knew he needed a muse. Inspiration. Something to hold onto and breathe life into him, into his work. But until then, he would continue to pluck away out the keyboard until he wrote something worthy.

Her warm breath trailed up the column of his throat, causing his eyes to shoot down to her face. Shadows criss-crossed her features, highlighting the sharpness of cheekbones, the strength of her jaw. Her nose was small and upturned, the smallest nose he had ever seen, really, but it somehow fit her face. Her brows were thick but feminine, framing her eyes and adding a delicate curve to her brow. Her lips were slightly parted and he wanted to trace their outline, if only to see if they were indeed as soft as they appeared. He reached out, as if to do just that, his index finger extended so close that her breath surrounded it, but he pulled back. He couldn't. What if she woke up? What if this moment was ruined? He dropped his hand to his lap and let out a breath.

The fact that she had fallen asleep in his presence was a big deal. Sleep was when a person was most vulnerable. It was probably one of the most intimate things a person could do with one another because all defenses were down. He wouldn't take this moment for granted. He knew he should carry her back to her bed and close the door behind him, so when she woke up she'd know she fell asleep but he was chivalrous enough to put her back where she no doubt wanted to be, in the safety the small room provided her. But he wouldn't. He knew he wouldn't. There was a good chance he would never have this moment again, and he refused to surrender it. He would hold onto it for as long as he possibly could, which meant he would not move, would not go back to his own bedroom. He would stay for as long as he could, for as long as she would have him.

It was a risk. If she woke before him to find herself against his shoulder, he had a feeling she wouldn't be ecstatic. In fact, if she didn't slap him, he'd call it a blessing. And then what would happen? He couldn't be sure if Emmy would retreat after finding herself asleep on the couch with him, guard her heart even more thoroughly than she had been. He didn't care. It was a risk he was willing to take. He wanted this time with her, and whatever the consequences, he would deal with them. For now, he just wanted to enjoy the feeling of a warm body pressed against his, the soothing sound of her even breathing, his newly-acquired dog asleep at his feet. There was a good chance he would never get this moment again. As such, he allowed his eyes to slowly close and he hesitated slightly before resting his cheek on the top of her head. Her hair was messy, immediately surrounding the majority of his face, but he smelled the cinnamon and vanilla, and felt the soft strands against his skin, and it wasn't long before he, too, was fast asleep. He knew, without a doubt, the nightmares couldn't touch him here.

CHAPTER 8

The first thing Emmy noticed after she woke up the next morning was the fact that she was not in her bed. Definitely not in her bed. Her head was resting on something firm but comfortable, as though the formation was made exactly for her face. There was warm pressure on her waist and she was warm. Not only warm but cozy. Her mind shut off, wanting to go back to sleep, so she pushed her face even deeper into her pillow and threw out her arm, hoping to coil it around something and pull it closer to her chest. Her favorite sleeping position was the fetal position, and she liked to enhance it by clutching something, like her baby blanket or a body-sized pillow. Her hand found something slender but when she pulled, she nearly toppled off whatever it was she slept on. Apparently she had underestimated its weight. Which meant whatever she was sleeping next to, with her head upon it, weighed more than a pillow.

Her eyes snapped open.

She knew.

How could this have happened? They hadn't even been talking last night, not that much anyways.

She must have fallen asleep. He must have fallen asleep. But who fell asleep first? And did that even matter?

She wanted to run, run, run back up to her room, slam the door shut behind her, and stay there for as long as possible. How could she have possibly let herself fall asleep with him? He could have done anything to her! He could have molested her or murdered her or –

Judging by the fact that you are still fully clothed and very much alive, we can conclude that he did neither of those things, a droll and very tired voice pointed out.

Emmy continued to breathe as normally as she could, even though her heart was racing as fast as a car on a track. She couldn't move. It was apparent that Jason was still asleep, what with his steady intake and subsequent release of breath, causing his chest to go up and down, her arm along with it. She was still clutching him though her grip was decidedly looser than it had been when she thought he was still a pillow.

What did she do now?

She couldn't just leave. She figured the pressure on her hip was Jason's arm, and he was holding her to him. In fact, the more she twitched different parts of her body as though to check what position they were in, she realized her legs were entangled with his, like some sort of pretzel one might buy at the mall. If she disengaged herself from him, he'd wake up. There was no doubt he would wake up. Which meant that he would see their current predicament and –

Emmy blinked.

She had no idea how he would react. That was what she was hoping to avoid the most. Maybe if she could get herself to fall back asleep, he could wake up and stumble over apologies and it would be him who happened upon the fact that they fell asleep together and not the other way around. She would blush and wave him off, reassuring him that it was all right and they were both tired and it wasn't surprising that after all of that and a warm drink of hot chocolate that they wouldn't get drowsy and fall into slumber right there.

But she knew such a thing was futile. Once she was up, she was up. Perhaps she could fake being asleep. He wouldn't be able to tell, would he?

It was only then, as the sun's rays cascaded through the window and touched on the two figures on the couch, that Emmy looked up and saw Jason. This light was much more different than the firelight but just as revealing. As he slept, he looked serene, peaceful, much younger than before. His face was void of most of the lines that trailed on his skin and his dimples were nowhere to be found. His lips were closed but they came together in a caress rather than a long, thin line. There was more color in his face now. He wasn't as pale as he had been last night. His hair fell into his forehead in light wisps like the wings of a butterfly and Emmy itched to touch them, to see if they really were as soft as they looked. And, if she so dared it, to run her fingers through his tresses, just feel them on the skin between the digits.

Her face flushed at the thought but she didn't immediately banish it away. Not just yet.

At that moment, Jason let out a grunt and curled his arm tighter around her waist, pulling her closer to him so his chin rested on top of her head and her chest was pressed against his, her lips deathly close to the column of his throat. Both were on their sides, his back pressed against the back of the couch, and she, teetering off the edge. She might have fallen if he hadn't held onto her the way he was.

Emmy held her breath, waiting for him to notice something wrong with his sleeping quarters and wake up. After a moment, though, she realized his breathing had never changed, and though she couldn't see them, she had a feeling his eyes were still sewed shut. She swallowed. Now she was in a compromising position and she wasn't sure what to do. The rational part of her brain was telling her to stay exactly the same way she was, without moving, without shifting, and just wait for him to wake up. A more daring part of her wanted to explore things she never would when Jason was conscious. For whatever reason, the magnetic pull of her darker side was winning out, and before she knew it, she was lifting her free arm up from in between them and, after a soft bout of hesitation, tentatively placed it flat on his chest, between the folds of his robe, where the thin material of his dark grey thermal acted as a barrier between his skin. Warmth soaked her fingers, her palm, wrapping its desperate coil around her and drew her to press down even more so she could feel his heart beating against her palm.

It was official. He was human.

Another minute, and she felt herself relax. He still hadn't stirred. Keeping her hand where it was, she decided to try something else, something dangerous, something she would never do if Jason was awake and she wasn't as blinded by temptation as she was now. Her heart slowed down but continued to pound against her chest. Her breathing got shaky, and try as she might, she couldn't quite steady it. Clenching her jaw, swallowing, Emmy took a deep breath through her nose and then tilted her chin up just a fraction so her lips innocently brushed the side of his throat like a bee caressed a flower. She didn't press them down, didn't kiss him, per se. All she wanted to do was see what his skin felt like on her lips. She didn't taste him, but as she righted her head, her tongue darted to see if there was any residue of him that permeated her lips.

He sighed.

She tensed.

Had he felt her? Did he know?

She waited another minute, but Jason still appeared to be asleep. He turned his head and buried his nose in her hair. Her face heated up and she wished she had washed her hair while showering last night. Not that it mattered, of course. He was asleep.

A bark snapped her thoughts in half, and suddenly, Jason was stretching, somehow keeping his arm still locked around her. He was definitely awake now.

Emmy used that as a good excuse to stand up, and with a small hint of regret that she pointedly ignored, she disentangled herself from his body and stood, heading over to the backdoor in order to let out Rumpel. He was close behind her. When she caught sight of him, she couldn't stop her quick laughter.

"What?" he asked in his soft-spoken voice. His voice was deeper than normal, probably because he was still tired.

Her eyes traced the outline of his hair, and she shook her head, looking down at the socks on her feet. "Your hair," was all she could say.

"My hair?" He took a deliberate step towards her and reached out pulling a part of Emmy's on tresses out in order to show her. "You should see your hair."

Emmy giggled as he released his hold on her. He didn't step away, though, and his eyes – those eyes she was now certain could see through the layers of her body, into her heart, through her soul, until she was stripped of everything, with absolutely nothing left – looked past his nose in order to catch onto hers. His lips pursed into a lopsided grin so that only one dimple popped up.

"How did you sleep?" she asked him, and then bit her bottom lip. Perhaps that wasn't the smartest of questions, considering they had slept together on a couch and the question might have a double meaning that she wasn't sure she wanted to discover just yet.

"Well," he said, his voice so soft it probably wouldn't be considered a whisper, so tender that her insides exploded with fireworks and she was suddenly happy though she couldn't explain why. "I don't think I've slept that well in a long, long time." A beat, a slight cock of his head. "Although, I should probably invest in a new couch."

Her smile deepened as she nodded her head.

"What about you?" he asked as he stepped away from her, heading back to the kitchen to make coffee for the two of them.

Emmy wasn't sure how to respond to that. If she was being honest, she would have to agree with him. She didn't know the last time she slept better than last night with him crammed together on an old couch. It didn't make any sense, but it was the truth.

"Well."

He glanced at her over his shoulder, and his eyes were the same sea-blue color as they had been last night. "Good," he said, sounding sincere. "I'm glad."

The moment Rumpel stepped back into the house a loud clap of thunder snapped at the sky, causing Emmy to jump. She nearly let out a yelp, not expecting it to rain, let alone thunder.

"Storm's coming," Jason said. This time, he was smiling and both dimples were on display as a result of it.

Emmy shut the door and locked it, as though this was a good shield against the turbulent weather. A firm chorus of chuckles told her Jason had seen her apply her logic and followed it too, but he didn't tease her, he didn't call her stupid for doing it. And he didn't unlock the door either.

"What do you say to pancakes?" he asked as he handed her a cup of coffee. "I'll make them."

Emmy tried to fight a smile but it escaped her effort and slid onto her face. "I would love that," she said, meaning every word.

"Good." He placed both hands on her shoulders, taking her by surprise, and turned her so she was facing the living room. Before she realized what he was doing, he gently pushed her out of the kitchen. "I'll take care of everything. You enjoy twenty minutes to yourself."

Emmy opened her mouth, prepared to argue, to offer to do something, but he was already heading back to the stove. Rumpel followed him, dodging Jason's legs expertly before coming to a sit. He tilted his head up, waiting for Jason to offer him something.

Emmy knew Jason well enough to know that Rumpel would not only be getting dog food but some pancakes as well.

She sighed, deciding to concede defeat, and turned back around, wondering what she was going to do. She could take a shower, but she didn't want the pancakes to be cold by the time she got out. Plus, Jason always took showers in the morning and she didn't want to steal his hot water. She decided to change out of her pajamas and into some clothes, killing about five minutes of the designated twenty. Today's outfit consisted of another pair of skinny jeans, this one the color maroon, and a goldenrod long-sleeved shirt that dipped in the front and clung to her torso without being too tight. She ran a brush through her hair and brushed her teeth, hoping to rid herself of any and all morning breath.

By the time she came back down, Jason still refused her presence in the kitchen so she was forced to find something else to kill time. Then her eyes locked onto that small bookshelf in the living room, and without being aware of her body's movements, her feet led her directly to them. She had yet to read a Jason Belmont book. Her grandmother had been a fan of his before she passed away. She loved suspense and mysteries, especially when they took place in a foreign country. Apparently, the books that made Jason all his money was the Stephen Carlyle series. Stephen Carlyle was a Scot who worked for the CIA on international cases that took him everywhere from France to Russia to Japan and New Zealand. There were nine books in the series, and while Jason hadn't published anything since before his wife's murder, his fans were still waiting for a new Carlyle thriller.

Emmy couldn't help herself as she stepped onto her toes and grabbed the first book in the series, *One Knight Stand*. It was a first edition hardcover and looked as though it hadn't even been read. She took a seat on the couch and flipped the cover open. When she reached the dedication page, she merely saw, *For Stacey For everything*. Her fingertip traced the letters of her name. He seemed to love her, what with the wedding picture he kept even now, the fact that he dedicated his first book to her. What happened between them? Why did she feel she had no other option but to cheat on him? Why couldn't they work it out?

Forcing herself to continue on, Emmy turned the page.

CHAPTER 9

She was halfway through the page when her name from the kitchen caused her to pause. After tucking the page in the flap of the book jacket, Emmy closed it and sat it on the coffee table. It wasn't bad so far. She would have to continue after breakfast.

* * *

HE HAD FELT her lips on his skin. How could he not? He knew when she woke up since he had been awake before her. As an expert at controlling his breathing, he managed to feign slumber well enough to goad her into thinking he was still asleep. He wanted to have her for a little longer and, as selfish as it sounded, he wanted to see what she would do knowing they had spent the night together. He was hyperaware of every little thing she did, every breath she took, every touch she either knowingly or unknowingly branded onto his skin. He wanted to take a picture of every movement, sear them into his mind so he would always remember them.

When her palm trickled up to rest over his heart, he was afraid she might feel it skip and ruin his façade. He was lucky. The edge of her fingers had danced dangerously on the edge of his thermal and his skin. In fact, he could still feel her fingers there, even now, as though she had branded him. Maybe she had. She applied a soft sort of pressure against him, and it felt as though she was holding his heart hostage, giving it the air it needed to breathe but the threat of her abandoning it, releasing him to a life of solitude, caused rain clouds to drown it so its beating slowed back down. The only good thing he could make out of this was the fact that she never pulled away. She continued to leave it there, reassuring it that for now, while she held onto him, that he was whole.

Her nose continued to breathe in and out, in and out, tickling the light hair just underneath his collarbone. It caused his insides to run into each other and his fingers, still gripping her waist, itched for the familiarity of a soothing cigarette. But he wouldn't give this up for anything.

If he thought he was surprised by her exploration of his body, he was sorely mistaken when she tilted her head up in order to kiss him like a ghost on the corner of his neck, just above where his shoulder and throat joined. Jason couldn't stop the goosebumps from springing up all over his body if he tried. He hoped, if anything, she would assume he was cold, not that he was reacting to her kiss.

Although, if he was being honest, it wasn't really a kiss. She didn't purse her lips with the intent to kiss him, and she didn't press them against his skin. It was just her lips brushing his neck and nothing more. However, he was absolutely certain that she did this on purpose. Her head tilted up and the contact was made. She had wanted to almost-kiss him. Why? He couldn't be sure and refused to speculate. It happened, and that was all that mattered. He couldn't contain the sigh if he tried. In that moment, he was truly content. He didn't want to leave just yet.

Since she had tested him out, Jason decided it would only be fair if he attempted to do the same thing. As such, he turned his head, tightened his grip on her so she was practically on top of him, and buried his face into her hair. He was suddenly surrounded by cinnamon and vanilla and, at that precise instant, decided that it was his favorite scent and if she continued to smell just so, he would always be content. The strands tickled his face, and perhaps it was time for a shave, especially now that he had female company. He should try to look more... put together now, even though they were never going to go to town together and any notion of something romantic happening between them was plain ludicrous. However, it was nice to have a reason to try to look nice again, even if nice meant a clean pair of sweats and no robe rather than a suit and slicked back hair.

The moment was shattered, just like the glass of wine in the kitchen, after he confronted his wife about her affair, when Rumpel told the seemingly sleeping pair that it was time for him to be let out Jason needed some time to himself, and as such, offered to make breakfast. Even as the mix of Bisquick, milk, and eggs was frying over the stove, all he could smell was vanilla and cinnamon and that was okay.

When she came back into the kitchen after he informed her that breakfast was served, he noticed that his book was in her hand.

"I hope you don't mind," she asked, tucking a strand of hair behind her ear as she took her seat, "but I didn't really have anything to do, and I was interested in reading it."

He felt a soft smile play with his features as he took his seat across from her. He handed her the maple syrup, knowing she would soon be lathering her breakfast in it. "What do you think so far?" he asked, spreading butter on his own pancakes. Syrup was too sweet for him.

"Well, I've only read the first page," she said. As he predicted, Emmy poured a generous amount of the sticky substance on her pancakes. It baffled him that someone so small could eat as much as she did. "But it looked..." She paused, searching for the right word. For whatever reason, he felt compelled to hold his breath. When she finished with, "promising," he couldn't help but be relieved.

Which was just silly, since it shouldn't matter what she thought of his writing. That particular book was published around the time she was born, if not before. It was written just after he met Stacey actually.

They ate breakfast in relative silence, the only sound of the tapping rain and the soft slobbering of Rumpel as he ate the extra pancakes Jason gave him. Every now and then, he would catch Emmy looking at him from the corner of her eye, but he couldn't say why that was. He didn't know if he should feel insecure or flattered. Her face gave nothing away, her eyes as guarded as she could muster. Maybe someday soon, she would lower the guard, even if it was for a short time, just so he could see her look as vulnerable as she had looked while sleeping.

"Emmy," he said after swallowing his last bite. He straightened his shoulders and locked eyes with hers. "I wanted to ask you your opinion."

Emmy knitted her brow and pushed her lips together before nodding her head in assent. She did not speak.

"I was thinking of cutting my hair," he said, and before he could ask if she thought it was a good idea, her mouth dropped open, her eyes got wide, and she interrupted him with, "No!"

He watched in mild amusement as her face turned pink and her eyes shot down to her plate. She began to coil a strand of her long hair around her finger, a nervous habit he noticed. "I just mean," she said before biting her bottom lip. He loved when she did that. He couldn't explain why, but it looked intoxicatingly innocent and thoroughly seducing at the same time, and he was absolutely positive she had no idea the sort of effect she had on him or anyone else who might witness the duplicitous gesture. She tilted her head to the side and, surprising him, was able to look him in the eye. "I like your hair the way it is. The way it falls into your face." She looked away again, this time to watch as she cut up another piece of pancake. "At least, that's what I think. It's your hair. You can do whatever you want." And with that, she shoved the forkful of food into her mouth so she wouldn't have to speak anymore.

Which was fine with Jason. He didn't need to hear her say anything else. He had no idea how she did it, but she managed to say exactly what he needed to hear without lying to him or sugar-coating anything. She never spoke more than she had to and always said what she meant. If she didn't know what to say, she remained silent. He liked that. He liked that very much.

And, more than that, the fact that she verbally admitted that she liked some sort of attribute of his, even if it was merely physical – especially if it was merely physical – made his contentment transform into a raindrop of glee. He would not cut it then, not if she liked it as much as she seemed to.

Another clap of thunder startled Emmy, causing her to nearly choke on her food.

"You live in Frisco," Jason pointed out. "Shouldn't you be used to thunderstorms by now?"

"Actually, I lived in Fountain Valley my whole life," she corrected. "I came up to San Fran a couple of years ago when I found out my grandfather was having trouble paying his medical bills. So no, I'm still not used to this weather."

"It's why you took the job," he murmured as he watched the pieces tumble into place.

"What?"

"Your grandfather."

"Oh." A pause. "Well, yes. I was going to college down at San Francisco State, living with him while I did so. He had his retirement, but I worked two jobs to be able to contribute. He won't let me actually give him the money. He's too prideful for that. I just grab the bills before he has a chance to get to them and pay them before or after class."

"And now?"

"It just got to be too much." Her voice had grown softer as more emotion touched her tone. "His leg, which he injured in World War II, still bothers him, and he has to take various medication... I couldn't do it anymore, and I don't want him to have to use all of his savings on medicine when he's saving up for a boat." A transparent smile. "He loves sailing. It was one of the reasons he came up here. The weather and the sailing. So I decided to take a semester off and come work for you, which would have me make more money than my two jobs combined."

"Are you almost finished with school?"

"This would have been my senior year."

Jason took a bite of his food even though he wasn't hungry anymore. It gave him an excuse to remain silent as he took in her words. He had no idea what it was like to be in her position. He had come from a well-off family who supported him and his crazy dream of writing. He had no idea what it was like to sacrifice a higher education in order to take care of a family member. She was much more mature than her young years would otherwise suggest, and while that made him admire her all the more, it made him a bit sad that she wasn't out partying, stressing out over finals, and falling in love with the wrong guys. Guys, he knew, could never deserve her.

"You should call him," he suggested after he swallowed his food. "Your grandfather."

"You think so?"

"Tahoe storms always get worse before they get better. I'm not sure how long this one is going to last either. I just want to make sure you get to talk to him in case the power gets cut and the storm lasts for a few days." He offered her a smile. "Go ahead. I'll take care of the dishes."

"Thank you," she said as she stood up. He knew she meant it.

Jason gave any leftovers to Rumpel and proceeded to handwash the dishes. He heard Emmy, his book tucked firmly under her arm, pad into the living room, lift the phone receiver, and call her grandfather. The minute he heard her start to speak, he turned off the faucet in order to listen to their conversation. It was wrong, he knew, to eavesdrop, but he couldn't help but be curious.

The rough side of the sponge scrubbed at the syrup Emmy left on her plate, but Jason's head was cocked at an angle that best allowed him to hear her voice. Already he could detect an unfamiliar genuine happiness when talking to her grandfather. It was a tone he had never heard while speaking to him, and while he couldn't exactly blame her for it, he hoped one day perhaps she might grant him the honor of allowing him to make her happy.

"Hi, Papa. It's me."

A pause. More scrubbing.

"Yeah, I'm okay. It's raining, though. Jason says the power might go out so I just wanted to call you and let you know I'm okay, just in case the storm lasts for a few days."

Another break in conversation. Jason finally looked down at the plate and found that he was scrubbing something that was already clean. He put it just off to the side of the sink so it would be ready when it was time to dry it. Picking up his plate, he realized there wasn't much to clean, but his fingers needed a task if his mind was consumed with Emmy's discussion.

"Jason's good." A beat. "He's different."

Another pause, and Jason knew that her grandfather was asking her what she meant by that, of that was a good thing or a bad thing. He sucked in a breath and stopped his pointless ministrations so he wouldn't mishear her response.

"In a good way. I didn't expect him to be so... Well, I'm not sure what I expected, but it wasn't this." Another beat. "He surprises me, Papa. Yes, in a good way. I didn't expect it, but I'm glad. He's not as bad as everyone makes him out to be." A pause. "I will, but I don't think anything like that's going to happen. I just... I don't know. It's just this feeling I get." He could hear his heart ring in the silence. "I'm always safe, Papa, but I don't think I have to worry. You don't have to worry either."

He set the plate down. His smile was too loud for him to hear the rest of the conversation. He picked up a clean hand towel and started drying the dishes. He thought he heard her tell her grandfather she missed him and inquire as to how Bingo was, but it didn't matter. Nothing mattered because she was beginning to trust him. It was a cautious sort of trust, but it was something. And that was all he wanted, really, because he could work with something. It gave him a small amount of hope that he never expected to have.

He remembered the feeling and decided to bask in it and not think of the future, of the fact that there was a good chance he would lose this hope just as quickly as he gained it. Instead, he focused on what he did have. That, and drying the plates without dropping them.

CHAPTER 10

The storm lasted three days and three nights. The cabin lost power after the first night. Just because the weather was bad didn't mean Rumpel couldn't go out. Interestingly enough, it was Emmy who volunteered to walk him in the rain. They were short and the pair didn't go too far, but she actually did immerse herself in the storm, always without an umbrella.

Jason watched her go one day, leaning against the door frame so as to not get the full throttle of the water falling. His eyes could clearly make out Emmy and Rumpel, the only breathing beings out and about. She seemed to be enjoying herself, what with the wild arm gestures, the jumping up and down (that ultimately led to Rumpel getting excited just as much as she apparently was) and leaning her head back in order to taste the rain on her tongue. It was in these moments when he realized that while she was much more mature than he expected, there was still an uninhibited part of her that appeared every now and then. It was hard not to be charmed by her.

When she came in, she was soaked to the bone, her hair sticking to her face, her clothes holding onto her in a way he probably never would. He met her at the door with a towel and the instructions to take a hot shower while he dried off Rumpel, but he kept the vivid image of her in his mind. Her eyes sparkled and she smiled as big as he had ever seen. She was beautiful soaking wet. She was beautiful when she was blissfully happy, and it would appear that rain inspired such happiness.

His fingers twitched. He had something to write about.

* * *

AFTER EMMY HUNG up the phone after calling her grandfather to tell him the storm had passed and power was restored, Jason came bounding down the stairs in a simple grey-white thermal and loose, dark jeans. It was the first time she had seen him dressed since they first took Rumpel for a walk and she caught herself taking in the sight. He was a rather fit man, however lean he might be. His shoulders were broad and there was actual muscle, especially on his arms. His gaze had the power to garner attention from everyone occupying the room he walked into. This, of course, made him look more powerful than he actually was. That, and Emmy had a soft spot for men in thermals.

"I was thinking we could go to the store," he said when he reached her.

"You're actually going to the store with me?" she asked in disbelief. Jason rarely, if ever, left the house. In fact, the only instances she could remember doing so was when he tended to his garden, when he walked Rumpel, and that one time he picked her up from the trolley station without a car.

"Well, I'm not going to go *in* with you, but I figured I could drive you," he said, shoving his hands in his pockets.

"You don't have to do that," Emmy said. "I can walk. It's fine."

"The storm just ended. I don't, exactly, trust the trolley system with slick roads and irresponsible tourists who think they can drive in bad weather. Plus, if it starts raining again, I don't want you caught in the storm, your arms filled with groceries."

Her mouth dropped open, prepared to argue with him, but she shut it. Who was she to tell him to stay inside? The fact that he was willing to drive into town – whether or not he actually got out of the car – was a big step to reintegrating himself with society. It was a step in the right direction, and she didn't want to dissuade him. As such, she offered him a smile and said, "Okay. Let me go change and we can go."

A few minutes later, she, Jason, and Rumpel were loaded into Jason's old Honda and they headed into town. The drive was quiet, and Emmy proceeded to look out the window and observe how the locals reacted to the weather. She was glad Jason decided to drive since the trolley driver's maintained the same routine despite the bad weather, including the speed and the sharp turns they had to make as the circled the mountain. They were either really reckless or really familiar with their vehicle. Jason's driving was steady but cautious, and she felt secure.

"I'm almost finished with your third book," she said, turning to him. She felt her eyes light up while speaking. She had dived head-first into the world he created and she found it too irresistible to come up for air anytime soon. When she wasn't cooking, cleaning, doing laundry, or walking the dog, Emmy was reading. Luckily for her, she was currently living with the author and could ask him questions about Stephen Carlyle whenever she wished, but for some reason, he had been sparse the past few days. "I'll probably finish the series by next week."

"Really?" He smiled at this, and he gave her a quick glance before replacing his eyes back on the road. "I'm glad you enjoy them."

"I do. I really, really do. But I know you haven't written anything for a while and I was wondering... Does that mean you're finished with the Carlyle series? Or are you working on another one?"

"I can't tell you that," he said, his eyes crinkling with amusement.

"Why not?"

"If I said it was the end, you'd expect everything to be resolved at the end of the ninth book," he explained. "But what if I left a cliffhanger as the end of the series? What would you do then, hmm?"

"I'd probably be furious."

"Exactly. And you're living with me at the moment. I don't want to answer either way in case you build expectations that aren't filled and then decide to poison my food."

Emmy tried to suppress a smile as she shook her head, but failed. "Will you at least tell me if Stephen and Rosie finally get together?" she asked.

"Emmy," he said in a mock-lecturing tone. "Where would the fun be in that?"

"What's the fun of living with the writer if you aren't going to tell me anything?" she asked, her brow pushed up as her cheeks pinched from smiling.

"Once you finish the series, you can ask me whatever you want," he said, "and, if you've found that I have concluded the series, I'll answer. But if you've found that there will be another one, I'll only answer what I can without spoiling it. Deal?"

"I suppose I have no other choice," Emmy mumbled as Jason pulled into the Raley's parking lot.

"I'd suppose you're right," he said.

Once he slid easily into a stall, he rolled down the back windows even further for Rumpel and pulled out a crossword puzzle book. Emmy got out of the car, list already out, and after murmuring a quick goodbye, headed into the market. Since she had the car with her, she decided to get as much as they needed and then some since she wouldn't have to carry them with her, especially when it came to the heavy things like dog food, milk, and laundry detergent.

Emmy was about fifteen minutes in and nearly three-quarters finished with the list when she nearly ran into Linda Carson. How was it possible that she ran into Linda at the same grocery store twice in the span of a month? Her entire body tensed as she stopped the grocery cart. Maybe if she turned around, Linda wouldn't notice her.

Emmy expected that this ploy wouldn't work out. It never did, not in the television shows, the movies, and the books she had come in contact with. But somehow it worked. She did a little skip to celebrate and managed to finish her shopping and pay for her groceries without another run-in with the woman.

It was only as Emmy was heading out of the store did she encounter Linda again. And she had been so close to the exit, too.

"Emmy?"

Emmy stopped but kept her body facing the exit. She closed her eyes and released a breath through her nose, hoping that might inspire patience. She could hear the click-clack of Linda's telltale heels as they hit the tile, and they got louder and louder until they reached Emmy's side. Emmy moved her cart off to the side so she wouldn't be in anybody's way, and turned so she was now facing Linda who, for some inexplicable reason, had a look of utter confusion chiseled on her face.

"Yes?" Emmy asked, her voice tight. She wanted to go back to the car. She wanted to go back to the cabin. She did not want to be here with Linda in a grocery store. People still looked at her and whispered as she walked by. It happened whenever she shopped, and the more she encountered it, the more she wanted to snap at these people. How could they continue to talk badly about Jason and pray for her welfare when it was obvious he hadn't done anything to her and probably wouldn't.

Oh my.

The thought struck her like a bullet to the heart. She was so surprised by it, she had to take a step back.

When had that *happened?*

Did she trust that Jason wouldn't hurt her? The thought would have made her laugh upon first receiving the job because of *course* there was a good chance harm would befall her when everyone knew he killed his wife and her lover. Now, the thought was funny because Emmy had this feeling that Jason would never harm her. At least, he gave no indication of wanting to, and somehow, someway, she trusted that feeling more than what everybody said supposedly happened.

"It's just," Linda continued, her blue eyes sketching Emmy's features, searching for something. She took in Emmy's face, her neck, even the clothes she was wearing. They were nothing compared to Linda's short summer dress, tights, and ankle boots – was the woman not aware that a storm had just ended? – but as far as Emmy was concerned, there was nothing wrong with them. Finally, after seemingly being unable to find what it was she was searching for, Linda's eyes made it back up to Emmy's face. "I just thought you'd be, like, hurt or something. If you were still alive at all."

Emmy pressed her lips into a thin, white line as she wrinkled her brow. "What?" she asked, sharper than she originally intended. "I don't quite understand what you're trying to say, Linda."

"I thought it would be obvious," Linda said in a tone that insinuated Emmy was an idiot for not knowing. She took a step forward and lowered her voice so nobody would overhear. It was actually thoughtful since Emmy knew that while everyone appeared to be minding their business at the checkout, they were all trying to listen in on Emmy's conversation. "You're living with Jason Belmont."

This explained nothing.

"So?"

Apparently, any patience Linda had had gone out the window, because she snorted and then rolled her eyes. "Please, Emmy, you can't be this stupid." This time, her voice was its regular, projected self. She had one grocery bag dangling from her manicured fingers. "Jason Belmont. The guy who killed his wife. Is it really a stretch for me to assume that he killed you too, or, at least, I don't know, beat you or cut off your finger or something?"

This time, Emmy did laugh. Linda made a grunting noise, indicating that she had taken offense to Emmy's laughter, but, quite frankly, Emmy didn't care. The thought of Jason slicing off her finger was too hilarious not to react.

Linda took a step forward and tilted her head close to Emmy. "Seriously, Emmy, this is serious," she said, as though Emmy didn't know. "How could you be laughing at something so serious?"

"Linda," Emmy said, placing a hand on her hip. "It's not as serious you're making it out to be."

"What are you talking about?" Linda asked in a firm voice.

"You aren't living with Jason Belmont so don't pretend like you know what's going on in his home," Emmy replied. Her eyes narrowed. This wasn't funny anymore. "Stop acting like you do. I don't care what you've heard about him and I don't care who you've heard it from, but I guarantee you're wrong. He didn't kill his wife. He didn't kill her boyfriend. And he's not going to kill me or hurt me or slice off my finger."

"Do you even realize what you're saying, Emmy? I know you can't afford cable at your grandfather's home, but I'm sure you got the local news channel and I'm sure you heard the top media analysts talking about how the evidence against Belmont was overwhelming and a Guilty verdict was almost guaranteed. Then, lo and behold, he winds up getting away with murder. Do you understand? *He got away with murder.* Not just one, but two. *Two,* Emmy. Yeah, legally, he wasn't guilty, but that doesn't mean he's innocent. Everyone knows he did it. Why do you think he hides away in his cabin in the woods? Because he can't face the town. Because he knows what he did and he knows we know."

"He doesn't come to town all that much because everyone assumes he committed the murders even when he was found not guilty," Emmy corrected. She tilted her head up in order to look down at Linda. "No one will even give him a chance."

"A chance?" Linda took a step forward so they were less than a foot apart. "You want to give a murderer a chance? What is wrong with you?"

"There's nothing wrong with me. I've actually spent time with Jason and I think I can say I know him better than anyone else. Why would you choose to listen to people who've never even met him over a girl who's lived with him for the past month?"

Linda looked as if she was about to argue and then something akin to realization spread across her delicate features. "Oh," she said, dragging the word out longer than what was necessary. "I get it."

Emmy pushed her brow together. "Get what?" she asked. "I have no idea what you're talking about."

"Stop playing dumb, Emmy," Linda said, her voice flat. "It's not a good look for you. This whole living situation with Belmont, the fact that you're defending a known murderer, it's all so clear now." Emmy couldn't reply. She still wasn't sure what Linda was trying to say and was getting frustrated because the girl just wouldn't spell it out. "You're sleeping with him."

Emmy would have laughed at the suggestion had Linda not been so serious.

"That's it, isn't it?" she continued. "You're sleeping with him and that's why you're defending him. I knew you were weird, but I didn't think you were twisted. I mean, not only did he kill the guy, but he's got the face only a mother could love" –

Emmy didn't know where it came from. It amazed her how fast it happened and her mind didn't catch up until after the fact. She wasn't even a violent person and yet, somehow, Linda had made her so furious that she couldn't help but sock her across the face. It was only when her hand started to throb did she realize it had actually happened.

Linda let out a startled scream, her hand immediately going up to cover the side of her jaw. "I see he's already rubbing off on you, you whore," she said in a low, dangerous voice.

That was when Emmy heard the loud murmurs, the new rumors that would be spread throughout Tahoe in an hour at the most. People didn't even attempt to hide their staring now, not after what she did to Linda.

She had to get out of there. Now.

After grabbing her cart, she all but dashed out of the grocery store and only allowed herself to breathe after reaching the familiar sea-foam colored car. She knocked on the trunk, hoping Jason would understand she needed him to open it. Once it popped open, she all but threw the bags in and shut it before sliding into the backseat flushed, out of breath, with her hand throbbing.

"What happened?" asked a bewildered Jason as he proceeded to start the car and back out.

"I'll tell you back at home," she replied. She was trying to drown out the pain that she didn't even notice that she had used the term home as though she belonged there instead of 'the cabin.'

* * *

EMMY STILL WASN'T OFFERING any explanation so once the groceries were all put away, Jason took a seat at the round dining table and looked up at her through the lenses of his bottle cap glasses. Before he could open his mouth to ask her again, he noticed her cupping her hand, holding it tentatively. It was swollen, red. Something had happened to her. Something had happened to her to the point that she had to punch somebody in the face. His blue eyes immediately snapped back to her face, wanting to make sure she wasn't marked or in pain anywhere else. From what he could see, however, she was okay. She didn't seem to be favoring one leg over the other and her breathing looked even.

"What happened?" he asked. He tried to keep his voice gentle, but there was a firmness that all but demanded she answer as honestly as possible. If anyone had hurt her, he wanted to know so he could take care of it.

"Oh," she said, glancing down at her hand. Jason stood up and headed to the roll of towels, prepared to wrap ice cubes in it and help her soothe her wound. "It's nothing, I" –

"That isn't nothing," he said, indicating the swollen hand. He took her other one and gently tugged her over to the table. When she reached his recently-vacated chair, he placed both hands on her shoulders and eased her down before turning to the freezer for some ice. "So?" he asked over his shoulder.

"It's embarrassing," she murmured, but even her voice revealed she knew she wasn't going to win this battle. "Okay, well I was finished with my shopping and five feet from the exit when I ran into this girl I went to college with."

"Ah," he said as though that explained everything. Once he had the paper towel bounded together, he put a squirt of water on it and then knelt down. Without waiting for her permission, Jason took her wounded hand in his and placed the ice on her knuckles. She gasped when it touched her, and though her intuition was to pull away, he made sure she didn't. "Go on."

"I, uh." A pause. Jason looked up at her, wondering what caused her to stop. He was surprised to find her watching him with an intensity in her eyes he had never seen before. "We were friends, actually, but as it so often is with girls, a boy came between us. I told her I liked this guy Cody and I was almost certain he liked me, but almost immediately after that, I hear she and him are going out, and from then on, I didn't talk to either of them. It's silly, I know. So high school."

"So you punched her in the face as a way to get back to her for stealing your crush?" he asked. She giggled because he sounded so convoluted when he was confused.

"No," she said, shaking her head. "I'm not a violent person. At all. My grandfather taught me how to throw a punch back when I was in sixth grade one Christmas, just in case, but I don't like fighting except in hockey, and even then, I tend to get worried about both players, whether or not he's from my team.

"Anyway, do you remember the time I went to the store for you? Where you asked about it, and I said I defended you?"

"Of course." How could he forget it? It had been one of the kindest things anyone had ever done for him in a long, long time.

"Well, she was there. And she was the person I defend you to. Not that no one else was saying anything or giving me odd looks, but she was the only one who actually had the courage to say it to my face.

"Today wasn't any different." A pause. "Well, that's not true."

"Obviously not," Jason said with a tiny smirk. He continued to hold the towel against her knuckles. Every now and then, he would lift the ice up and blow on her hand. "You socked somebody this time." He had been hoping his teasing would make her smile, but she looked at him with such a serious expression on her face that he almost thought he had offended her.

"No, it's not only that." She bit her bottom lip, knitting her brows together. He knew that look; she was trying to string the right words together and needed a little time to do so. "It's us."

Jason licked his lips, an anxious habit, and managed to look her in the eyes. Instead of seeing them guarded like he expected them to be, she looked almost... shy. It was an expression he never expected to see and he found it endearing.

"Us?" he asked in a soft voice as to not scare her away.

She nodded her head. "I know you now," she explained. "A lot better than I did then. I can handle people whispering about me and looking at me like they feel sorry for me or they think I'm crazy or for any hidden marks on my body that you may have caused. I can deal with that. But for some reason, Linda just made me snap. She said some things about you and I nearly got into a shouting match with her over it. And then she said that we - Well, there's no need to repeat it, but I wound up socking her in the face. And then I ran out of the store."

Jason watched as her face turned pink to a shade of crimson, darker even than his tomatoes.

"What did she say that set you off?" he asked. He didn't want to push her, but curiosity was getting the better of him.

"I, it's..." He knew she wasn't going to tell him but something in his expression stopped her. He didn't think it was possible, but she flushed even more and looked away. "She said we were sleeping together."

"Oh." So she was upset someone thought she was sleeping with him? It was a suckerpunch in the gut, but he understood her point of view. If the whole town thought she was only defending him because they had a sexual relationship with an alleged murderer, he could rationalize feeling the need to punch someone due to the damage it did to her reputation. "Yeah, I get where you're" –

"That's not it." Her words were fast so they jumbled together, but Jason was able to decipher them. He picked his eyes up from her knuckles – her hand was about half the size of his – in order to meet her eyes once again. "I mean, I don't want people to think we're sleeping together because we aren't. And I'm not that type of girl. I don't go around sleeping with guys I'm not in a relationship with." He wasn't sure why she felt the need to clarify, but he was glad she did. "She just said some stuff about you, along with the statement. That was insulting. And I was insulted. For you. I had been standing there, listening to her talk about you – a person, by the way, she doesn't even know –and I just lost it. I lost it. I have no idea what came over me, but I socked her in the face. I probably won't ever be allowed back into that store because everyone started talking after I did it. Not just whispering, but talking. Sorry about that. The store, I mean."

"There are plenty of grocery stores in Tahoe," Jason assured her, but her words were still sinking in. He needed a moment to wrap his head around them. "So..." He pressed his lips together, tilting his head slightly to the side. "You punched someone in the face. For me."

Emmy let out a shamed whisper, tucking her chin down so her hair fell into her face. He was certain if he hadn't been holding onto her hand, she'd be burying her face in them. "I'm sure you hear this a lot in a much different context, but I really am not that girl," she said through a mumble.

Jason couldn't help but smile. Without even realizing it, he began to trace designs into her skin with his fingertips. She rubbed her lips, her eyes descending to watch his ministrations. When he became aware of what he was doing, he stilled, unsure if he had crossed a boundary. Then, a miracle happened. With delicacy he wasn't aware any human was capable of possessing, she squeezed her fingers around his. She closed her eyes, muffling a groan of pain, but she didn't let go until after a few seconds.

He wasn't sure what he was doing at that point. He extended his torso so his knees were keeping him up in order to look Emmy in the eyes. She looked back, not breaking contact even when his index finger resumed tracing her skin. He was so close to her that if he turned his head to the side, his lips would be pressed against hers and hers would be against his, not his neck, but his lips, and if he pushed his lips, he'd be kissing her, actually kissing her. When her tongue slid out of her mouth to dab her bottom lip, to moisten them, he nearly did it too.

But he hesitated. He couldn't. Not yet. He wanted to kiss her, more than anything. But now, he would wait. For the right moment.

Instead, he reached up with his free hand and cupped the side of her neck. Her skin was warm and as soft as it looked. He extended his fingers up so he could feel the silky strands curl around them of their own volition.

"That boy," he said, his voice softer, huskier, as though they were clogged in the back of his throat and he needed to force them out because she needed to hear them. "The one you had a crush on? He's mad, daft, a downright idiot for going with her when he had you standing right in front of him."

Gently, he used those fingers in her hair to push her head towards him so he could rest his forehead against hers. His nose was long, pointed, and perfect hers was short, petite, a smooth slop that turned up and somehow they fit when his bridge brushed hers. It was an odd piece in their puzzle, bridges of noses touched together in such a way that felt right, together, a match. He would have closed his eyes to relish it if he wasn't saying something serious to Emmy. "You were the right one, Emmy. You *are* the right one, and he'll regret it for the rest of his life."

Her eyes looked so big and hopeful, like she wanted nothing more than to believe everything he was saying. If he had to remind her every day of what a wonder she was, then he would. He could promise that and be lucky to have the opportunity.

They stared at one another. He wasn't sure what was going to happen now. All he could think of was that she wasn't pulling away from him, she was leaning into him, her hand was soft and warm and maybe sometime soon, he could interlock his fingers through hers, bring her hand up to his lips, kiss every knuckle and simply hold her hand. When was the last time he held someone's hand?

He pulled back. He didn't know why, but he pulled back, dropped his hand from her neck down into his left, and resumed his kneeling position. However, he kept a steady hand on her injured one, making sure the ice was still in position. From the corner of his eye, he could swear he saw a hint of disappointment flash in her eyes, but it happened so fast there was a good chance he was mistaken.

"How's your hand?" he asked. His voice was like a crack in the sidewalk, searching for sunlight.

"It'll survive," she murmured.

"A leftie, eh?" He picked his eyes up and locked them with hers. "Well, you rest it for the rest of the day. I'll take care of everything.

You can hang out on the couch and read all day. How does that sound?"

Even without hearing her say it, the look on her face clearly stated that she was about to object. He pushed his brow up, indicating the matter was not up for discussion. A lovely smile slid onto her face and he felt himself smiling in return.

"It sounds wonderful." She stood, as did he, keeping the ice on her hand. He barely blinked when she placed a chaste kiss directly on his cheekbone before scurrying off without looking back.

A smile broke out onto his face. He could still feel her lips lingering on his skin.

CHAPTER 11

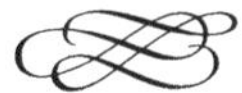

There was a light drizzle that lasted four days. Rumpel was disgruntled at the lack of exploration and exercise but he wasn't willing to venture farther out into the rain if he didn't have to. Emmy, as usual, didn't mind taking strolls in the rain. It helped clear her mind and the bitter air helped clear her thoughts. She noticed a changed had taken place in her body and in her mind regarding her current whereabouts and the person she was with. She actually slept through the night now, and when she woke up, her body wasn't as tense. She wasn't waiting for Jason to walk through the door and attempt to murder her any longer.

She trusted him.

It was scary the first time she realized it, truth be told. This man was intimidating if she had seen him in the street without the chip permanently on his shoulder. The fact that his wife and her lover were found murdered and he was the prime suspect just added to his mysterious drifter air. Once you got deeper, however, the man was gentle. Sweet. Kind. Warm. Completely unlike his public persona. The only reason she originally felt uncomfortable being with him was because there was a good chance he killed his wife, despite his acquittal.

Emmy stopped walking, swallowed. She looked out at the woods from the outer limits of Jason's backyard. Before taking the position here, Emmy had been so sure Jason was guilty, that the justice system had failed the minute he was able to walk free. He got off on a technicality, and now, even if he had committed the crimes, he would never stand trial for either one of them again. Now, however, her thoughts had shifted. She believed he was innocent. But a small part of her worried she only believed in his innocence because she needed him to be innocent. She had physically harmed someone in defense of that innocence. She was comfortable around a would-be murderer to the point of being attracted to him.

Because she was. Attracted to him. And if it turned out he did kill his wife and her lover, she would hate herself for the rest of her life. Emmy, for the life of her, had no idea what happened or when things changed. But they did, and she couldn't go back to the way things used to be. She got butterflies in her stomach and her legs were like yogurt whenever she was around him. Her eyes were glued to his form when he wasn't paying attention. She did not know how it was possible that someone so intimidating could be so beautiful. Truth be told, he looked like a red neck when he was in the public - plaid and jeans and boots. His dark hair was in his face. Covering his eyes. This made no sense to Emmy because his eyes were probably his best feature. They were a dark color. Initially, Emmy believed they were a brown. However, upon further inspection, she realized that she was wrong. They were blue, an incredibly dark blue like the bottom of the ocean. When he caught her eye, it was hard to look away, and her breath caught in her throat and she couldn't breathe, like she was drowning.

She didn't want to think about him being guilty. She wanted to believe the best in him, even though there was no reason for it and he didn't necessarily deserve it. She shook her head, her hair matted to her face. It was starting to rain harder, and there was a good chance there might be another storm coming.

Rumpel yipped, his tail wagging in the rain, his tongue hanging out of his mouth through a wide smile. Emmy could not help but chuckle at the excitement the dog was showing.

When she turned to see what had riled him up, her heart jumped into her throat and remained lodged there. She couldn't move, couldn't breathe. She was rooted to her spot, and there was no chance of her moving anytime soon unless Jason walked out to her and swooped her up in his arms himself.

And she wanted that. Badly.

Because he was the reason Rumpel was so excited in the first place. Jason Belmont was standing in the pouring rain in actual clothes and not his robe, getting soaked to the bone. And he was the most beautiful thing she had ever seen before.

She wasn't thinking when her feet proceeded to hurry in his direction. Her thoughts were on mute. She wasn't acting rationally, and even worse, she didn't care. Her hands were shaking but she couldn't distinguish if it was because of the cold rain or if it was because of what she was about to do. Her heart was slamming in her chest the way a child jumped up and down on a bed - enthusiastically and without pattern.

Jason's eyes were on her - so dark and difficult to read. She almost stopped herself due to the fact that she didn't know how he would respond, but she pushed through like it didn't matter. He looked puzzled, unsure what she was doing and why she was approaching him. In all honesty, she had no idea what she was doing either. She was acting on pure instinct, and even if her consciousness intervened, she highly doubted she would be able to stop if she tried. Rumpel was running with her, yipping happily over the falling rain. He only stopped to shake the rain off his fur as best as he could. It did not help, of course, but he tried all the same.

When Emmy reached him, she threw her arms around his

shoulders and sprung up on the balls of her feet so she could kiss him without any inhibitions. Her eyes closed on impact, but her hands moved from his shoulders to his hair, and she buried her fingers in the now-dark tresses.

Jason seemed surprised at her show of affection, but that shock lasted only momentarily before his own arms wrapped around her waist, pulling her even closer to his body. There was no space between their torsos, much like their mouths. They couldn't breathe but they still continued to kiss. Jason made the first move to deepen it by using one hand to clutch her cheek, bending his thumb so it tilted her chin back and gave him better access to her mouth. His tongue slipped between her lips, tentatively at first, almost as though he was waiting for her to reject him, for her to demand he retreat and keep the kiss passionate but close-lipped. She did nothing of the sort, and instead, opened her mouth to give him better access.

Emmy's thoughts were muddled and foggy, probably because the rain was masking her better judgment. But she didn't care - goodness, she didn't care - not when his hands held her face and her waist as securely as his did, the roughness just adding to the safety she felt when he touched her. Not when his lips were claiming her mouth as his own, when his tongue burned every fragment of flesh it came in contact with. She didn't know kisses could feel this way. She didn't know Jason could kiss this way - that anyone could kiss this way. It astounded her, and as her thoughts continued to get heavy and difficult to decipher, she could not help but think why in the world any woman in their right mind would cheat on a man who could kiss like this? Maybe she deserved it...

The thought instantly made Emmy choke. She pulled away from Jason, suddenly glad the rain was falling hard. She needed to wash that terrible thought away from her mind, from her person. Regardless of the type of person Stacey was, she and her lover did not deserve to die that way. Nobody did. Not even Linda Carter.

"What?" Jason asked, and his deep blue eyes filled with concern, like he was some sort of lost puppy, worried he had done something wrong and that his master wouldn't love him anymore. "I, I'm sorry, I shouldn't have" -

Emmy held up her hand, immediately silencing him. This was not what she wanted to hear though she was certain if he said anything else, anything sweet or romantic, it would be just as bad. She needed silence, she needed the soft drumming if the rain, she needed the absence of everything so she could clear her head and give her time to breathe.

It wasn't difficult to figure out, she realized. She didn't need that much time. Despite the fact that Jason was tried for murder, despite the fact that he was a writer that created realities that shocked his audience, despite the fact that she barely found out she liked him as a human being, she wanted him. She wanted him more than she should, more than she wanted anybody before. She wanted to feel his hands on her curves, his mouth on her neck, her fingers through his hair. She wanted to breathe the same air as he did and hear him moan her name. Just thinking about it caused her upper thighs to moisten, caused her pelvis to pulse in just the right way where she felt both pleasure and pain simultaneously.

The reason she pulled away was because her thoughts were becoming inappropriate. Despite her feelings for Jason, Stacey and her lover did not deserve to die. They could be the worst people in the world, but they did not deserve to die. No one did. Even if they were the most awful people on the planet, they did not deserve to go the way they went. And her desire for Jason did not give her the right to justify his actions - if he committed them in the first place. She needed to break apart from him in order to remind herself of that fact. She couldn't lose who she was and what she valued because she wanted to have sex with someone.

When Emmy picked her eyes up to look back at Jason, she realized he was waiting for a response from her, any kind of response. She didn't know if he realized it, but he was holding his breath. She smiled softly at the sight, not realizing she could possess such power over someone's emotions the way she did with him. More than that, she found she liked it, and her confidence continued to grow.

It was for that reason why she was able to step to him again, clutch his face within her watery hands and pull him down so she could meet lips with him once more. From there, she released his face so she could cross wrists behind his neck, and his own hands pressed the flat of her back close to his so no air could sneak through. It was as though he was breathing fresh air by kissing her, by holding her to him, by allowing himself to lose his control with her. She didn't know how long he'd been holding onto it, how hard he's been keeping it at bay, but once she gave him permission to let down his defenses, he didn't waste a moment. The rain started to fall harder, but somehow, Emmy wasn't cold. Heat radiated from her body, meshing with Jason's own heat, mingling together to create steam. The goosebumps on her skin were because of her feelings Jason was stirring within her rather than her temperature.

Somehow, Emmy ended up with her back against the wall of the house. Her arms were raised above her head and kept together at her wrists by one of Jason's hand. The other gripped her waist the way a dog gripped a bone - possessive and insistent, with no intent to let it go anytime soon.

Emmy felt a spark shoot straight through her pelvis, between her thighs, until it twisted into a throb and she couldn't help but moan against his mouth, a desperate sound that pierced the cold silence. The rain still landed in fat plops on the wooden cabin, the noise a symphony. She wanted more of him, and judging by the way his teeth nipped at her bottom lip and how the lower half of his body was pressed so tightly against hers, he wanted her just as much.

"Inside," she told him through the kiss, that blip of a moment where she could speak and catch her breath at the same time.

He nodded, and without releasing his grip on her, began to lead her inside. Their mouths were still connected, their bodies still molded together, and it was amazing that neither of them was tripped up of their way inside.

Jason knew his house well, so without looking up, he was able to find the doorknob and open the door. Emmy could feel Rumpel dart between her feet to get inside where it was warm, but she couldn't give the dog much thought. Not when she was wrapped up this way. She barely heard the door slam shut. Her hands were gripping his hair, her chest was pressed hard against his. She didn't realize she was cold until she was out of the rain and in the surprisingly warm cabin. It didn't even matter, though, not when Jason kissed her the way he was. All other thoughts, all other feelings, were tossed casually aside, left for another time. Not now. Not when she was in this moment.

The back of her knees hit the couch, and she buckled underneath it. Jason was quick to get on top of her. It didn't seem to matter to him that they were both soaked, which meant his couch was getting soaked.

Emmy's fingers let go of Jason's hair and proceeded to run down his back. She could feel his muscles twitch underneath her touch, and a surge of power coursed through her. The fact that she had such power over this decidedly masculine person was enough to want to go even further, to make him twitch even more. Her mouth yanked away from his and proceeded to find homes on his jawbone, the place on his throat where his pulse kept time, the column of his neck, and the connection point between his neck and his shoulder. With every kiss she placed on his body, his breathing caught in his throat and a small groan was emitted instead. The noise was unlike anything Emmy had ever heard before, and she found she liked the sound of it so much she wanted to hear it again. And again. And again.

He pressed himself down onto her. Emmy could tell he was being careful with his distribution of weight. Somehow, she was able to feel his entire length on her without being crushed by his girth. He never stopped kissing her. Not when he shifted his weight to position himself appropriately, not when she reached up to wrap her arms around his neck. It was like she was his oxygen, and he wanted to breathe as much as he possibly could. His lips sought after hers, kept track of them the way a father kept after his daughter. He would not let up. His tongue was possessive, laying his claim on her mouth, branding her as his now for as long as he wanted.

Emmy was familiar with the art of making love. She'd had a couple of boyfriends in high school and one in college, but none of them made her feel the way Jason was making her feel right now. Her pelvis throbbed with desire. It pulsated painfully against her inner wall, and if he didn't fill her soon, she was going to sob. There was a need for him, a need she didn't particularly understand. It was as though her life depended on being with him in this way. Her body craved him the way she craved chocolate once a month. She needed him desperately, and this uncontrollable urge to be with him physically scared her because it was completely unexpected. He was the last person she ever saw herself with. He didn't go to college, he didn't have a stable job, and he had been married before. On top of that, he had been tried for the murder of his wife and her boyfriend. A jury didn't even say he was not guilty; Jason got off on a technicality.

The thought thrilled her. It was the worst thing she had ever felt, and she knew she would probably feel nothing but guilt afterward, but the thought that the hands currently touching her right now, the mouth currently kissing her, had done something so terrible, so cruel, so awful...

The danger thrilled her. And she hated herself for it. But not enough to stop.

His hands gripped her waist like he never planned on letting her go anytime soon. Like he would have his way with her as many times as she wished. And she wanted that too. God, she wanted that, too.

She could feel his hand press against her hip and she gasped. He swallowed the noise by capturing her lips with his once again. His hands started to travel, from her waist up to her stomach. His fingers, callused and rough, touched her bare skin, her flat stomach, and it traveled up until it reached the hem of her jacket.

"Take it off," she said against his lips, she said without thinking.

Jason snapped back so his butt rested on his ankles, and he looked at Emmy with wide, searching eyes. It was almost as though he wanted to be hopeful but didn't want to risk it. From the dark shade of blue, she knew he wanted her. Badly. She wondered if her eyes reflected the same desire, the same need for his body, because she certainly felt it.

Regardless, he listened to her. He took his shirt off in that masculine way where men reach behind them to pull up their shirt and contort their torso so it was easier to slide it up and off. Emmy couldn't stop herself from reaching for him, putting her hands on his skin and pulling him back to her. He was beautiful - a stocky body type, toned and in shape for his age. Her fingers twitched over his abdomen and she felt him flinch, like her touch sizzled and he couldn't handle it. It made her feel powerful and she found that she wanted more of that power over him, wanted to make him beg and moan and plead and say her name in a throaty voice.

His mouth found hers once more, like they were positive and negative atoms, like they didn't have a choice to but to attract. He was rougher this time. He tugged at her bottom lip with his teeth, eliciting a surprised moan from her mouth. He wanted his power back and she was happy to give it to him for now. She likes being in control but she would give it up for a minute or two but only to him. He could dominate her, do whatever he wanted with her, to her body, because she trusted him and she knew he would shower pleasure over her. Her pelvis throbbed painfully just thinking about it.

His lips descended to her jawbone. Emmy wasn't sure how it was possible, but there was something sensual about the jawbone, about the attention he lavished on it. From there, he trailed his lips downward, to her neck, where he pulse best against her skin the way boxers beat against a sack of meat. He slobbered on her skin which should have been gross but wasn't. He nipped and tugged and pulled and she was sure he was going to leave multiple hickeys on her neck but she didn't care. She didn't care, not when it felt so good. She felt like a teenage boy - or, at least, she could imagine this incessant need to have sex with someone to the point where it didn't matter what stood in her way, she was going to get him inside of her no matter what it took.

Emmy could feel the strength in his hands, how they clutched at her, pinched her, pressed into her. Yet she could feel the restraint on top of that as well. His strength overwhelmed her but his gentleness consumed her, and the mixture of the two made her moisten between her thighs. He could hurt her if he really wanted to. He could force her to do this by his mere physicality alone. But there was more to him, a softness buried deep beneath the jagged edges that made him who he was. It was a softness she wanted to take over, to immerse herself in, to solely call it hers. She wanted to tease it out of him, slowly as to not overwhelm him and not rush it. She liked the chase, she liked the work she put into it, she liked the torture it caused within herself to wait, to anticipate. They had all the time in the world. It was raining outside, the dog was upstairs, and there would be no interruptions for an indeterminate amount of time. Why rush when they could slow things down, take their time, and explore everything they each had to offer.

As her hands roamed his back, they came in contact with distorted skin. He flinched again but this time, he pulled away. Emmy searched his eyes, wondering if she had pushed too far, touched too much. He looked wary, stiff, and she wasn't sure what to do. Was the moment broken because she stumbled upon something so secret, so personal, she doubted anyone really knew about it? They were scars. Multiple. Deep. Permanent. Indicating abuse. And Jason, her beautiful Jason, was ashamed of them.

"Hey," Emmy said, her voice gentle. She reached up to cup his cheek with her palm. He leaned into it desperately. "It's okay. We can stop."

"The last thing I want to do is stop," he breathed, and she swallowed because his voice did things to her insides she wasn't fully prepared for.

"Do you have a...?" She let her voice trail off, pressing up her brow. She was a grown adult and she still had trouble saying condom. It was kind of embarrassing.

"Oh," he said, pushing off of her. "Yeah. Upstairs. In my room." He paused. "Should we head up there anyway? So the first time can be in a bed?"

Emmy giggled. "First time?" she said, teasing. "We'll see how you do tonight and then we can decide if it's worth doing again." He blushed and Emmy stood up on her toes to kiss the tip of his nose. "Come on! Let's go so we don't lose the momentum!"

They bounded up the stairs, laughing and giggling like teenagers. Once they got to the bedroom, Rumpel ran off as though he knew what they were going to do and wanted no part in the spectacle. Emmy and Jason barely noticed. The minute they were inside, Jason pushed Emmy into the wall and captured her mouth with his once more. His pelvis pressed into hers and she could feel his desire for her and it only made her throb with her own. She found he liked to be in control, liked to have all the power, which was fine with her because she liked how vulnerable she felt.

It wasn't long before he began to discard her clothes. In fact, as he did so, he began to lead her to the bed, leaving a trail of her sticky wet clothing behind, like a raunchy version of Hansel and

Gretel. When they hit the bed, they were completely naked. Jason's eyes burned through her skin, taking in every inch she had to offer, like she was a goddess and he had come to worship her body.

"You're beautiful," he said when his eyes finally reached her face again. "You're fucking beautiful."

She wasn't sure how to respond. She had been called beautiful before by previous boyfriends but none who meant it with every ounce of his being. She felt beautiful. And he was, too.

She reached out and touched him - her fingers fluttered across his abdomen, making him twitch. Her hand trailed lower and lower until she found him, and with a boldness she didn't realize she possessed, she wrapped her fingers around him. He gasped, his eyes rolling into the back of his head. His knees buckled and he nearly fell to the bed, but his last ounce of strength was spent keeping himself upright as she began to explore him and how he reacted to her touch. If she thought she had power before, it was nothing compared to this. So she continued to explore him, continued to caress and pull and tug and twist, all while being gentle. The noises he made were like an addictive resource she needed to fuel her drive, and she refused to stop until he grabbed her hand and all but begged her to.

"Not yet," he choked out, his voice desperate. "Not until I get to feel you from the inside."

She swallowed at his words. The pulsing inside of her got more insistent, more desperate, until it felt almost painful against the walls of her pelvis. He took his hands and traced them downward, outlining the curves of her body, trailing down the length of her legs. Gently, he pushed them open so he was between them and his eyes took in everything her body had to offer. He was gobsmacked at her beauty and she was too much in awe to be embarrassed at how thoroughly he was staring. She watched as his Adam's apple bobbed up and down, indicating he was just as nervous as she was. It made her feel better, as though they were now in this together.

He looked at her with midnight blue eyes, a question residing in the irises. She knew exactly what he was asking her. She bit her bottom lip and tilted her head back, arching and giving him the answer she hoped he would understand. His eyes flashed dark and a primal instinct took him over. His grip reached her waist until he was holding her tightly. His hands seemed to fit her hips perfectly and he held her like he was staking a claim on her body. She didn't care. She was his, hands down, white flag waving, all of her.

He positioned himself above her and slowly entered her slick lips with his sheathed cock. He was dragging this on painfully slow and she wasn't sure if it was for her benefit or his. She could feel how badly he wanted her, could feel him twitch as he inches inside of her. A whimper broke free from her mouth, one she couldn't stop from escaping if she tried, and that was all he needed before he threw slow to the wayside and completely thrust himself inside of her. She let out a cross between a gasp and a scream - a sound she had never heard herself emit before - and her head knocked back into the pillow as her eyes rolled back at the complete feeling that exuded throughout her form at the presence of him inside of her.

At first, he was slow, feeling her from the inside out, teasing her, exploring her. He wanted to go slow, it would seem, so he could feel her wholly and completely. There was no reason for them to rush, not when they've waited so long. Not when they had all the time in the world. Which they did.

Her hands clutched at his arms and it was almost tortuous, how slowly he was dragging this out. Her eyes were wide, pleading. It was as if this had built up in her so fast that she needed immediate release but the look on his face said he didn't particularly care; he was going to take his time and she would have to deal with it.

Emmy had never been with someone who could make her come without her own assistance. She didn't mind it because she knew her body better than anyone else. However, from the angle of her hips, Jason hit her just right. She didn't even have to do anything. Her breathing got short as the tingling built up - more and more and more. Her head started to get light, chin tilted back, and without warning, he claimed her exposed neck with his mouth the way a wolf would snap the neck of its prey.

That was her undoing. Her vision exploded in fireworks and she didn't even have time to tell him let alone say anything except his name. He thrust in, keeping time with her spasms before he finished as well. He grunted, moaned, made all sounds that shouldn't be attractive but came out masculine and sexy and -

She wrapped her arms around him tight as he finished and when he finished, he collapsed on top of her without placing his weight on her.

"Oh my God," she said, feeling sweat accumulate on her brow.

"Yeah," Jason agreed.

It wasn't long before they fell asleep.

CHAPTER 12

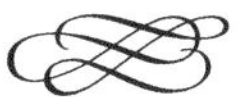

A smile nothing short of blissful featured on Emmy's face as she was aroused from her slumber. She could not fight off the smile nor could she force herself to feel a sense of guilt that was not there. She had slept with Jason Belmont. A few times, if one was technical about it. And it was the best experience she had ever been a part of in her entire life. It was as though her body was on fire and she was still simmering hours after the fact. Even now, she still wasn't able to breathe properly, still wasn't able to open her eyes entirely. She could feel electricity brimming from her fingertips and was certain if she touched herself, sparks would fly and she'd be shocked.

She could feel Jason breathing behind her, his hot breath tickling the hairs on the back of her neck. Her tummy felt like bowling pins being knocked into by bowling balls, and it was difficult to get her breathing adjusted. She was afraid to move, afraid to be anything but still because she did not want to shatter this moment. She was afraid that if they were both awake, one of them might regret what had happened. Worse would be if they wanted to do it again.

And Emmy wanted to do it again.

Even thinking it caused her face to flush with heat and she was certain she turned as red as a cherry on top of an ice cream sundae. She buried her face deeper into the crook of Jason's arm as though to hide her shame - though who she was hiding from, she did not know. She had no idea things would progress in such an unpredictable way, and now that they had, there was no way to change back to the way things had been. Emmy wasn't sure if that was what she wanted. In fact, she didn't know what she wanted at all, and the thought frustrated her because she always knew what she wanted. However, her head and her heart were at odds with each other, and while she knew what she wanted on an emotional level, she wasn't sure that desire was logical for her to pursue. She closed her eyes right, trying to keep up with her conflicting feelings.

On the one hand, Jason had legally been acquitted of murder - of both murders. He was single. He was warm, gentle, and sweet. He was a decent cook and made jokes that weren't all that funny but he tried. He was also concerned about her comfort level, about how people treated her due to her affiliation with him, and how her grandfather was doing. His written work was brilliant and captivating, well thought out, and deep. He knew what he wanted to say with his stories and how he wanted to say it. She liked that he was quiet; he didn't go out of his way to prove anything and he really didn't need to. His body of work, as well as the court decisions, stood for themselves so there was no reason for him to comment. And he was an excellent kisser and an unselfish lover. Just thinking about that caused her pelvis to tremble. She was sore but she wanted more of it, more of him.

On the other hand, there was still a part of her, a small fraction of what had been inside of her when she first got to Jason's place, that believed there was more to the story than anyone knew. That maybe Jason was holding back on something that needed to be shared with the public.

What that was, she didn't know. And, to be frank, was it really important? He was legally acquitted. That was all that mattered. And he never threatened her, never scared her. He was the perfect gentleman.

That was how they all started out, though, wasn’t it? It wasn't as though murderers were easy to spot, it wasn't as though violence rolled off the shoulders of men and women in waves that made it easy to decipher who to get close to and who to avoid. Stacey and her lover met an unfortunate end. She wondered, at that moment, if anyone took the time to ask Jason what he felt, if he was okay. If he didn't commit the act - which the law said he didn't - he was just a victim as well. Not only did he lose his wife to another man, but she was taken from him before they could decide whether or not they were going to repair their marriage. That unto itself was a tragedy, and Emmy felt her heart cracking at the thought.

Even though she had just had sex with him, even though she wanted to do it again, she could not help but be surprised by the twinge of sympathy she felt for Jason. It was as though the media had trained her to regard him as a villain and any compassion for him was regarded as compliance in his crimes.

She shook her head. That perception of him needed to change. She needed to see Jason not as a murderer and not as a victim. She needed to see him as a man who was starting over in life, who was kind and quiet, warm and reserved. A man she could end up loving if she wasn't careful. A man she might already be falling for...

"You think any louder, you're going to wake up the whole forest," came a mumbled reply.

Emmy felt her lips quirk up in a grin, as she shifted her eyes so they rested on Jason's upturned face. His eyes were still closed and his messy hair littered his face, but even she could not deny how beautiful he was. That was the one consistent thought she had about him during the entirety of her stay.

He was clothed in nothing but a pair of boxers, and for some reason, he hated the covers, choosing to sleep on the blankets rather than under them. This was fine for Emmy because she loved the blankets and was known to hog them in her sleep. Even during the hottest nights, she still needed something covering her, even just a plain, cool sheet, so she had the facade of protection against the night. She had always been this way, and it didn't appear as though it would change now.

Because of his hatred of blankets, Jason was exposed to Emmy's eyes, and seeing him stirred her appetite. There was a surprisingly fit body underneath his robe, and judging from the weights in the corner of his room and the pull-up bar in his doorway, he worked out on a daily basis. It would explain those arms she had no problem getting acquainted with last night. She loved touching them, squeezing them. Loved knowing she was responsible for the way they tensed up underneath her touch.

"Tell me," he said, and now he opened his eyes - a surprising shade of blue, clearer than she had ever seen it before. Like the sky after a storm. "What's on your mind? And don't say nothing."

Emmy smirked. She didn't realize he knew her well enough to read her mind or predict the words that would come out of her mouth. She turned to him and placed her head in her hand so she could look at Jason clearly - as clearly as she could for just having woken up. She could feel her lips turn up into a soft smile - she couldn't stop smiling and she genuinely felt foolish at her inability to control the facial inflections she was emitting to the world - and she knew the reason for it was Jason. It was something she never experienced before - uncontrollable smiling - and the fact that this man in front of her was the one responsible for it was even more unbelievable.

"I'm not really thinking of anything," she told him, and she was being honest. "I'm just looking at you."

She could tell her comment made him uncomfortable from the way his face tightened and his eyes looked away.

"Now why would you want to do that?" he asked in his indecipherable mumble.

"Because you're beautiful." His eyes snapped into hers, and he almost looked angry. Angry that she was say something so sweet and so unbelievable because there was no way it could be true. But she did not blink, did not look away, did not flinch under his penetrating gaze. In fact, she moved - keeping her eyes locked with his the whole time - until she crawled on top of him, straddling his waist, letting him see her in all her bare naked glory. She would not be shy in front of him; she would not feel shame in front of him. "Because I like looking at you."

She watched his Adam's apple bob up and down after he swallowed, and she tilted her head at him. "What?" she asked. Her fingers began to trace nonsensical patterns on his chest, and she could feel the skin underneath her tighten at her mindless ministrations.

Jason didn't answer. Instead, he lunged for her. Before Emmy knew what was happening, Jason flipped her on her back and pinned her beneath him. His mouth was on hers and he didn't seem to care about morning breath because he opened her mouth with his tongue and explored it as though it was the first time and he already wasn't familiar with it. This caused Emmy to lose track of all rational thought to the point where she didn't even worry about what her breath must taste like, couldn't even detect a problem with his, not when her thoughts were fogging up and fire began to spread through her veins.

She clawed up at his face. There would be scratches there, on his back, everywhere. It wasn't as though she could help it. He brought out this uncontrollable need in her, where she had to have him no matter what the cost, no matter what that meant. She liked seeing her scratches on his flesh because it meant that last night happened, that it was real and not just a dream. It reminded her how badly she wanted him. It didn't matter that her body aches. It didn't matter that she smelled of sweat, sake, and sex. She needed him inside her, and she needed it now.

Jason seemed to be on the same page. His fingers were like irons, searing into her skin. No one would be able to touch her the way he touched her from this point on. He had ruined her, totally and completely, and there was nothing she could do about it. She didn't want to do anything about it. She wanted him to ruin her again and again and again.

It was much faster to connect than it was last night. Both were naked, both were ready, and both wanted it badly. Jason's hold on her was much more confident, like he knew she wouldn't break under him. Like he knew she could withstand the torturous pleasure he would give her.

Before she could catch her breath, Jason flipped her over so she was on her stomach and he was behind her. She felt vulnerable and exposed. Her muscles tensed with anticipation, waiting with baited breath to see what he would do, and how. Clearly she trusted him, for her to allow him to have access to her body. No limitations. No fear. Nothing that would inhibit her from saying no. Not even his reputation. Not even the fact that he could be a murderer.

Somehow, she could feel his eyes - those deep dark pools of blue - penetrating her skin as they took the sight in. She wasn't sure what he saw, but she wasn't shy about her body. She knew that like every woman, she had flaws. But her assets made up for them and tended to make up for it. They distracted her lover to the point where she was utter perfection in their eyes. It made sex much more enjoyable not worrying about little things like that and focusing all of her attention on the pleasure she expected him to instill on her body.

--

Jason couldn't breathe. He had never had a reaction to a

woman's body before, save for the moment he enjoyed his first Playboy as a thirteen-year-old. This was completely new and more than a little enjoyable. Emmy was his dream girl incarnate, in the flesh, ready for him to do whatever it was he wanted to her. This was a dream, a fantasy, everything he ever wanted right underneath his fingertips.

Her nipples were like soft pink rubies, and he caught one in his mouth because - how could he not? They beckoned him to her like a lighthouse in the dark. His survival depended on going to her. She arched her back up, releasing a moan from between her lips. God, he loved the noises she made. They were genuine and clear and all because of him. He wanted more of them, fixated on them, like an addict needed more of his addiction. With his left hand, he fondled her other breast. It was easy to pick up what pleased her and what didn't.

Jason appreciated how open she was regarding her sexuality. She wasn't afraid to tell him what she liked and what she didn't. She knew herself well enough to know how to communicate her desires to him. She was sensitive to his touch, reacted to his rough skin like a cow to a brand. He didn't realize he could affect someone this way. Not even Stacey was this enthusiastic when they would -

But she was the last person he wanted to think about right now.

Jason was not the sort of guy who was arrogant or overtly confident. He was quiet, usually kept to himself, preferred to watch with his own eyes and listen with his own ears than have to converse with someone who might be trying to manipulate the situation and lie straight to his face. Jason could tolerate a lot but bullshit wasn't one of those things. He didn't make much noise, not during sex, not during the day and only spoke when he had something he needed to say that he seemed important enough to make the effort to speak. It was something Stacey constantly complained about, how he wasn't talkative, how he never complimented her, how he was so quiet it was weird. He was cold, he was distant, he wouldn't talk about his scars, he wouldn't even make noise during sex. Didn't he enjoy it? She just wanted to know he was enjoying it. And then, when he caught her with another man, he distinctly remembered her telling him, "You never talked to me. What did you expect?"

And he lost it.

Like it was his fault she slept with another guy multiple times behind Jason's back. The thing was, Jason never hid the fact that he was reserved. He wasn't a social butterfly and didn't like to push his boundaries. It was why he refused to do book signings and be on social media. He hired someone to do that for him, to market his books. All he wanted to focus on was his writing. He was introverted and that was okay with him. Stacey wanted to change him into something he wasn't. It was her fault she couldn't understand and accept that he was who he was. She would force him to open up so he would stop talking all together. It was why he never talked to her about his scars. It was why he stopped talking to her altogether. So she found someone who would.

In a way, he couldn't blame her. She did come to him with concerns and he refused to entertain them. He understood now her frustration with him then. The problem was, she didn't know him at all. She didn't know that he wasn't going to change just because she wanted him to. She didn't know that if she pushed him, he would withdraw even further until she wouldn't be able to reach him anymore.

Was it right? No. But it was who he was.

She didn't need to cheat on him. She could have filed for divorce. He would have given it to her; he didn't love her anymore. It was the embarrassment, the lack of respect, that enraged him. And he had every right to be enraged. If she didn't want to be with him, fine, but to betray him in such a way? That crossed a line.

He grabbed another condom from the dresser and tore the

plastic. He hadn't had sex in a couple of years. Hopefully, the condoms weren't expired. He knew he would have to get more anyway, with the way they were going at. Inwardly, he grinned. He felt like he had when he was a kid in school and couldn't stop staring at tits and asses. With Emmy, he couldn't stop staring at her in general. Everything about her was a well of beauty and he wanted to drink her in as much as he could. He would not let himself take her for granted, would not allow himself to let one moment escape where he wasn't touching her, breathing her in, feasting on her with his eyes. She was everything he wanted in a woman. She was younger than he was used to and it almost made him self-conscious. He wanted to make a good impression; if she didn't want to be with him, fine, but he wouldn't let her forget their moment together.

He must have made an impression on her because she was insatiable. She wanted him more and more, her desire for him insurmountable. He worried he didn't have the stamina to keep up with her but refused to linger on that thought until he needed to. For now, he felt the same way about her, unable to keep his hands off of her, unable to tear himself away.

Once the condom was on, he grabbed her waist and flipped her over so she was on her stomach with her ass in the air. He stared at her, drinking her in. She got him hard just looking at her.

Fuck.

His instincts worked in double time with her. Before he could mentally process it, his body was already doing the work. His hands pressed in her hips and he was almost certain she would bruise because of it. She didn't seem in pain at his touch, however, so he wouldn't - couldn't - lessen it. It would fascinate him to see his mark on her. It would make him want to consume her body again.

At that moment, he thrust into her. She hissed at his roughness but after last night, he knew she liked it. Which surprised him and turned him on at the same time. He watched as her fingers curled into the sheets, her knuckles turning white at how tight she gripped them. Fuck, she looked good. And she felt good, too. He didn't understand what he had done in his life to deserve her, to deserve this moment, but he would not let it go without him taking full advantage of it.

She was wet. God, she was wet. For him. He caused this response in her body. He had that ability over her and he wanted to use more of his power to his advantage. The way he felt inside if her must be what Heaven felt like. It was indescribable. He couldn't find the words and he was a writer. This didn't make sense. He didn't want it to.

This morning was nowhere near last night. He refused to take his time. He wanted instant gratification. He wanted it hard, fast, right now. And fuck, she was giving it to him.

He could hear her moans. It ripped right through him and caused him to bleed out. His hands gripped her waist - he had this fascination with holding her waist; his hands fit perfectly in the curves and it made him feel as though they were specifically made for him to hold - and continued to thrust, in and out, in and out.

Fuck, she was so good, so wet. There was a good chance he would bruise her, simply because he was holding so tight. He didn't know any other way to hold her. He tried to be gentle about it but that didn't work, not when she looked the way she did. Not when she sounded the way she did.

From the corner of his eye, he caught sight of a movement. She was doing something with her left hand. When he realized what that was, he nearly toppled over and missed a beat. She was touching herself, keeping her balance with one hand and increasing her pleasure with the other. Her moans got louder. If he had neighbors, they would have heard. With his history, they might even have called the cops. He didn't give a shit. Not when she looked like this. Not when she sounded like this. Not when she felt like this.

"You better hurry," he told her, "because I'm going to come soon and I can't stop."

Her cunt twitched around him in response to his words. He was surprised she liked to be talked to that way though the fact they were in an intimate setting probably helped. He made note of it and continued to thrust, faster and harder. He wanted her to get off but he wasn't lying when he said he was going to come soon. She had to have expected it, when she was so tight so wet for him.

Fuck. She would be his downfall.

She took her left hand and placed it between her thighs, keeping her weight balanced on her right hand. He couldn't see her fingers on her clit, couldn't see them push back and forth helping her reach her climax. Her moans got louder and louder, however, and he knew the exact moment when she reached that point of no return. He remembered from last night.

The sounds she made, God, he had no idea how he'd be able to take it. They were like wind chimes in the wind. They were like his favorite song on the radio after a lull in playing it. She was saying his name like it was a prayer, like he was some kind of holy being granting her pleasure and she wanted him to rain down on her and save her very soul. Which was crazy to him, because she was his goddess, a woman to be worshiped with every piece of him, everything he could possibly offer, and somehow, she still wanted him, wanted him inside of her, fucking her, taking her any which way. She looked so sweet and innocent but wasn't. She was pure but she knew what she was doing. She knew how to take it. She knew. She knew.

And that knowledge gave her all the power in the world, but he didn't care. Jason didn't care because he wanted her to have it all. Because she only used it for good. She was responsible enough not to take advantage of him.

Her breathing got shallow and there it was. She convulsed around him like she had no choice, like she couldn't stop it if she tried, and he finally let himself release into her, filling her up and letting him go and it was literal bliss. This was Heaven. He was dead. And it was beautiful and perfect and he never wanted to go back to his old life ever again. Not when she was here. Not when she wanted him just as badly as he wanted her.

When he finished, he held himself inside of her as long as he could before he started softening and slipped out altogether. She collapsed onto the bed and placed her head on the pillow, completely spent. He discarded the condom before crawling back into bed with her. Now that he had her in the most intimate way, he didn't want to be away from her. Not when she was warm and perfect and hopeful. Not when her goodness enveloped him and made him forget. Made him forget about all the bad things he had done. All the bad things he might do if this was ever taken away from him.

He couldn't lose her. He wouldn't lose her. Not now. Not ever. Not if he could help it.

--

Jason hadn't realized the two had fallen asleep until a knock on his door woke him up. He pressed his brows together, waiting. He never had visitors. Something was off. Something was strange. The knock resumed, this time, more insistent. He felt Emmy stir next to him until she cracked her eyes open. When she focused on him, her lips curved into a smile. Jason felt his heart skip at the sight of it. It was a smile he felt he didn't deserve. It was a smile he wanted to keep locked in his memory for the rest of his life.

"Is someone at the door?" she asked through a yawn.

"It would seem so," he said. "Should we answer it?"

Emmy shrugged but sat up. The two threw on clothes: for him, a t-shirt and sweats; for her, one of his shirts. He could tell if anyone would answer the door, it would be him. He didn't mind. She looked so damn good in his old shirt and the curve of her thighs and the length of her bare legs were causing fantasies to spark his mind into waking up even further.

"Let's get this over with," he murmured to himself but Emmy caught it and smirked.

They headed down the stairs and Emmy went to sit on the couch while Jason went to the door. He furrowed his brow when the visitor was still there, hands on his hip, brow furrowed with obvious impatience. Jason had a knot in his gut. He shouldn't answer the door. He should let this stranger leave on his own accord. But there was no reason for his gut feeling and he knew Emmy was waiting for him to make pancakes. Jason intended to get rid of this guy as quickly as possible.

Jason opened the door a crack, furrowing his brow. It used to bother him that people would be intimidated simply by his physical appearance. Perhaps his reputation played into it now. He hoped this guy would actually back off upon seeing Jason, whatever he thought of him. Jason was satisfied when the guy's eyes widened a fraction at seeing him in front of him, in the flesh.

"Yeah?" Jason asked roughly, just to emphasize his prickly demeanor. "What do you want?"

The guy was younger than Jason, probably around Emmy's age and good looking in a pretty kind of way. He had short dark blond hair and crisp blue eyes, angles in his face that revealed a masculine nature, and while he wasn't as tall as Jason was, he was lean and compact. The guy probably ran; he looked like the sort who was in good shape. He wore a simple t-shirt and jeans. There were goosebumps on his arms due to the heavy fog that usually occupied Tahoe winters in the early morning, so either this guy wasn't from here or he left without remembering to grab a jacket.

"I need to speak to Emmy," he said and Jason had to hide a smirk at the fact that the guy's voice wavered just a bit.

"What do you want with her?" Jason asked. He didn't like that a man had showed up to talk to his girl. A man shown up at his house to talk to his girl. It wasn't right.

The guy furrowed his brow, annoyed. That was surprising. He didn't continue to stay afraid of Jason. "I need to talk to Emmy," he said, rather forcefully. "Emmy? Emmy?" He was shouting. Jason wasn't sure whether to be annoyed or amused. "You kill her too, you sick son of a bitch?"

"You want to say that again?" Jason asked, standing at his full height.

Jason had to hide a smirk seeing the man flinch. He narrowed his midnight blue eyes and clenched his jaw so it popped. It didn't help that his hair fell into his face, hiding a portion of it, making him all that more intimidating. He wore a sleeveless shirt and pajama bottoms, his arms long and well-defined. Jason might have been a recluse but he still kept in shape as best as he could, and now, muscles were coming in handy.

"I'll handle it," Emmy murmured, squeezing Jason's hand before stepping in front of the door. She had thrown on a pair of her jeans at some point, as well as sandals. He watched as her eyes widened in recognition and then narrow suspiciously. He could feel tension rolling from her body and knew there was more to the guy than his asshole behavior.

"Emmy," he said and Jason furrowed his brow. He didn't like the way this stranger said Emmy's name - warm and familiar - like they had been acquainted with each other before, in the most intimate of ways. Like he was one of the reasons Emmy seemed so experienced in the bedroom. The thought made Jason's skin crawl.

"What do you want Cody?" she asked, her tone clipped.

There was a history there between them, Jason realized. He couldn't say if it was romantic, sexual, or platonic, but something was definitely there. It hung on the lines that connected them, like dirty laundry out in public for everyone to see.

"I" - His eyes shifted to Jason before looking back at Emmy.

"Whatever you can say to me, you can say to Jason," she told him.

"What are you talking about, Emmy?" the kid - Cody - said, aghast. "Don't tell me you're actually friendly with this guy, this murderer? He killed his wife and her lover. You know that, I know that. Hell, he knows that. What's to keep him from killing you if you mess up or piss him off? He got away with it once. He probably thinks he can get away with it again."

"Cody, what do you want?" she asked again, interrupting Jason from growling some smartass retort. "I haven't seen you since college and now you show up at Jason's door like you have the right."

"Don't tell me you're friends with this guy, Em," Cody said, still not answering the question. "Or, God forbid, you're fucking him or something."

"That's none of your goddamn business," Jason said through gritted teeth.

Cody swallowed but stood his ground, his eyes only on Emmy. "You can't have a life with him, Em. Not with his baggage. People will talk. They'll discriminate against you - not because you did anything wrong but because of your relationship with him. You'll be isolated. You'll be a recluse. Your grandfather would disown you" -

"Don't talk about my grandfather like you know him," Emmy said, and it was the first time she actually sounded mean. "You don't know him. You never did."

Cody ignored the interruption. "You wouldn't have a life," he finished, looking at Emmy with big, pleading eyes.

Jason held his breath, his gaze burning into Emmy, waiting for her to respond. Then, "Is that all you have to say?" she asked.

Cody opened his mouth and then shut it. "Yeah," he said, almost helplessly.

Emmy nodded. "Don't come back here again," she said and shut the door in Cody's face.

CHAPTER 13

"He's right, you know."

Emmy's head snapped behind her, and she shut the front door, locking it before looking at him once again. Her brow furrowed and she pursed her lips together, tilting her head to the side. Her heart was beating against her chest like a baseline in a rap song. She wondered if it was loud enough for him to hear. She certainly could hear the echo of it ring in her ears.

"What do you mean?" she asked, crossing her arms over her chest. Jason couldn't possibly be talking about the vile Cody had been sputtering about before she slammed the door in his face. He had just defended her, defended them and their relationship, whatever their relationship was. It had been a few hours since they started sleeping together, but neither felt any reason to bring whatever this was up. It was unspoken, something that did not need any more analysis.

"He's right about everything," Jason went on, and she saw a flash of frustration, of anger, of danger, in his eyes. It lit them up, taking them from an indecipherable dark color to a clear dark blue. It was hard not to stare into them, but hard to lock eyes only because of how penetrating they truly were. "You. Me. Us."

"Stop it." Emmy closed her eyes and clenched her jaw. He could not be serious. Jason was lashing out. He was upset at Cody's words, certainly, but there was no way he actually agreed with him.

"No," Jason said. His eyes continued to bore into her, as though they were a weapon unto themselves. And, in truth, they were. She was rooted to her place, and she could not look away, not even if she were to try. "You need to hear this. What Cody said about everything was right. You deserve better than this shack, than me and my life and my baggage. Whatever this is" – he gestured between the two of them – "you don't deserve to be stuck with it."

Emmy opened her mouth, ready to argue with him, but something made her stop. Cody and Jason were talking as though she and Jason were serious, that this was the rest of her life, being with Jason secluded from the world in their own piece of Heaven. She knew such a thing wasn't possible, and to be honest, she didn't know if she was ready to make such a defining commitment to a man she liked but didn't love just yet. Cody was being a dipshit, Jason was being insecure, and Emmy was caught in the middle with a feeling that neither was right and neither was wrong. What she needed to do was get on more stable footing about what she wanted and where she saw her life. She knew she wanted to be with Jason but not at the expense of isolating herself from the world, from her grandfather, from the possibility of travel.

Traveling was important to her, and the only thing that held her back from it was her grandfather's various medical issues. Even money wasn't an issue because if she knew her grandfather was one hundred percent healthy, she would have no problem scrapping together some money for a plane ticket and backpacking throughout Europe. If Jason did not want to see the world then she knew she couldn't be with him long-term.

"Listen," she said, after another pause. She was digesting her feelings, trying to figure out the best way to handle the conflicting emotions warring inside of her while still remaining true to herself. "You and Cody can't tell me what's good for me and what's not. You can't tell me what I deserve and what I don't. These decisions are mine and mine alone. We haven't even talked about what this is" - her hands gestured between them, flopping around carelessly - "and you're already making decisions about it without discussing it with me first."

She hadn't realized her eyes were shut until she opened them once she was finished speaking. She found Jason smiling at her, one of his small, amused grins that caused her heart to speed up and the blood rushing through her veins to slow down so her cheeks turned a weird shade of pale and pink combined.

"What?" she asked, her voice small but curious. Back to normal.

Jason shook his head, the ends of his hair dancing on his shoulders. "You're right," he said with a shrug. "We should probably figure out what this is before we make decisions based on it."

"Exactly," Emmy said with a nod. "You go first."

Jason chuckled, then reached up to cup the back of his neck with his hand. It was such a boyish gesture, her body could not help but explode with warmth at the sight of it.

"I like you," he said, and Emmy was surprised that his confession and with his eyes looking directly into hers. From her time with Jason, she knew he didn't talk much about his feelings, especially feelings that exposed his vulnerability and left him open for rejection. The fact that he was able to write books using his real name and not a pen name - when books were so easy to criticize and exposed the author straight through to their core - amazed Emmy. It didn't surprise her that he could emit anger and frustration, annoyance and amusement, but the fact that he admitted to having romantic feelings for her with such ease... "I like you a lot."

Emmy waited a beat, and then another. When he continued to remain silent, she gave him a smile. "What?" she asked. "Is that it? You like me?"

"What more d'you want me to say?" he asked, pushing his brows up so they disappeared behind his long hair.

Emmy pressed her lips together to keep frustrating words at bay. Being frustrated and giving him attitude wouldn't help the situation. Instead, she decided to lead by example. "I like you, too," Emmy said, and she looked him in his eyes the same way he did for her. "I don't know what these feelings mean. I have no idea what it would mean for us, what it means at all, and maybe that's okay for now. But I know I want some clarity so I'm not confused. I want us to know where we stand with each other." She cleared her throat, trying to figure out where to go next. She was lucky he wasn't the type to jump in and interrupt. Finally, "I know I don't want to be with anyone else. I can tell you that I'm a monogamous person, even if we're just... doing what we're doing."

"Being with me isn't going to be easy," Jason said. "Let's not pretend I don't have baggage, and I don't want to pull you under any more than you already are. Your reputation is in tatters; it'll be ruined if we're together romantically. Even though I wasn't convicted, people still think I'm guilty. They'll put that on you, just for being with me. They'll call you every name in the book and I won't be able to protect you from it all."

"I don't need you to protect me," Emmy told him. Her voice came out shaky despite the fact that she tried to control herself. He just spoke about the murders, the trials. He didn't go into detail but he mentioned it. To her, that was a big step. Maybe even the biggest. "Everyone has baggage. I have baggage. The person that I'm with will have to understand that my grandfather comes first. I know that's not like your baggage but not many guys can handle that. When it comes to you, I can't tell you I know what I'm getting myself into or that I'll be able to handle whatever comes our way because we're together. But I'm willing to try." She gave him a smile, feeling confident at her own words. "We can take it day by day, so there's no pressure on us."

"You would do that?" he asked. He swallowed, glancing away,

out the window, before looking back at her. He didn't believe her. Not yet. But he wanted to. "Just to be with me?"

Emmy rubbed her lips together. She wanted to wrap her arms around him, to reassure him that she wanted nothing more than to be with him, that everything would work out okay. That there was nothing to worry about. But something stopped her. She couldn't baby him. She couldn't be the place he constantly ran to whenever he was afraid. He needed to be able to handle things on his own, especially if they were going to be together. It wasn't a fair burden to place on her, and she didn't think it was fair to him, either. If she was willing to go through the ordeal of being with him, he needed to figure himself out in order to be with her. He needed to be the man she ran to, just as much as she was the woman he ran to.

"What are you so afraid of, Jason?" she asked, her voice hesitant. She didn't want to force him to tell her things he wasn't ready to share just yet, but it was important to her that they communicate what they each expected from this and where they stood. It wouldn't work if they weren't on the same page.

"I" - He stopped himself, looked away.

Emmy ignored the hurt that spread across her chest, tried to be understanding. If the timing wasn't right for him, she couldn't force it. And she wouldn't force herself to wait for it, either. Perhaps it was something that should have been discussed before they had sex multiple times. Not that she regretted it. She didn't regret sex with Jason at all.

"After everything that happened with Stacey, it's been hard for me to trust someone," he said. He looked like a deer caught in headlights, ready to dart away into his room and lose himself in his writing. But he stayed. He was talking. That had to count for something. "But it was so easy to fa-, to trust you. I don't know how you did it. But I trust you. I do. But my scars from the whole ordeal are still ripe."

"You miss her," she said, nodding her head once.

"I don't," Jason said. His tone was sharp, reprimanding, but Emmy knew the hostility was not directed at her. She pressed her teeth together and held back anything that might come out. Instead, she chose to listen. "Stacey betrayed me. Once she did that, something inside of me snapped. I don't give a shit for her. At all. I don't feel sorry about what happened to her."

Emmy wasn't sure how to feel about his admission. Regardless of their history and what happened between them, it was a little harsh to not care that his wife was murdered. To be honest, it sounded like something a cold-hearted killer would say, and Emmy knew Jason wasn't cold-hearted. The thing was, she didn't know if he was a big softie at heart or if she brought that out in him. If it was the former, then the chances of him killing his wife and her lover were slim. Plausible but not likely. If Emmy was special, it meant that this warmth wasn't common for him, which meant he would never harm her but it didn't guarantee someone else the same thing. It was a catch-22. Emmy liked being special, liked knowing she was responsible for Jason's slow socialization, but at the same time...

Her thoughts trailed off and she did not chase them. She wouldn't think about his past now. Maybe later but not now.

Jason looked remorseful. Emmy couldn't tell if he regretted his words or his feelings. Maybe he regretted both. But his dark blue eyes pooled with concern and he had to look away from her.

"Look," he began. He picked his eyes up from the floor and forced them back into hers. "I know it's not a nice thing to say. But I don't want to lie to you. I won't ever lie to you. You can ask me anything and I promise you, I'll be honest.

"You want to know about Stacey? I fell in love with her perfume before I fell in love with her. She was a publicist for my publishing house and on the rare occasions where they called me in for meetings, she was in the room, taking notes and pitching ideas. I hated all of her ideas. I'm not the type that likes to be in the public eye. I like to hole up in my room and write."

Emmy felt her lips curl up in a smile. "I know," she said.

"But she was pretty and she would always smile at me and make me feel special. I couldn't look at her for a while because I was so shy. But she cornered me one day and forced me to get her a coffee. And we talked. And we started dating. And life was good." His eyes darkened as memories flitted through his mind, memories he had buried a long time ago. Memories he wanted nothing more than to forget. "Until it wasn't. Stacey was a social animal. She was constantly going out after work and having drinks with friends on weekends, which is fine. She can do whatever she wants, especially since I'm not the type to do that with her. As long as she came home at a reasonable hour and didn't drive drunk, I didn't care. What I care about is mutual respect and understanding. If I didn't complain about her free time, she shouldn't complain about what I do with mine. But she did. Constantly. I tried going out with her a couple of times and she tried staying in with me, but we hated it. We were both miserable."

"So she tried to change you but wouldn't change for you," Emmy said slowly, trying to sort this all out.

Jason nodded. "There were other things," he said. "We both wanted kids but once we were married, she changed her mind. She liked the city, I liked the quiet of Tahoe. We were just different. Opposite. Too much."

"Yeah," Emmy said, nodding her head. "There's this myth that opposites attract, and that's true to a point. You can have independent interests from your spouse, certain activities you choose to do alone rather than together, but no one broke up because they were too alike and spent too much time together. As long as your core values line up - whether you want kids or not, how to raise your kids, religion, politics, what you believe in - you should be set for a happy, healthy relationship. Now, I'm not saying it's impossible to have differences. My mom was a republican and my dad was a democrat and they were crazy for each other. But then again, they had the same view on the world." Emmy watched as his lips curled up into a gentle smirk. "What? What did I say?"

He shook his head. "You talk a lot," he said in his mumbly voice. "I like it."

She gave him a flirty smile. "Oh yeah?" she asked, perking her brow.

He took a step toward her. "Oh, yeah," he said. When he was close to her, he placed his hands and her waist and pulled her closer to him.

"Can I tell you a secret?" he asked, tilting her chin up so he could caress her jawline with his lips.

She sighed in contentment at the feeling, her eyes fluttering shut. She was gorgeous, an angel.

She couldn't speak, so she nodded her assent, swallowing as his lips descended to her throat. She had no idea how he was able to know her body so well already but he did. He knew exactly how to touch her. He knew exactly how to kiss her - and where. She wanted him, again. She was almost embarrassed by the fact that she wasn't satisfied with him, that she wanted more and more and more. He felt like home, like this was where she was meant to be live the rest of her life. She needed to feel him inside of her in order to feel complete. She needed him now, she needed him all the time.

"I hate that Cody guy," he told her. He nipped her neck almost as a punishment. She gasped at the feeling, finding that she enjoyed it. Probably too much. "I don't even know him but I hate him because I hate the way he looks at you, like you're his, like you had something, some past of yours that I don't give a shit about and don't want to be reminded of." His fingers started playing with the hemline of her shirt. "You're mine, Em. You're mine and no one else's and I wanted to let Cody know, I want him to know that you belong to me and he isn't welcome here. If he ever touched you, I'll beat him to a bloody pulp. And that's a goddamn promise, you hear me?"

His lips vibrated across her skin, making her body respond but her lips unable to. Instead, she nodded but all she cared about was feeling him inside of her again.

He took her arms in his grasp - not too tight but with enough firmness for her to know that he was in charge and she was going to do whatever he wanted her to. His mouth found hers and he kissed her with a hunger she didn't know existed. Her head got light. She thought she might faint. She knew her lips would bruise - there was no doubt about that, not with the way he was working a number on her mouth, her tongue, her teeth.

She had never been kissed this way before. Didn't know what it was like to be wanted so badly. She loved it. She craved it. Now that she had it, she couldn't live without it.

When he backed her into the arm of the chair, he tugged the button of her jeans free and proceeded to pull down her pants. She had to help due to how tight they were but the pause in passion wasn't awkward. Jason kneeled on the floor to help peel the denim off of her legs and she used him to steady her balance. Suddenly, the air sizzled with promise, crackled with desire. When her jeans were off, Jason reached up from his position on the floor and with his two hands, ripped the slip of underwear she wore so he didn't have to go through the hassle of taking those off as well.

Emmy made a grunt of protest and he glanced up at her with a smirk. "Don't worry," he said. "I'll buy you five more."

Emmy's look didn't fade, but when Jason eased her down on the arm of the couch and spread her legs wide open, any protests she might have had died on her lips. Her eyes were wide and she couldn't help but watch him, stare at him, drink him in. She watched with utter fascination as he picked his bottom lips and then pressed his face against her mound.

"Oh my God," she gasped.

She knew what was going to happen. She knew what he was going to do. She wanted him to do it. No one had ever done it to her before. She didn't want them to. It was too much, too intimate. She hadn't trusted anyone that much to allow them the privilege of doing something so personal to her.

But Jason was different. God, he was different. He was perfect. She wanted this so badly. She didn't realize just how much she wanted it, truth be told. But now that she knew, she didn't want to stop until she got it. Until she felt this and understood and -

"Fuck."

She didn't normally swear but when his tongue was on her this way, she couldn't help it.

He looked up at her with his blue eyes - they looked so dark she almost believed they were black - as he moved back and forth with his tongue against her clit. She had no idea how it was possible, but somehow, he knew exactly what type of pressure to put on it and what direction his tongue needed to go and how fast. Guys usually had no idea what they were doing, if they were willing to do this at all. Most guys wouldn't. But Jason wasn't most guys. Jason was his own level of perfection.

Emmy dropped her hands to her breasts and began to tug her nipples. She loved the sensation of any and everything on her nipples as long as it wasn't too rough. She didn't mind an occasional nibble but she was extra sensitive so even the lightest touch would do the job.

"That's right, baby," he said against her. The vibrations rippled across her slick mound, only pushing her closer and closer to her brink. "Touch yourself."

She did. Fuck, she did. Her head was thrown back - she didn't know if she did that on her own or if it just sort of happened - and she felt herself start to grind against his face, helping herself along.

And then, without warning, Jason slid his index finger into her cunt and curled it. She gasped, her eyes snapping open and her hips rolling in time to meet his thrust. He continued to fuck her with his hand, never losing time with his tongue. Her fingers caressed her nipples faster. Her eyes rolled back. She was so close, so close...

And then, there it was. The free fall. The release. It was like she stepped off a cliff, right before gravity pulled her to earth. She came around his finger, the muscles squeezing him tightly, rocking against him like her whole body was the San Andreas and this was the big quake everyone kept talking about.

When she finished, she had to push his face away from her because it was too much. She was too sensitive and it was too much for her to handle. He remained on his knees, staring up at her, but she couldn't move. She couldn't even hold her eyes open to stare at him. The only thing she could do was smile. So that was what she did. She smiled as her bones turned to jelly and oozed throughout her body. She had no idea how she was still able to function, how she wasn't in a pile on the floor.

Finally - it could have been hours, it could have been seconds - she picked her head up and met his eyes. Her lips curled into a small smirk. "Your turn," she announced in a way that left no room for argument.

Jason's mouth dropped open. He shouldn't have been surprised. Emmy was more sexual than he expected her to be in the best way. She dropped to her knees, completely naked. He was already good to go but just the sight of her caused his cock to throb with desire. It was almost a painful feeling that, if he didn't get it taken care of soon, he was going to explode.

But Emmy wasted no time. She took her hand and trailed her fingertips up and down his length. She was teasing him, he knew. She was teasing him and he loved it. Fuck, he loved it. He watched her with dark, hungry desperate eyes and was surprised when her own eyes found his. She wasn't shy with who she was, with her body, with the pleasure she bestowed upon him. With her eyes firmly stuck on his, she put her lips - her full, soft, slightly bruised lips - on the tip of his cock and flicked her tongue to moisten it.

"Oh, shit." His knees buckled underneath him. Literally. He had to sit on the arm of the chair or else he would have lost his balance and fell. And that would have been so embarrassing but it would have been so worth it.

Emmy grinned - the minx fucking grinned up at him like she knew what she was doing to him (she probably did) - and slid down his length, getting it wet and -

"Oh my God." He wanted to keep watching her. He wanted that image seared into his mind so he could remember it the moment before he died. A slice of Heaven he experienced while on earth. But he couldn't keep his eyes open. They rolled to the back of his head and stayed there.

With the absence of one sense, the other four were heightened, especially his sense of touch. Oh, Christ, his sense of touch was heightened. She started to move up and down his cock, as far down as she could go, at least, but she was skilled in getting him moist and wet by using her hand and following her mouth up and down. Her fingers were tight without being suffocating and they had a grip on his cock that rivaled his during his loneliest nights. The difference was, her hands were small and soft and touched him with this warmth he had never felt before. The fact that she used both her mouth and her hand to jerk him off made no sense to him but was absolutely perfect and there was no way in hell he'd be able to put into words.

And then, she did something no one had ever done to him before. Never. She moaned. His eyes snapped open and he stared at her. He found her eyes looking at him with that coy grin on her face and he lost it. He wanted to last longer. He wanted to hold on and enjoy. But the vibrations of her moans on his most sensitive area, the way she was looking at him, grinning at him, touching him, tasting him...

He couldn't do it. No way. She was a real-life fantasy.

"I'm going to" -

He wanted to give her a warning. He wanted her to be able to use her hands the rest of the time if she wanted to. He couldn't get the words out to let her know except what he already managed on top of quick breathing and grunting.

But she kept going. She didn't remove her mouth from his cock. In fact, she took her hand and started twisting it as she moved up and down, and with her other, she began to fondle his balls and -

Oh shit.

He was gone. He was done. He felt his orgasm behind his knees, charging through the bones of his fingers all the way to the tips of his toes. He was done.

But he wasn't because instead of Emmy removing her mouth and finishing him up with her hand like every other woman before Emmy, she kept going and when he released himself into her mouth, she lapped him up like a puppy lapped up water on a hot day. He couldn't contain the moan, he was certain his face was contorted into some kind of grimace mixed with utter and helpless pleasure.

She took all of him. She didn't let one drop go to waste. When he thought he was done, she kept squeezing more out of him, just in case, until he couldn't take it anymore and had to get a grip on her shoulder and squeeze. It was too much. He was too sensitive.

When she finished, she wiped her lips with the back of her hand, staring up at him with a devious grin. "I don't," she began, sliding up to stand over him. He looked at her with helpless, hooded eyes. "I don't know if I like it. The taste. I'll have to try it again."

"Fuck," Jason said.

There was no before Emmy. Before didn't matter to him. Before was going through the motions. Letting life happen to him. Now, he was alive. He was living. Emmy made him feel alive. The spark that started his fire. No one mattered before her. It was a blur, not worth remembering.

There were no words to describe her. No words that would adequately paint a picture of her. Instead, he remained silent, comforted by the peace and stability she brought to his otherwise lonely life. Now that he had this, now that he had her, he couldn't give her up. No way, no how, no nothing.

He positioned himself on the couch so he was comfortable and she crawled over to him, slipping next to him, practically on top of him, so she was comfortable. He wrapped his arm around her waist, locking her securely to him. It wasn't long before he could feel her steady breathing. It wasn't long before he joined her into a blissful slumber.

CHAPTER 14

Emmy woke a few hours later to darkness and her phone vibrating. She furrowed her brow, surprised there was even cell service.

"Hello?" she asked, slipping out of Jason's grasp and heading to the dining room. She didn't want to wake him up.

"Yes, may I speak to a Ms. Emmy Atler?" a woman with a pleasant voice said on the other end.

"Speaking." Her eyes flickered to the cabinet. Jason still owed her pancakes.

"Yes, hello. My name is Nurse Belle Pritchett. I'm here to talk to you regarding your grandfather, Oral Brown. He's just been admitted" -

Emmy did not realize she had dropped her phone until it landed just next to her foot. She heard the crunch – she could still hear the crunch hours after it happened – and blinked once. Then, twice. The crunch was more than the phone hitting the floor, it was a crack. A break. It was the screen on her phone, she realized. She had cracked the screen on her smartphone, something she had never done before.

How clumsy of her. This was unlike her.

She blinked once more, and then a garbled sound caught her attention. Someone on the other end of the phone was still speaking to her. With shaking fingers, she knelt down and grabbed the phone. She dropped it again.

"Wait!" she exclaimed to the phone, still on the wooden floor beneath her feet. "Wait." Her voice cracked. It came across as shaky as her fingers, and she curled them up into tight balls where her nails left crescent marks in the palms of her hands. Even the pain did not steady her. She needed to breathe, to control herself, but she could not. She could not seem to do anything.

"Hello?"

Her eyes looked up from her hands, still shaking, and saw Jason on her phone. His eyes were on her and the concern pooling from the depths of the blue was her undoing. The tears started flowing the same way water sputtered from a broken sprinkler with no signs of stopping in the near future. He was speaking to the nurse. Bless him, he was speaking to the nurse on her behalf because she couldn't.

"I'm sorry, the news has put her in shock. Can I give her a message?"

She heard the nurse – Emmy suddenly felt sorry for nurses who had to make these terrible phone calls, who were indirectly responsible for ruining lives. Who could want a job such as this? Why would anyone do this? – speak something to Jason. She saw Jason nod twice and then remember that the nurse could not see him.

"Yes, I'll let her know," he said. "Thank you for the call."

And there was Jason, thanking this nurse for the terrible phone call she made, and Emmy was certain she could hear the nurse suck out a breath of relief that she did not have to deal with anger or sadness. He reached out, handing her back her phone, unsure of how to handle her emotions, worried that if he touched her she might shatter. And she very well might. She did not know what would happen in the next breath, in the next blink of an eye.

She did not know anything anymore. She neededsomething to help her refocus. She needed to be strong, but she did not know how to do that. The only thing she could do was breathe. In. Out. In. Out. So she did.

When she caught her breath, she reached out and accepted the phone. It felt like a deadweight in her hand, and her arm dropped to her side. She blinked once. Was this real? Again. It had to be. People didn't lie about things like this. She looked up and saw that Jason was speaking to her, but she couldn't hear him over the blood rushing to her ears. Was it weird that it sounded like the ocean?

She shook her head. She needed to focus.

"What?" she asked.

Jason stopped speaking, then reached out to comfort her. For some reason, instead of letting himself touch her, he dropped his hands to his sides, as though he thought better of it.

"He's okay," Jason said. "He's passing a kidney stone. He might need surgery but he'll be fine. He's sleeping now. But the nurse says you can come visit when you want since you're his only kin."

"I want to go now." Her eyes were wide and her voice was firm. She hoped she didn't come across as rude, but right now, she didn't care. Couldn't care. She needed to get to Papa. That was all that mattered.

He nodded once, his blue eyes dark with thought. "I figured you'd say that," he said. He nodded his head to the front door. "Come on. I'll drive."

Emmy's eyes widened and she continued to stare at him. "But they won't let you in to see him," she said. "You'd have to wait. Either in the lobby or your car, but you couldn't go in." She was babbling now, but she couldn't stop. Words were pooling out of her mouth too quick for her to stop, and she had to physically put her hands over her mouth to restrain herself. She knew she looked ridiculous, and perhaps even a bit immature, but she didn't care right now. She couldn't.

"I know." He gave her a small smile. "Grab your stuff. I'll drive."

"But you normally don't go out." She sounded stupid. She knew it. It was just, she couldn't comprehend any of this.

Thank God Jason was so patient with her.

"You're right," Jason agreed. "Because I didn't want to deal with the looks, the whispers, the rumors. I realized, though, that by working for me, by being with me, you deal with it. It's not fair for you to deal with it alone." He shrugged, suddenly getting a pinched look on his face, revealing his discomfort. "Plus, we're together now. And we make sacrifices for the people we care about." Emmy felt herself blush at his words, but before she could think too much on it, he nodded to the door. "Now let's get going before I change my mind."

The two headed to the car without further incident. Emmy was so consumed in her thoughts that Jason had to reach over and buckle her seatbelt for her. She turned to him and gave him a quick smile before looking out the window. It was dark - she couldn't make out the trees in the woods surrounding Jason's cabin. She couldn't tell where darkness began and where shadows ended. Even the sky reflected her mood. The moon was new - almost black - and the bright stars that shined so brightly were blotted out by the tops of the trees. Everything looked dark. Everything looked bleak. Her hands shook, so she took them and pressed them flat against her seat before placing her thighs over them, hoping that would inspire them to stop.

It didn't.

Her head was so filled with thoughts, she couldn't distinguish between what she wanted to focus on and what she didn't, so she chose not to focus on anything. She didn't bother trying to sleep - the hospital was a good hour away without traffic, so she knew she was in for at least a sixty-minute drive - she wouldn't be able to quiet her mind, and she definitely didn't want to talk. She was glad Jason wasn't trying to talk to her either. Emmy didn't understand friends who wanted to distract someone from their circumstances. That was what movies and tv and music and books were for. Friends were supposed to sit with you during the bad times so you didn't have to sit through them alone, not pretend they didn't exist. Even though Jason was silent, he was here with her. He was risking ridicule and harassment by going out in public, but it didn't matter. He was still here, his priority Emmy and being there for her in whatever way she needed him.

Her heart swelled. She could love this man.

Her breath caught in her throat and her eyes immediately sought out Jason, almost as if he could read her mind, afraid he'd be able to hear her thoughts, but his eyes were focused in front of him, keeping steady on the road. She clenched her jaw and looked away, not wanting to give him any indication that such a thought crossed her mind. She gulped and rested her forehead on the glass window. She hoped the cold window would shock some sense into her thoughts, but nothing shifted, as of yet.

It made her feel guilty, to be honest. She should be focused on her grandfather. She should be worried about him and trying to think of -

Trying to think of what? There was nothing she could do. He was at the hospital and she wouldn't get any other information besides that until she got there. For now, she would have to wait. She wouldn't think about Jason, either. She didn't want to make any decisions based on her emotions during this time. It wouldn't be right, either. So she cleared her mind and stared out the window, trying not to think of anything.

"When they called me about Stacey," Jason began, his voice as tight as a guitar string, "I didn't know how to react. So I didn't react at all."

Emmy remained silent, her ears tickling with meaning. This was important, probably the most important thing he might ever tell her. Except, possibly, that he was in love with her. If he was in love with her. If it ever got to the point.

"I didn't feel anything," he said, keeping his eyes focused in front of him, not exactly sure where he was going with this. However, Emmy hoped he knew he needed this confession just as much as she needed to hear it. "Like I said, once I found out about her, I didn't care about her. I didn't care about us. There was nothing she could do to get me back because I didn't want her. Couldn't look at her the same way. Once you commit to someone, you commit and that's it. If you're unhappy in a relationship, talk about it. It's not that difficult."

Emmy rubbed her lips together. She was afraid to breathe lest the noise distract him from himself. She was at full attention, even though her posture left a lot for wanting, but she could hear every word that came out of his mouth no matter how mumbled, no matter how indecipherable.

"People took my lack of reaction however they wanted." He shrugged his shoulders and quickly glanced at her from the corner of his eyes. "I don't care what people think so it didn't bother me. We all handle death, loss, and things of that nature differently. I guess what I'm trying to tell you is that however you choose to handle this with your grandfather, whatever this turns out to be, I'm here for you. No matter what."

Emmy pressed her lips together but she couldn't stop the smile from eclipsing her face. It felt weird, to smile under these circumstances, like it was the first time she smiled ever, but she didn't think too much on it. Instead, she let his words wrap them self around her body, coating her in his warmth. She couldn't stop herself from reaching out and taking his hand in hers, before placing it back in her lap. She could swear she saw a flicker of a smile tease the corner of his lips, but he kept his eyes fixed firmly ahead and she didn't press.

Her heart burst at the seams, spilling out confetti and rainbows and red velvet cupcakes. She didn't know why his words made her so happy. It probably had to do with the fact that she shared something personal, something intimate, with her of his own volition.

"Thank you," she said, because she hadn't yet, and she wanted to. He needed to know it meant a lot to her, that it meant a lot to have his support in whatever way he could give it.

"No need to thank me," he said, casting another look in her direction. It was quick, and his eyes refocused on the road in front of him. "I'm yours. You're mine. It's what we're supposed to do for each other."

* * *

"I DON'T LIKE HOSPITALS," Emmy blurted out. They were a couple of miles from the one her grandfather was in and the silence was deafening. She needed to fill it with something. Anything. She needed a distraction.

"Me either," Jason said, glancing at her from the corner of his eye. "I don't know anyone who does."

"My parents," Emmy said, staring straight ahead of her. The only lights came from the headlights of Jason's Honda. It didn't make sense how good he was at seeing in the dark. It didn't make sense how much Emmy trusted him already. "When my grandmother was in the hospital, my parents tried to make visiting her fun. She had pneumonia and it was a slow death. She was in and out of there for about a year before she finally got over it and decided to die at home. My grandfather hated being there but he practically lived there. He didn't want to go home but he wouldn't let my parents pretend hospitals were a fun place. He always said she had the good sense to die at home. When my parents died in a car crash, I had to go to the hospital to see..." Her voice hitched, surprising her. She told this story numerous times before; she should be used to it. "My dad died instantly. He was the driver. My mom, my mom was still breathing. They rushed her into surgery but she didn't." Emmy stopped, looked down in her lap. Her eyes filled with tears and she didn't know if it was because of her parents or because of her grandfather. It didn't matter. "I hate hospitals. I don't want my grandfather to die there. He wouldn't, either."

"Hey." Jason squeezed her hand and rubbed her knuckles with his thumb. "Don't stress over something we don't know about yet. No one said anything about dying. Dry your tears. We're going to be there soon and you need to be strong for him."

Emmy nodded, blinking rapidly, trying to get rid of the tears. Jason was right. She needed to stop. She needed to breathe. She refused to be a blubbering mess when she walked through the sliding doors of the small town hospital. She needed to be coherent, capable of listening to the nurses when they discussed what was going on with him. She wasn't too concerned about looking good, but she did want to look put-together. She needed to be strong for her grandfather. He was too stubborn to admit it, but he needed her. She was all he had left and she wouldn't drop the ball when he needed her the most.

She grabbed the vanity mirror to make sure her makeup wasn't running and her eyes weren't red. Jason kept his hand on her thigh, which she needed. He was her lifeline, her reminder to take a moment for herself and just breathe. When she adjusted herself, she closed the mirror and unbuckled her seatbelt. Jason had just pulled into the half-filled parking lot. He turned off the engine and waited. He didn't push Emmy, didn't even ask if she was ready. He simply waited. And that made her heart swell with joy. She wasn't rushed. She called the shots. And he supported her. And it meant the world to her.

They walked into the hospital hand-in-hand, fingers intertwined. Emmy held on tight to Jason but her face was as relaxed as she could make it. The hospital itself was small, and since it was just after eleven o'clock in the evening, it was quiet. Their footsteps echoed on the cool tile and a nurse looked up from the reception of the quarter-full emergency room and offered them a small smile. She didn't seem to recognize Jason, and if she did, didn't gave any indication of it.

"How can I" -

"I'm here to see my grandfather," Emmy said and winced when she realized she interrupted the nurse. "Sorry. I got a call an hour ago, maybe. They told me he was rushed here by ambulance. His name is Oral Brown."

The nurse's fingers flew across the keyboard. "Mr. Brown was rushed in after complaining of severe stomach cramps," she said. "It appears as though he's currently in surgery. I'll let the doctor know you're here. What's your name?"

"Emmy Atler," Emmy said. "I'm his granddaughter."

"Great. Once he's out, the doctor will come out and speak with you. Please have a seat in the lobby." She gestured at the purple plastic chairs.

Jason led Emmy to the very back, where they could be practically alone. In a way, she was grateful this was a small town. It wasn't terribly busy - especially in the winter in the middle of the night - with only a few people sitting, waiting to be called on. Emmy barely paid them any mind and they kept to themselves for the most part. An old television hummed in the background, playing an old western television show no one was paying attention to. Once they sat down, Emmy glanced over at magazines stacked neatly on a low plastic table. She knew it would be a while and gossip magazines was a favorite way for her to pass the time, but she knew she wouldn't be able to retain the information nor would she be able to think about anything other than her grandfather.

From the corner of her eye, she noticed a couple of boys - they might have been twenty but that was pushing it - start looking at Jason. Suddenly, they began whispering, not loud enough to decipher what they were saying but they weren't hiding the fact that they were talking about him. Emmy clenched her jaw and forced herself to look away. She felt Jason tense but a cursory glance at him showed that his face was cool and indifferent. Like he didn't care.

Emmy knew better. Of course, he cared. He hated dealing with people. He was an introvert at best and an isolated writer at worst. He didn't like going out if he could help it, yet here he was, sitting in the lobby of an emergency room, like a caged animal in a zoo on display for the masses. Emmy was positive a Jason sighting would go viral through social media.

"You know," she whispered to Jason. "You can go home. I'll call you when I'm ready to be picked up."

Jason said nothing but he shook his head and took her hand once more.

Her heart screamed with bubbles. She was floating. In this awful, terrible, horrible situation, she was air. This didn't make any sense to her. Jason didn't make any sense. Why would he choose to deal with something that made him so uncomfortable when he didn't have to. She was giving him an out. He wouldn't take it. Instead, he took her hand and squeezed it, like he was reassuring her. It boggled her mind. No one had ever done something like this for her before. She was almost uncomfortable about it, almost felt like she owed him. But she knew he wasn't doing it because he wanted something in return. He was doing it because he cared about her.

He genuinely cared about her.

It was a while before a doctor emerged from the ER doors. Emmy passed the time by flicking her eyes over to the old television or dozing on Jason's shoulder. Ever since she started touching him and holding him, she couldn't stop leaning on him in some way. It didn't matter where, either. Her head fit his body perfectly, like they were from the same puzzle. Like they were molded from the same clay.

It was an odd thing to think about. These feelings for Jason had cropped up unexpectedly. She wasn't exactly sure what to think. She didn't know if it was because Jason was so beautiful in his darkness or if it was because she allowed herself to trust him just a little bit. She didn't know if that made her foolish or optimistic. She supposed it didn't matter at this point. She had made her choice, and the more she thought about it, the more she realized it had been before that fateful night in the rain when she couldn't deny it any longer. In fact, she knew exactly when it occurred. The minute he opened the door to his cabin to her and her breath was stolen from her in such a way where she couldn't expect for it to ever fully return.

There was something there she hadn't noticed, hadn't put much thought into. Perhaps it was something she unconsciously dismissed because there was no way she ever expected to fall for someone like him. Not that there was anything wrong with him, exactly, his whole murder trials not withstanding. But he had baggage, a history she did not yet have due to the difference in their ages. It wasn't a bad thing. Not really. When she was with him, she never thought about his age or his past. She only thought about the way he made her feel, the way he looked at her. In fact, she didn't think much about their future together, if she was being honest. Did they have a future together? Was that even feasible? And what did future mean, anyway? Marriage? Babies? Emmy didn't even know what she wanted to do as a career much less figure out who and what she wanted to support. She was just having fun in the moment.

But. She pressed her lips together. She did care about him. A lot. And she didn't see a reason why they wouldn't be together in the near future. And for now, that was enough.

"Emmy Atler?"

The doctor's voice broke her out of her swirling thoughts and caused her to stand. Without thinking about it, she tugged Jason over to the doctor with her. Her heart pounded throughout her body like it was on a loudspeaker and the vibrations thrummed through her nerves. She tried to study the doctor, hoping to decipher if what she was going to say was good or bad, trying to garner her grandfather's status based on how her facial features responded.

"I'm Dr. Reslen," the doctor said, introducing herself in a smooth voice. Her dark eyes slid over to Jason - recognition flashed in her eyes and she involuntarily swallowed before looking back at Emmy - and took a breath. "If you'd like to follow me, I can let you know what's going on with your grandfather."

Emmy narrowed her eyes. She knew what the doctor was trying to do and she wasn't going to have any of it. "Whatever you need to tell me, you can tell my boyfriend," she said pointedly. She didn't even feel bad that her tone was harsher than she originally intended it to be. It was important that the doctor know that such behavior would not be tolerated, regardless of the doctor's personal feelings regarding Jason. He had been acquitted for both murders. He should be allowed to return to a normal life without constantly being judged. That wasn't fair to him.

Dr. Reslen's eyes widened at Emmy's admission and even Emmy had to remember what she said that was so surprising.

Boyfriend, a voice reminded her. *You called him your boyfriend.*

She would have to deal with that later. Right now, she was here for her grandfather. They could talk about labels and the depth of their relationship at a later time.

"All right," Dr. Reslen agreed, shifting her eyes back to Emmy. She was still wary but she couldn't argue. This was Emmy's decision and she had to respect it. "Your grandfather, when he was admitted, was passing a kidney stone. Because of his age, we had to help him pass it with surgery, just to make sure it did not tear anything internally and cause bleeding. He's out of surgery now and is currently resting but he looks like he's in good shape. If everything remains consistent, he'll only have to stay for a few days."

"Few days?" Jason asked. "Besides a night of observation, don't you get discharged the next day for just passing a kidney stone?"

When Reslen looked at Jason, her eyes were hard and cold, almost as though she was offended that he was questioning her in the first place. Emmy felt her jaw lock and her eyes narrow. She started to get defensive and had to curl her fingers into tight fists and squeeze, causing pink crescent moons to appear in her skin. She did not like when Jason was dismissed simply for asking a question. She knew it had to do with who he was, what people thought he was, and she had to bite back a response. She honestly had no idea how Jason was able to handle this disrespect whenever he went out, probably every time he went out. He had more patience than she ever could.

"Can we see him?" Emmy asked, trying to keep her tone under control. She apparently didn't do a good job because Jason reached out to squeeze her hand, trying to offer her support in any way he could.

"Actually, no," Reslen said. Her eyes flickered to Jason before shooting back to Emmy. Emmy didn't think Reslen did it on purpose; it was a tic. She revealed her hand. "We don't allow visitors past eight at night" -

"That's bullshit," Emmy said through a snarl. Reslen's mouth dropped open and her eyes widened. Emmy felt Jason look at her with a similar reaction but she kept her focus on the doctor in front of her. "I've been here before at this time and I was let in to visit him once he was stable from surgery so don't tell me I can't see him. We both know what you're doing and I'm not going to tolerate it. You can't discriminate against people based on race, religion, ethnicity, sexuality, and income level. You do not get to dictate my visiting rights based on who I'm dating. If I want him here with me, you can't tell me he's not allowed."

"Em," Jason said in a rough murmur. "It's okay. You go ahead and check on your grandfather. I'll stay here."

"It's your choice, Ms. Atler," Reslen said, her eyes hard and distrustful. She was looking at Emmy the way she looked at Jason. Filled with suspicion and dislike, even though she didn't even know Emmy.

"So I am allowed back there even though it is past eight?" Emmy asked through gritted teeth.

Reslen pushed her brow up but says nothing. It was almost as though she were challenging Emmy, and Emmy did not respond well to challenges. "Yes," she finally said. "You can go back." She shifted her eyes back to Jason, giving him a hard, long look before looking to Emmy. "Check in with the front desk and they will bring you back." With that, she spun on her heels and disappeared back into the ER.

Emmy opened her mouth, ready to vent out all of her frustrations, when Jason intervened by placing his finger over her lips. "Wait," he said, his eyes locked with hers. "You're pissed. I get it. You have every right to be pissed. But this isn't the time to be stubborn. Not when it involves your grandfather. Go to him. I'll be here. I promise I'll be here."

Emmy clenched her jaw. She wanted to argue but she knew he was right. She nodded once and gave him a quick kiss on the cheek. "Thank you," she whispered before heading over to the front desk. Before she went through the emergency room doors, she cast one last look at Jason and gave him a smile.

Even in a dire situation such as this one, Jason somehow still made her feel like the luckiest girl in the world.

CHAPTER 15

He was getting better. Papa was getting better.

Emmy and Jason would visit him every day in the afternoon for lunch. Well, Emmy would visit. Jason would sit out in the lobby on his phone, writing. Emmy had no idea how it was possible to write a book using just his phone, but he did it diligently every day for the hour she spent with her grandfather.

To be honest, she wanted to introduce Jason to her grandfather. They hadn't really had the chance to talk much regarding how she was and what sort of work she had to do and what sort of man Jason was, and the times when her grandfather was awake and coherent in the hospital was filled with reading his favorite book - *To Kill A Mockingbird* - or listening to the nurse talk about possible medications and treatments and how this would affect him in the long run. What Emmy noticed was absent from both him and herself was the lack of discussion about how this was going to get paid. Emmy was afraid to bring it up on the off-chance that her grandfather might refuse treatment if it cost too much or put stress on Emmy. She wasn't sure why he hadn't brought it up yet, but every time she and Jason returned to his cabin in the woods, she knocked on the wooden door, hoping her luck would last at least another day.

Jason never asked why she knocked on the front door, which she appreciated. The more time she spent with him, the more she realized that he was accepting of her in her entirety. It was something she had never experienced with anyone else before, whether they were friend, lover, or even family. It was as though the world was filled with puppets, and everyone pulled on strings. Nothing came for free; everything had a contingency.

But somehow, Jason liked her for exactly who she was. It didn't matter that her hair frizzed up at the slightest exposure of moisture. It didn't matter that she drooled in her sleep and didn't know how to put on makeup or babbled to the point of being incomprehensible when she got excited or frustrated. It didn't matter that she was reserved in her affection, cautious during their time together before sex and after. She still didn't know who to be or how to act in a real relationship. Though, to be fair, it was still new, still undefined, still mysterious and uncertain and precious. She changed her mind constantly, but her heart never wavered in regards to her feelings for the man. She liked him, she liked being around him, and she definitely liked when they were connected. She kept telling herself that love might be too strong of a word right now, but she was on the precipice of falling and nothing could stop her. He was growing to become the second most important man in her life, which was why she felt it was important for both he and her grandfather to meet.

The thought caused her breath to get light and her stomach to get dizzy. To say she was nervous would be the understatement of the century. It was important that her grandfather liked Jason. Perhaps he would be wary - what overprotective grandfather wouldn't be - and perhaps he didn't trust Jason was innocent despite the outcome of his trials. In fact, the more that Emmy thought about it, the more she realized her grandfather had never given her his opinion on her choice of work. He told her to protect herself but never told her whether or not he thought she was safe. She wondered if it had anything to do with the fact that she was going to do what she was going to do, regardless.

It was two weeks since being admitted. His health had improved, and the doctor estimated another week before he could be released. This was good news – especially considering he was only supposed to be there for a few days at most. Emmy was happy. Relieved. Grateful. With every passing day, she saw color return to his face, his periwinkle blue eyes come back to life. He was sitting up on his own now, and complaining how salty the gravy on his hospital-issued meatloaf and potatoes was. He was returning to his old self again, and the sight of the transformation warmed Emmy's heart to the point where she thought it might burst right out of her chest.

Once they finished their lunch, Emmy's eyes drifted to the standard wall clock above the small television set in the room. She moved cleared the trash from the tray and moved the tray to the side. It was conveniently attached to the bed so she could push it away from him and fold it into a slot.

"You seem happy," he said, his eyes locked on her. He was smiling, his eyes crinkling, and she couldn't help but smile in return.

"You're going to be out in a week, Papa," Emmy said, folding her hands in her lap. "I'm ecstatic."

He waved her words away with a dismissive hand. "That's not what I've meant," he said. "You're different, Em. Happier. Why?"

“You’re questioning my happiness?” she teased.

“O’course,” he said with an abrupt nod of his head. “It’s my duty as your grandfather.”

“I...” She stopped, pressed her lips together. Her eyes descended to her lap, and her thoughts swam into each other. This was the difficult part. Telling her grandfather everything. Well, maybe not everything. If she wanted him to come home sooner rather than later, she didn’t want to tell him just how close she and Jason had gotten. Secrets were meant to be kept, and a lady never kissed and told. "There's a guy." She looked back at him and was surprised to see a blank look on his face. No reaction whatsoever.

"So?" he asked, quirking a brow. "I figured sooner or later this was coming. Do you realize how beautiful you are, Emmy? I'm surprised this wasn't sooner."

"Yes, well." She cupped her bicep with her right hand and squeezed. "This one is different."

"That's what they all say." He paused. "How are you able to see someone with your job? I figured you don't get out much, and..." He let his voice trail off and his eyes widened. He knew. He just knew.

"Papa" –

"Are you telling me this boy is Jason Belmont?" he asked, and while he wasn't yelling, his tone got clipped.

Emmy started to feel her breathing get shallow, that it took extra effort to get oxygen to her lungs. She could feel his disapproval from where she sat; it rolled off of him in harsh waves crashing into the surface. She wasn't used to disagreeing with him, to having some kind of tension between them. To be completely honest, she had no idea how to handle it.

"Now, Em," he said after clearing his throat. She could hear the no coming, could see it dancing on his bottom lip. "I don't know" –

"Papa." Even she was surprised how curt her tone was. How she interrupted him. She forced herself to look into his eyes. If there was nothing wrong with Jason, with what she was asking her grandfather, then there was no reason for her to feel ashamed of her choices, her actions. She already knew she did not regret Jason in any capacity, and just because her grandfather didn't approve didn't mean she was going to start now. "He's sitting out there right now."

"Just because he's sitting out there doesn't mean I'm obligated to meet him," he returned, his voice a tad defensive. She wondered if it was as difficult for him to disappoint her as it was for her.

"That's not what I meant," Emmy said. "You know what people are saying about him. You know what people are saying about me just for working for him. Papa, he drives me here every day so I can eat lunch with you. He sits in the lobby with other people, reading magazines. He endures the looks, the whispers. I'm not sure if anyone said anything to his face – he hasn't told me – but I wouldn't put it past them. But he does it for me, because he cares about me. And whether you like it or not, I care about him. He knows you're always going to come first. Always. And he respects it. He hasn't argued or complained. I'm not saying you have to like him. But, in my opinion, he deserves a chance, at the very least."

Papa was silent. Seconds ticked away like hours, and the sound kept time with her heartbeat. She held her breath, kept it lodged in her throat until it choked her, and then she released it slowly, through her nostrils little by little.

"Tomorrow," he said finally. "He can come tomorrow." He stuck out his finger and pointed at Emmy. "You make sure he looks presentable, Em. I'm not saying I'll like him, but I won't let him sit down if he comes dressed sloppy. You know I won't."

Emmy couldn't hear him over her smile. Regardless, she leaped up from her seat and pulled him into a tight hug.

"I promise, Papa," she told him. "I promise."

A small smile begrudgingly popped up onto his face. "If *you* like him, I can at least give him the benefit of the doubt," he allowed. "But he only gets one first impression. Make sure he doesn't waste it."

--

"How do I look?"

Jason's voice caught Emmy off-guard and she nearly stumbled off of the couch. She managed to catch herself just in time, and as she stood, flattened the wrinkles that accumulated on her pencil skirt. If Jason had to dress up, she would as well. She didn't want him to feel like a sore thumb; they were partners, they would look like fools together. Dressing up to go to the hospital wasn't something people normally did, especially in the outskirts of San Francisco.

When she turned so she could get a look at him, her breath caught in her throat. He looked... Well, Jason could definitely clean up. He wore a simple white shirt and black jeans with a pair of boots on his feet. He combed his hair but still let the strands fall in his face. Emmy had to resist the urge to keep from brushing them to the side. He shaved, making him appear almost boyish. The clothes fit him well. She could tell he ironed both articles of clothing, which amused her to no end. His biceps clung to the sleeves, popping out in such a way - like burlesque dancers strategically hid certain parts of their body while revealing others. She had to grip the sides of her skirt as subtly as she could in order to refrain from reaching out and squeezing them.

She was excited. Giddy even. Emmy wasn't quite sure as to why. Her grandfather had met guys before. If she dated, he insisted on it. But Jason was different. This was different. And deep inside, she knew that.

"You look very sexy," she said, feeling her cheeks pinch with redness.

Jason blushed. She grinned inwardly. She liked making Jason blushed.

"Sexy is not what I'm going for to meet your grandpa," he said, his voice particularly mumbly. Emmy noticed this only occurred when he was nervous about something. It was kind of cute.

"You look great," she said. She couldn't stop herself from reaching out and squeezing his hand. She had to touch him. Had to.

"So do you," he said, looking her over with a predatory look in his dark eyes. "You should wear one of your big sweatshirts so you don't distract me that much."

Emmy giggled. "Jason," she said when she finished, her tone

serious. "Thank you. For coming, I mean. You have no idea how much I appreciate it. I know it's not the most comfortable experience, especially being an introvert, but it just makes me feel amazing knowing you would do this for me and for my grandfather. So thank you."

Jason's face turned even redder, which Emmy thought was impossible.

* * *

THE DRIVE over to the hospital was lighthearted and easy. Traffic was minimal. Winter was slowly starting to creep into spring, which meant snow was starting to melt. Winter tourists were leaving but it was still too early and too cold for summer tourism. As such, Tahoe was emptier than usual, which made driving easier. Not that it had been overtly difficult in the first place.

They stopped at her grandfather's favorite restaurant - a mom-and-pop diner that served meatloaf, potatoes, and gravy he absolutely loved - to grab takeout and then make their way to the hospital. It was slightly busier than usual, and Emmy felt Jason tense behind her. Because he carried the plastic bag filled with their food, Emmy reached behind her and took his free hand in hers, squeezing to offer what reassurance she could. They stopped at reception and Emmy gave the now familiar nurse - Jan - a smile before heading to the elevators and heading to the second floor.

"I must really like you," Jason mumbled once they were safely within the confines of the steel elevator. "To put up with this shit." He snapped his head in her direction. "I don't mean your grandpa. I mean... You know." She looked at him, a soft smile on her face. "But I know you must feel the same way about me because you put up with the same shit."

The elevator pinged and the doors slid open. "I do," she assured him. "May I ask you a favor? Please refrain from swearing around him. He was in the army and is familiar with it but if someone swore in his company and they weren't one of his buddies, he'd take it as a sign of disrespect."

Jason said nothing but he grinned.

When they reached her grandfather's room, Emmy felt her heart start to race. She was nervous and excited at the same time, which was something she had never felt before. Her eyes slid over to Jason; he was giving her a lot of those first-time experiences and they all seemed thrilling and scary at the same time. He looked beautiful, standing next to her with his shoulders squared to the door, as though he was going to battle. His jaw was locked, determined, his eyes on the closed door in front of him. His hair still fell in his face - that was something it didn't appear as though she could change - but at least it was combed. She took his hand in hers - it was cool but clammy, another nervous tic - and she pressed a kiss into his shoulder.

She was in love with him, she realized. She didn't know how it happened or why it did without her being cognizant of it, but she was in love with this man. It didn't matter that he was acquitted of murdering his wife and her lover. It didn't matter that he was the best and only suspect and was only released on a technicality. She was in love with Jason Belmont. She was in love with him wholly, completely, fully. And now, there was no going back.

"Papa," she said with a grin as they stepped through the curtain and to the foot of his bed.

Warmth flooded through her body when she saw that while he was still recovering from surgery, he was sitting at a table looking out the window in tan slacks and a red polo shirt. His thin grey hair was combed and his periwinkle blue eyes were sparkling. He looked better. And more than that, he was trying just like Jason was. The two most important men in her life were finally meeting.

"You must be Jason." Her grandfather got to his feet with more effort than it normally would have taken him. He gripped the corner of the table, putting his weight into standing up. Emmy had to press her lips together to keep herself from expressing something akin to sympathy. He would hate that.

Instead of trying to help her grandfather up, Jason remained at Emmy's side, simply watching the old man. There was no judgment in his eyes, no sympathy either. He had no emotions, to be honest, but he wasn't empty. He regarded the old man like his equal, like a man, and based on the firm stare her grandfather had for him in return, Emmy knew he appreciated it.

"I am, sir," Jason said.

"I've heard a lot about you." Her grandfather extended his arm and the two hands. They were both prideful men and Emmy was certain the handshake would tell them exactly what they needed to know about each other. It was some weird guy thing that Emmy didn't fully understand but refused to question it.

"All good things, I hope."

Emmy's mouth dropped open as she set the food on the table and she looked at Jason with wide, sparkling eyes. He made a joke. He made a joke. That was actually funny. He rarely jokes. He was typically a quiet person, losing himself in his work. In fact, the only time he really makes an excessive amount of noise was when they were engaged in intimate behavior. She beamed at him. Of course, he ignored her. His attention was on her grandfather which was where it should be, but Emmy knew he knew just how much that meant to her.

Her grandfather chuckled but said nothing. When he saw the food, he took a seat. Jason pulled out a chair for Emmy and grabbed the small stool with wheels - the one the doctor usually sat in while on their computer in the room - and moved it over so he was sitting in between the two.

"Have you had Lucille's before?" her grandfather asked Jason. Emmy started handing out the styrofoam containers while Jason passed out the drinks.

"I have not," Jason answered.

They decided to eat first. There was little to no discussion among the three unless chewing counted as a form of communication. When they finished, Emmy stood up and disposed of the trash before resuming her place in between both men.

"Jason," her grandfather said, his eyes like bullets heading straight for Jason. "Do you mind if we cut the crap and get straight to the point?"

"I'd prefer it."

Emmy looked back and forth. Her heart was still jumping on a trampoline. Sometimes it landed in her throat, sometimes it landed in her gut. But it never landed in the same place twice.

She was nervous. She knew that. What she didn't understand was why she so badly wanted these people to get along. It honestly didn't matter what their opinions were regarding the other. She was still going to be in love with Jason. She was still going to put her grandfather first. But she wanted them to like each other. She still had this innate desire to obtain her grandfather's approval. It wasn't likely that that would change anytime soon. But she had this fire inside of her that only grew when she was around Jason. He set her on fire and kept the flame burning. She doubted it would ever go out completely.

She rubbed her palms on her thighs. Her hands were always cool - never warm - which was the worst in the winter. Never were they clammy or sweaty or filled with perspiration. Until now. She could feel the tension between the two men but it wasn't overwhelming. They were both open to giving each other a chance.

"What are your intentions with my granddaughter?" he asked.

Jason didn't flinch. He did not look away. That had to be a good sign.

"I don't really like the word intention, sir," Jason said. "For me, it seems to imply that I'll make decisions regarding Emmy without her knowledge and her opinion. I have no intentions regarding her. What I want, though, is to be with her. I want to be around her because she's this shining light and I can't look away from her. She's good and pure and genuine and that's so rare to find nowadays that I recognize how vital she is to someone like me. I love her but if she didn't feel the same way about me, I wouldn't condemn her to life with me. I just... I just..." He shrugged. "Whatever she wants from me, I'll gladly give it. I want to be with her for as long as she'll have me." He paused. "Does that answer your question?"

"I'll allow it," her grandfather said after a moment. "Son, do you mind if I talk to my granddaughter alone? You can wait outside of my room. It won't be long."

"Of course," Jason said with a nod of his head.

When the door clicked shut behind him, Emmy's grandfather turned to regard his granddaughter for a long moment. His arms were crossed over his chest, resting on his stomach. Emmy felt herself squirm under his gaze but she did not want him to know he was getting to her. Instead, she tried to breathe in and then breathe out, calming her nerves and hoping the shakiness was all in her head.

Finally, he said, "Do you love him?"

"W-what?" she asked, surprised by the simplicity and the directness of the question.

"Don't play dumb with me," he told her. "Do you love the guy? And be honest. I know you want to please me. I know you want to make me proud and you're afraid of making choices that you think I might not agree with. But the only thing I'm concerned about is your happiness, no matter what my opinion is on the matter. You are all I care about. So, tell me: do you love him?"

Emmy swallowed but nodded her head. "Yes," she said. "I do."

Her grandfather nodded, as though he expected this. "Emmy, more than anything in the world, I want you to be happy," he told her. His periwinkle blue eyes twinkled and she knew he was being serious. "I don't know if this guy is capable of giving that to you. Then again, I don't think anyone on this planet is capable of giving that to you. I don't care about Jason. I care about you. I may have my reservations about him but I trust you. I trust your decisions about your life, including the type of people you want in it. I asked him to come here because I wanted to see if he was the sort of man I could like. Even if he didn't show, that has no bearing on your feelings for him. You don't need me to like him to be with him. And I don't have to like the guy to support you." He paused and swallowed. "I still don't know if I could like the guy based on his past, which I know isn't fair. But I also realize he's here for you. He's already scrutinized and I'm up close and personal. I have to respect him for that. I just want you to know that I'm here for you and I love you and I want you happy. If he makes you happy, well, he's all right by me."

Emmy didn't realize she was crying until a tear dropped from her eye and hit her cheek. Without warning, she leapt from her chair so she could throw her arms around his shoulders and press her face against his chest.

"Now, now," he said, patting her back. "Why don't you let him back in so we can finish our lunch?"

"I love you, Papa," she murmured into his shirt.

"I love you too, baby doll," he said. "Now, come on. The poor guy is probably getting harassed standing out there. Let's get him back inside."

"Well," her grandfather said, "you're in for a treat."

EPILOGUE

People were fickle. They also loved a good redemption story. When Jason Belmont decided to head back into the spotlight, the general population welcomed him with open arms. It didn't hurt that when he made his re-debut at the Montgomery Writing Ball, hc had Emmy on his arm, a young woman with a college degree and a pretty smile, who looked good enough to be considered beautiful without overstepping the fine line between bimbo gold digger idiot.

The couple was at their cabin in the woods, and they were running late. Originally, Jason had wanted to do a signing before the ball and awards were announced, but then changed his mind and decided against it. Twenty minutes before they were supposed to leave, he changed his mind again and Emmy had to hastily throw her hair up into a simple bun instead of curling it the way she wanted to. However, as she stared at herself in the mirror, she realized the simplicity of her hair, makeup, and accessories really emphasized the dress, making it stand out. Emmy could not help but smile to herself. She looked beautiful, and she knew it.

The dress itself was a subtle white color that contrasted nicely with her dark hair and dark eyes. For this reason, she decided her makeup would be subtle and earthy, with warm Browns and nudes. There were no sleeves on the dress, but lace flowed freely from it, and the cut was sweetheart, giving her more cleavage than she already had. It narrowed at the waist and hit her ankles the way a waterfall hit the water in a graceful, eye-catching way. She wore a simple pair of matching white high heels, and there were thin silver rings on her fingers, reminding her who she really was and where she came from. It was too edgy to be compared to a wedding dress, and Emmy refused to let herself worry over what might be written about her in fashion magazines and tabloids. It came with the territory, she knew, but she it was nerve racking nonetheless. At least knowing she was happy with her appearance gave her courage to step out into an audience waiting to judge her.

When Emmy made her grand entrance by walking down the wooden staircase to the living room, the look on Jason's face was enough to make her forget about any worry she might have had. His mouth dropped open - Emmy didn't think that actually happened - and he stared at her unabashedly, not even bothering to hide his wandering eyes nor mask the awe that was so clearly emanating from them. Before he could stop himself, he strode over to her and pulled her into a passionate kiss, using his hand to support the back of her neck as he dipped her.

"You're going to get lipstick on your face!" she chided him, giving him a playful smack on the shoulder once she was able to breathe and he had released his hold on her. "And mess up my makeup."

He shrugged, fixing the lapels of his black jacket. "Don't care," he said. "When you look like that..." He let his voice trail off and shook his head. "You can't blame me. It's not my fault."

Emmy pressed her lips together and felt herself blush. They had been together now a little more than half a year, and somehow, Jason had the ability to make her blush regardless. She didn't understand it, couldn't question or analyze it. It was something so uniquely him that any further research into the matter would turn up with a headache and slight annoyance.

"Are you going to slick your hair back?" she asked, reaching out to run her fingers through the locks of copper-brown.

"Nah," he said. "I don't mind if they fall in my face. Nothing much to see."

Emmy rolled her eyes and decided not to comment on the fact that after all this time, she still believed him to be the most beautiful thing she had ever seen.

A knock on the door interrupted her thoughts, and she glanced at the staircase, past the metal baseball bat Jason kept next to the door just in case. Her brow furrowed on its own accord, and she paused. The only person who would choose to visit she and Jason would be her grandfather, and he knew they were going to the awards slash signing slash masquerade ball tonight.

"I'll get it," she said. Jason didn't respond, probably because he was still getting ready.

Emmy walked to the door just as the pounding started. She sprung up on her tiptoes to look through the peephole only to find Cody standing there. This confused her even more.

"Who is it?" Jason asked, fixing his cufflinks as he came out of the downstairs restroom.

"Cody," she whispered.

He furrowed his brow. "What's he doing here?" Jason asked as he stepped next to her. "And why are you whispering?"

"Because I'm not sure if I want to answer it or not," she replied.

He gave her a furrowed brow and an amused smile. "Let's just get this over with." More pounding on the door, and "I know you're in there!" Jason rolled his eyes as he reached for the doorknob. "He's never going to quit if we don't do something about this."

Just as Jason opened the door, Cody pushed it open, nearly knocking the wood into Emmy. If she hadn't taken a step back, the edge would have smacked her in the face. Jason's eyes narrowed as he caught the edge, watching Cody walk into the room without being invited.

"You almost hit my girl in the face," he snapped, turning his body so it faced Cody but blocked Emmy's.

"Your girl?" Cody looked from Jason to Emmy, his blue eyes filled with disbelief. "Your girl? Is he serious, Emmy?" His eyes suddenly took in Jason's suit, Emmy's dress, and they squinted. "Are you his girl?"

"I'm not going to dignify that with a response," Emmy said, standing on her toes once again so she could look over Jason's shoulders. "I have nothing to say to you, Cody. We're late as it is. If there was nothing you came here to say, you can leave."

"No," Cody said, shaking his hair. "No, I have something I want to say."

"Well, we don't really care what you have to say," Jason said, standing to his full height. He wasn't tall, but when he tensed his body, he appeared intimidating. Even Cody swallowed, though it didn't look like he was going to back off anytime soon. "You can leave."

"Not before I talk to Emmy," he insisted. His eyes shifted over to the woman in question. "Alone.".

Jason shifted his eyes so they rested on Emmy. She liked the fact that he didn't answer for her, that he trusted her well enough to make her own decisions and he would have her back, no matter what, even if he didn't agree with it. She nodded to him, letting him know that it was okay, that she could handle this. He nodded back to her.

"I'll be just in the kitchen," he said, more for Cody than for Emmy. The kitchen offered the best vantage point, where Jason could see but not be seen. It also had the best acoustics, so he could pick up everything that was said. He'd also be able to detect if she needed him right away as well. His statement also told Cody that if anything happened to Emmy, if he thought Cody was getting too aggressive, too belligerent, he would just be in the next room and wouldn't hesitate to control the situation if Emmy could not.

Cody paid him no mind, and instead, shifted his focus to Emmy. Emmy, meanwhile, smiled as she watched Jason leave.

"What is that?" Cody asked in a rushed whisper, raising his arm and gesturing at her face. "Why do you look that way at him?"

Emmy turned her attention back to Cody. "Because I love him," she said, making sure her eyes were locked on his.

"You love him?" he asked in disbelief. "You love this murderer psychopath? Are you out of your fucking mind, Em?"

"You don't get to call me, Em, Cody," Emmy said, taking a step toward him. Her voice was hushed because she did not want Jason to overhear him. He wouldn't like anyone talking to her that way, especially not Cody. "And you don't get to talk to me that way, either. Why are you here? What do you want?"

Without warning, Cody grabbed Emmy's hands in his and pulled her to him. "I want you, Em," he said as though it was the most obvious thing in the world. "Don't you see? Don't you understand that? I want to rescue you from this life. Come be with me. Come be *my* maid. You know I'll take care of you. You know I'll take care of your grandfather. You'll always have a roof over your head and food in your belly. You'll never have to worry about another bill ever again. Let me do this for you, Em."

Emmy yanked her hands away from Cody and stepped back from him. "I don't need you to do that for me, Cody," she told him. "I don't *want* you to do that."

"Come on, Em," Cody said. "I know you care about me. I know there was something between us. Don't deny it. Not now."

"Cody." Emmy's eyes narrowed. She was starting to get annoyed. Why did he think he knew her better than she knew herself? Why was he telling her how to feel. "I'm going to tell you one more time. I am in love with Jason. Like, crazy in love Beyoncé style love with Jason. You cannot change it. Back in college, I liked you. That's nothing - nothing - compared to my feelings for Jason. I don't care that you led me on. I don't care that you dated my best friend knowing I had a thing for you. I don't care about you and I don't care about her. You guys could both die tomorrow and I wouldn't care."

Emmy blinked, surprised with herself for her harsh words. It wasn't like her to be so forward, so blunt, so cruel. At the same time, it was true. She didn't care about Linda and she didn't care about Cody. If they died, she wouldn't care. She knew in her gut that she wouldn't care. Did that make it right to be so direct about her feelings - her lack of feelings - she didn't know. Perhaps she would make an effort to censor herself in the future but right now, she didn't care.

"Now, Jason and I have somewhere to be," she said after she cleared her throat. She went to the door and opened it. "I'll walk you out."

Cody looked surprised, to say the least. He looked hurt when she said what she said, but that hurt turned into anger and his eyes flashed into hers as he watched her open the door.

"Look at what his influence is doing to you, Emmy," he pointed out. He was allowing her to lead him outside which was a good sign. Maybe they'd make it in time for hors d'oeurvres. "You were never a cold bitch, Emmy. Sure, you had an attitude every now and then, but not like this. You're letting him change you into a person I don't even recognize anymore."

Emmy couldn't stop herself from rolling her eyes. She wanted to stop on the front porch and watch him walk to his car but she didn't know if he would stop with her. She decided to head to the driver's door while keeping a reasonable distance between him and the car.

"You never knew me then," she told him. "And you don't know me now. Stop insisting that we were a thing or that I'm changing when you don't know anything." She looked him dead in the eye. "I love Jason and there's nothing you can do or say to change that. Now, please leave. And Cody, don't come back here."

She watched as he clenched his jaw. He looked like he was going to say something, thought better of it, finally turned away. His hand slid into his pocket, probably for his keys, and he angled his body toward his car, as though he was about to go in.

"I came here," he said, then stopped. He looked away. Emmy tilted her head to the side. She did want to know why he was here, considering his presence made no sense whatsoever. Finally, his blue eyes clashed with hers. "I liked you, Emmy. Back then. Linda was a better fit on paper. I made the choice to be with her, but I made the wrong choice. When I realized you were with Jason, all my feelings came back and I thought I could rescue you, make you see sense. I realize now that you'll never see sense. Not anymore."

Emmy said nothing. There was no point. She did not want to argue with Jason. She had too much to worry about tonight. All she needed was Cody to drive off the property and then she and Jason could go. Without warning, Cody spun back around and lunged for Emmy, knocking her off her feet and causing her head to snap back and hit the ground hard. She saw stars.

Cody was saying stuff. Emmy couldn't make out what that was. She heard bitch a few times, then whore. To be honest, she was in a daze. It was hard for her to focus, to hear, to speak, to see. Maybe if she blinked... Once, then twice. She still saw stars but less of them.

It was only when she felt Cody climb on top of her did she get pulled back to the reality of her situation. He was still talking, still going on, but she couldn't hear him. His voice was like an instrument; he was making sounds but she couldn't understand what he was saying. Suddenly, his hands were on her body and all she could think about was, My dress, my dress is getting dirty and wrinkled and what if the fabric rips and it will be ruined before the ball...

Suddenly, hands were gripping her waist. No, not hands.

Claws. They were pressing down on her, keeping her still. Something about Emmy being a murderer's whore, something about wanting a taste since she gave it away so freely.

Then, it clicked. She could focus again. She understood.

Emmy refused to let him take advantage of her. She started screaming. Cody took his hand and covered her mouth with it. Emmy tried to bite it but couldn't. She struggled underneath him. She needed to move. She needed to keep moving. If he gave her an inch, if he gave her a centimeter, she needed to be ready to pounce on it. She needed to be ready to take it.

It didn't seem like he would. He was too heavy, like a bowling ball on her stomach, dragging her body down to the bottom of the ocean, keeping her there so air was not an option. He didn't care if he hurt her. He didn't care that he was ruining her dress, that this constituted as rape because she was screaming at him, screaming against his hand, that she did not want this, that he needed to get off of her, that he would be sorry. He didn't listen. She didn't think he would. He was lost in the lust of power he created for himself and by struggling against him, she was feeding into what he wanted. He started laughing. Like this was a goddamn joke. Like this was funny.

Where was Jason? She hoped he heard her. She hoped he was calling the cops. Because if not, there was no way she'd be able to get him off, to stop him from doing what he was doing.

She kept moving even though she didn't think it would do anything save for tiring her out. But she wouldn't let him take anything from her without a fight. Even if it did no good. Even if it exhausted her. She would not give him the satisfaction of succumbing to his strength, his sex.

Then, without warning, he was lifted from her body. She could breathe again. She was okay. But she didn't know what happened. Where did Cody go? Why did he stop? Maybe she shouldn't question it. Maybe God was taking care of her in His own way.

But no. She needed to get out of the situation. She needed to find Jason. Her dress was ruined. She would need another one. There was no way she could go to the ball looking the way she did. They would probably also need to call the cops. It would make sense to do that. She was assaulted, after all. She wouldn't let Cody get away with trying to rape her, for hurting her. For coming here and insulting both she and Jason. For assuming he could walk right up to her and think he could sweep her off her feet. She would not let it stand. Would not let it happen.

A crunching sound caused her to pause her thoughts. She turned and winced. She'd have to move her whole body, not just crane her neck. So she did. And her mouth dropped.

There was Jason, straddling Cody, punching Cody over and over and over again.

--

When Jason heard her scream, he dashed out the door. He didn't even stop to think about it. He nearly slid on the wooden floor - damn shoes, new and slick; he wasn't used to the black loafers yet - but he righted himself before he did and barely missed a step. He threw the door open and his blood froze. He was paralyzed. But only for a beat.

Cody was on top of Emmy - beautiful Emmy, his Emmy - tearing at her dress, trying to lift up the skirt. He saw red. He had never seen red before. Not even when he found Stacey in bed with her lover. But he saw red now.

Emmy was fighting back. He was proud. But he was furious she had to fight at all.

Jason couldn't stop himself. Didn't really care about the repercussions. Didn't even stop to think about them. All he saw was Cody on top of the women he loved, trying to take advantage of her. Hurting her. He would not let that stand.

He didn't know how it happened. One second, he was standing on the porch, taking it all in, the next, he tackled Cody off of

Emmy and straddling his waist before pummeling into him with his fists. He didn't think. His body was simply responding. He didn't even look to see if Emmy was okay. He was simply focused on the task at hand.

He was on top of Cody and beating the shit out of his face. Cody managed to roll him over. Got a few punches in. Good ones, too. Jason didn't hear Emmy screaming. She tried lunging at Cody, but he pushed her down without even looking at her. Jason could put up a fight but he wasn't as young as he had been before.

And then, a loud thwack rang out. It echoed in Jason's ears.

He could hear again.

Cody collapsed and Jason rolled him off of him, but Emmy kept hitting Cody with the bat. Jason could hear the bones crunch but he didn't stop her. She kept going and going and going -

There was no sound. Only Emmy's heavy breathing. Only his ragged breathing. His eyes dropped to Cody's face - what was left of Cody's face. It was so bloody, so purple, no one would be able to tell who he was. He was unrecognizable. No one would know who this was unless someone did a DNA test.

"Is he" - Emmy took a breath. "Is he dead?"

The bat slid out of her hand and clattered to the dirt.

It was then that Jason realized she was standing off to the side, looking at him with an indecipherable look on her face. She wasn't disgusted. She wasn't angry. She wasn't terrified of him, even though he was covered in blood and he was only now coming down from the adrenaline rush his body had just been immersed in. His right hand started throbbing and he could hear his heart start to beat in his head.

Her dress was ruined. Blood was everywhere. He couldn't tell if she cared about what she had done. She must still be in shock.

What had she done? There was no way Cody was still alive. Emmy had beat him to death. He looked over to her, suddenly scared she would scream, leave, fall out of love with him. He didn't even care that she might call the cops, that he might actually go to prison this time. None of that mattered if Emmy didn't love him anymore.

"Jason?" Emmy said, snapping him out of his thoughts. His knuckles hurt badly. He couldn't even move his hand. There was a good chance he broke a couple of bones. He looked at her. He still couldn't read her face, didn't know if anything thing had changed between them. "Is he dead?"

Jason nodded once.

He watched as she clenched her teeth together and looked away. More than anything, he wanted to know what she was thinking. More than anything, he didn't want to know at all. He didn't know how to feel. He didn't know what to do except slowly stand up and step away from the body.

"We need to figure out what to do with the body," she said finally, turning her gaze back to him.

Jason squinted up at her, not sure what to make of her reaction. She looked at him, not blinking, not judging him.

"Listen," she told him when he still didn't respond, "I don't care about your past. I don't care what you did and didn't do. In fact, I don't need to know either way. We need to think about now. We need to think about us and our present and our future. I was defending you. And me. He would have..." Tears filled her eyes. She had to look away. Finally, "What should we do with the body?"

Jason looked at her. "It doesn't matter," he said. "I already got away twice. The cops will do anything to make sure I'm convicted this time. And you – you're tainted. Being with me does that."

"I know," she said, surprising him. "I know me being a witness and a victim doesn't help. Me having defensive wounds, torn clothes, I get it. I highly doubt Cody told anyone he was coming here. He's an idiot but he doesn't talk that much."

"You don't know that for sure," Jason stated.

Emmy shook her head. "No," she replied.

Jason nodded and stood up. "Are you all right?" he asked her.

He went to touch her but stopped himself, not wanting to push her if she wasn't comfortable with being touched just yet. "When I saw him on top of you, I..." He shook his head and locked eyes with her. "I lost it."

Emmy nodded. "I'm okay now," she said but Jason could see she was still shaking.

Jason wrapped his arms around her, waiting to feel any indication that she wasn't ready, any sign that she would push him away. However, he felt her melt into him, clinging onto him for dear life, and his heart broke that she suffered already, that he hadn't been able to protect her. He tucked his chin on her head and held her even closer.

"I'm never going to let anything happen to you," he promised her. It was a promise he vowed to keep, no matter the cost.

"I feel the same way," she whispered back. "But." She cleared her throat so her voice came out stronger. "We have to get rid of Cody and we have to get rid of his car. We can't let anyone know he was here."

Jason nodded against her, keeping her wrapped up in his arms. "Okay," he said. "Okay. I'll take care of it. You get cleaned up."

"Do you need any help?" Emmy asked. Her voice was muffled against his chest, her breath tickling the exposed skin of his collarbone.

He shook his head. "I've done this before."

ACKNOWLEDGMENTS

I've been working on this book for years. I set it aside and didn't come back to it until early 2016. This is one of my favorite stories and I'm so glad I got to share it with you. So thanks for taking a chance on a dark, twisted love story.

Thank you to my family, especially my mom, for your support and your faith in my ability.

Thank you to my readers for your amazing encouragement. I'm astounded each and every time I talk to you!

Thank you to my beta readers – Diana L., Karen H., Heather B., Judes, Linda-Leah P., Leona, and Heather F. You guys are amazing and pick up what I couldn't. THANK YOU for helping me with my craft.

Thank you to my kickass launch team and everyone who wanted an ARC. Your feedback is so helpful and instrumental to my career.

Thank you to Suzanna Lynn of Funky Book Designs for my wonderful beautiful wickedly dark cover!

Thank you to JD, always my muse.

Thank you to Josh, Jacob, and Kylee for pushing me to be a

better parent and motivating myself to take myself seriously as an author.

Finally, to Frank, as always you're my reason for everything. Thank you for inspiring me.

DID YOU LIKE A BEAUTY DARK & DEADLY?

As an author, the best thing a reader can do is leave an honest review. I love gathering feedback because it shows me you care and it helps me be a better writer. If you have the time, I'd greatly appreciate any feedback you can give me. Thank you!

Want to find out when my next book comes out? Maybe you'd like to jump in on the giveaways, sales, and other fun stuff? Please consider signing up for my newsletter **here**.

ALSO BY HEATHER C. MYERS

Other Works by Heather C. Myers

ALSO BY HEATHER C. MYERS

Modern Jane Austen Retellings

Four Sides of a Triangle Matchmaking is supposed to be easy. But Madeline is going to learn that love can't be planned when she starts to fall for the last person she ever thought she would, who also happens to be the man her best friend claims to love as well.

Swimming in Rain Marion is a die-hard USC fan. Aiden goes to UCLA Law School. If only college rivalries were the worst of their problems. They say opposites attract. Well, some crash into each other.

ALSO BY HEATHER C. MYERS

New Adult Contemporary Romance

Save the Date As daughter of a man in charge of the CIA, Gemma knew her father was overprotective. She just never thought he would assign a man she couldn't stand to be her bodyguard under the rouse of a fake marriage.

Love's Back Pocket Holly Dunn didn't know that when she began studying at a rock concert, the lead singer would call her out on it. Tommy Stark didn't know he'd be intrigued by her odd sort of ways, which was why hew invited her to go on tour with him.

Foolish Games She was everything he didn't want in a woman and everything he couldn't resist. She thought he was arrogant on top of other things.

Falling Over You She wasn't supposed to see him, hear him, or feel him because he was dead - a ghost. She wasn't supposed to fall in love with him because she was engaged.

Hollywood Snowfall It's getting cold in Hollywood, so cold, there's a good chance the City of Angels will finally get snow.

ALSO BY HEATHER C. MYERS

Dark Romance

A Beauty Dark & Deadly He's the most beautiful monster she's even seen

ALSO BY HEATHER C. MYERS

Young Adult Novels

Trainwreck Detention is not the place where you're supposed to meet your next boyfriend, especially when he's Asher Boyd, known pothead and occasional criminal. But he makes good girl Sadie Brown feel something she hasn't really felt before - extraordinary.

ALSO BY HEATHER C. MYERS

The Slapshot Series: A Sports Romance

Blood on the Rocks, Snapshot Prequel, Book 1 Her grandfather's murdered and she's suddenly thrust with the responsibility of owning and managing a national hockey team. That, and she decides to solve the murder herself.

Grace on the Rocks, Slapshot Prequel, Book 2 A chance encounter at the beach causes sparks to fly...

Charm on the Rocks, Slapshot Prequel Book 3 When you know it's wrong but it feels so right

The Slapshot Prequel Box Set

Exes & Goals, Book 1 of the Slapshot Series Most people have no regrets. She has one.

ALSO BY HEATHER C. MYERS

Dystopian

Battlefield Just because they were, quite literally, made for each other didn't mean they had to actually get along.